ONE GOOD HEART

A J WEBSTER

SCARAB
PRESS

This is a work of fiction. Names, characters, places, and incidents either are the product of the author's imagination or are used fictitiously. Any resemblance to actual persons, living or dead, events, or locales is entirely coincidental.

Copyright © 2023 by AJ Webster

All rights reserved. No part of this book may be reproduced or used in any manner without written permission of the copyright owner except for the use of quotations in a book review. For more information, address: info@scarabpress.com

First paperback edition January 2023

Book design by Artificial Intelligence

ISBN 978-1-7392376-0-8 (paperback)
ISBN 978-1-7392376-1-5 (ebook)

Published by Scarab Press
www.scarabpress.com

For Sammy, who has the best heart

"The human heart has hidden treasures,
in secret kept, in silence sealed."
— Charlotte Brontë

WHO'S WHO?

Astrophel, sister of Jerry

Jericho (Jerry), brother of Astrophel

Dan Allen, mathematician turned gardener

Mary Allen, wife of Dan

Auden Everston, inventor and founder of EverTech

Jessica Everston neé Dryden, world-renowned cardiologist, wife of Auden Everston

Evie Hawkins, widower, her husband Harvey Hawkins was a police detective

Rufus Johnson, security guard for EverTech

Jack Lewis, medical school drop-out, turned surgeon

Daphne Morris, paramedic

José Perez, bouncer, turned security guard

Mia Svobodova, assistant to Jessica Everston

Molly Woodbead, school friend of Jerry

1

ASTROPHEL

Yesterday I was 14 years old. Today I have discovered that I am 33.

Don't worry though, this isn't some cute body-swap-coming-of-age drama, I'm just sharing this because up until this afternoon the most interesting thing about me was my name. Astrophel. Pretty weird, right? It means 'star-lover.' I've spent a lot of time looking up at them, but I think that's mostly because I have been lost, and I read somewhere that it was possible to find your way by the stars.

But this story is not about me. At least not yet.

However, if it were about me, I would make for a pretty ideal subject. Although apparently not actually a child, I think I should be considered one. As such, I should of course, be an orphan, because the children in stories are always orphans. Well, I can check that off. Ideally they should have lost their parents in tragic circumstances - tick (more on that later). But, I suppose if I really were the perfect candidate I would be living out a miserable life with a wicked aunt or cruel foster-family, which I am not. I'm sorry to report that Dan and Mary Allen, my parents through adoption, are completely lovely.

They are kind, caring and thoughtful, to the point where I almost stopped thinking about my birth parents.

Were.

They died.

At this point, a gaping void that so often leads the young protagonist into a dangerous adventure usually opens up.

But, as I have mentioned, this story is not about me.

This story is about a story that was left for me to find. And anyway, I'm not a child anymore, I'm a 33-year-old 14-year-old and that does not sound like a good fit for a hero of any kind.

That job goes to Jericho, my brother.

2

ASTROPHEL

I found out that I had a brother on Monday. Today is Saturday, so it has been a busy week, what with the second and last of my adoptive parents dying and the revelation that I am 19 years older than I thought and that I have another dead family member I didn't know about.

Dan Allen, my wonderful nearly-father died and within hours the world began to dissolve around me. I was alone in the house when the call came through from the hospice telling me that he had passed. They said it was a peaceful death, that his heart just stopped beating.

They asked if I was ok; if I had anyone with me; if there was someone I could call.

I told them that I would be fine and that I had lots of family around me.

I didn't.

I was alone.

Our little house was on a quiet anonymous road, in a quiet anonymous town, near to the seafront on the south coast of England. Dan and Mary had adopted me nearly a year ago after my parents died. Mary died almost the next day and I'm embarrassed to say that I barely even remember her.

Actually, that isn't quite true. I remember Mary in the way you might remember a whisper - she's like the memory of a ghost that flutters past your ear at a million miles an hour and is gone before you can even wonder what was said. And yet that breeze which swirls and kisses the outer edge of your ears on a cold day is, somehow, Mary. I didn't know her and yet I know deep within myself that she was a warm and kind person and I saw everyday how much Dan missed her.

Maybe his pain made me miss her too. Or maybe my loss and his got knotted up and I was confused about what I was hurting over.

In a year, I had never met a neighbour, though I think I might have seen someone through a hedge in the garden once, only for them to be quickly moved away by another unseen hand.

I don't go to school. Apparently I have 'episodes' when I do. I don't remember them, but Dan told me that school wasn't a building, it was a state of mind and he could help me build a library in my brain that any academic would be proud of. He was a bit corny like that, always telling me things that you might read on a postcard or a tea-towel, like "once you stop learning, you start dying", or "educating the mind without educating the heart is no education at all."

So, I stayed at home.

I didn't see anyone except Dan and Fandango. She is our dog.

My dog.

My favourite Dan-quote is actually from Mark Twain. I was never sure if he knew that I knew he wasn't making them up himself. "The more I learn about people, the more I like my dog."

Well now it was Fandango and me and there were no other people. Unless I was going to open the door and see what was waiting for me outside.

And that didn't seem like a good plan.

3

DAPHNE

Being a paramedic is one of those jobs where you see the best and worst of what humanity can serve up. Mostly the worst.

You're there for the sadness and pain, but worse than that, I always thought, you're there in the moments that are so urgent, there's no time for humanity. I look back across the time I spent racing around London in the rig in which Teddy and I built a life and I'm not sure exactly what I feel about it.

When we first met, I was to be Teddy's 5th partner in a year. I was warned that this was going to be some sort of rite of passage - something that I had to endure in order to progress. The head of our station was almost apologising to me, a newbie, for what I was about to face.

And my goodness she was right to do so! Teddy was an absolute bastard! He was rude, obnoxious, cold, meticulous to the point of compulsive and frankly, just not very nice! But if I could put up with him for 3 months, I could transfer to another bus and get a new partner, no questions asked.

I don't think I ever cried as much as I did in those first few weeks of working with him. I was still living with my dad at that point and bless him, he even threatened to go down to the station and give Teddy a piece of his mind. My dad was essentially a human teddy-bear, so I'm not sure exactly how threatening this would have been, but I was grateful to have someone willing to defend me against this man who I just did not understand.

Every callout felt like a disaster, but I hit rock-bottom about six weeks into our partnership. It was a simple gig, that even I should have been prepared for - 3-year-old boy, with a worsening barking cough and a history of croup. All I needed to do was take the sats, administer a single dose of dexamethasone orally and then stick around to do some obs.

The boy's mother was already in a state of wild fury as we entered her home and that threw me off my game. She glared at us as we as we asked the most basic of questions and she was hostile towards her son who was apparently keeping her awake when she had a very important meeting in the morning. The tension in the air was only amplified by the fact that she seemed to have the heating turned up to an absurd level, making the whole place feel airless and wet at the same time.

She huffed and puffed as I tried to take the boy's vitals, and my hands shook as I rummaged around my pack for the steroids he needed. I couldn't quite manage to tear the plastic cap off the vial and that's when Teddy and the woman snapped at me simultaneously. I had been kneeling down in front of this sweet, frightened little boy, but as they yelled at me, I fell onto my backside, spilling the dexamethasone as I did.

The mother roared as the few millilitres of liquid spilt on her carpet and Teddy yelled my name, before shaking his head as he started looking through his own pack for a new batch of the steroids I should have already administered.

I'm embarrassed to say that I ran out of the house and took refuge in the back of the ambulance. I wasn't exactly hiding - the back of the bus was, after all, basically my office, but it would take Teddy an extra 10-15 seconds to find me, once he realised I wasn't in the cab at the front. That would be a whole quarter of a minute less of his disapproving passive-aggressive silence to endure.

I heard his footsteps on the gravel driveway a few minutes later. Then the sound of the driver's door opening. I imagined him looking into the empty space where I should have been sitting and rolling his eyes. The door closed slowly, more crunching, gravelly steps and then the sound of the back doors opening. Our eyes met. I waited for admonishment. Up to this point, I had not been able to do anything right, but as he looked at me, a strained, strange look on his face, he said 'She was a real piece of work, huh?'

I knew then that I was in love.

4
JOSÉ

Tom Cruise nearly ruined my life! From the very first second I saw *Top Gun* I knew that the only thing I wanted to do was fly. I was certain that I was going to be a pilot for the RAF and that I would have amazing friends, incredible experiences and save the world from enemy attacks, one awesome dogfight at a time, whilst playing beach volleyball in my spare time.

As soon as I was old enough I bought a Kawasaki Ninja - the same bike he rides in the film. I remember how much heavier it was than I had expected. The roar of the engine vibrated through my whole body as I revved the throttle and my God I thought I was *the man*.

And then I failed the medical. Asthma. No good if you want to fly. My papá would probably be horrified to know that I cried a lot when I was told that my dream of flying was over. But then my papá disappeared when I was 2 years old, so I'm not sure I really give one single, tiny rat's arse.

Anyway, the dream was over and I was an 18 year old kid, in love with an idea that was out of reach. I messed around for a long while. I drank a lot, partied hard and worked as little as possible. Just enough to pay for me to waste every free moment I had.

Mamá was not proud of me during this time, but she saw that my heart was filled with sadness and she knew that she didn't have enough spare space in hers to help me. So she left me to my hurt and I left her with hers.

I had a lot of friends who spent a lot of time as wasted as me. I discovered that eventually you become one of two people - the lazy, spiritless drunk, or the angry drunk. I became the latter.

Bizarrely, this is what led me to the job that saved me. Though it nearly killed me first.

I was getting into a lot of trouble in the local bars and one night the bouncer took a real dislike to me (which was totally reasonable given what a complete muppet I was being) and grabbed me whilst I was squaring up to some guy who I thought had spilt his drink on my shoes (I had in fact pretty much thrown my drink on his shirt, on purpose, because, well, because that was who I had become).

So the bouncer grabs me and pulls me firmly, but calmly outside. He tells me I need to go home and I did not take terribly well to his direction. I punched him really quite hard on the nose. His co-bouncer Phil jumped in to take over, but I jammed an elbow into his chest and cracked two of his ribs. I know this, because Phil enjoyed telling the story to anyone who would listen for years afterwards, as this was in fact, unbelievably, the start of a beautiful friendship (though neither of us knew that until quite some time afterwards).

John (the broken-nose) and Phil were both out of action and then a third man rolls up to me. He was small, very round and he was the manager of the bar. He offered me a job as the bouncer, at least while the others recovered.

And that's how I got into the security business.

5

MIA

(RECORDED IN 2004, 10 YEARS AFTER THE INCIDENT)

Growing up in a tiny flat in Soho, filled with Czech poetry and Dixieland jazz, it's not hugely surprising that I spent my teenage years falling in love quickly and nursing a broken heart for months on end. My parents are beautiful people filled with soul that they desperately tried to pass on to me.

When I showed an aptitude for science they were surprised, but cautiously supportive. When an aptitude for, became a genuine talent they looked a little frightened. When I got my first job in robotics they looked like they might cry.

'How,' my mother asked in her vaulting baritone 'is a girl who can't get one note from a saxophone supposed to build a robot?'

She was right, in so much as my musicality extended to terrible shower-room singing and accidentally crashing keys on the piano that took up about a quarter of our living space, when I was cleaning it for my pocket money. But what my father the poet and mother the jazz-band trombone player worried about was not my job, but my heart.

They assumed that a scientist was a person who had lost their soul. Why would anyone trifle with God's creation when they could be exploring it and celebrating it with words and sounds? They did not understand that it was because I felt every tiny brush with love with an unbearable intensity, that I hid myself away in a job that needed only my mind. And I was good at it too. Not that this mattered very much to them, and indeed, for many years, to me. But it was a start down a road which I thought might lead to something. Something more. And it did. But I look back now and wonder if they were not right all along. I lost my heart to that work, and what's worse, is that I saw others losing theirs and I didn't do a damn thing about it.

6
JACK

Dear Mum,

I know it's old-fashioned to write letters, but there is something beautiful about pressing ink into paper in order to tell a story. And I do have story. I just don't really know how to tell it.

I suppose that this seems a ridiculous way to start a conversation after such a long time. I suppose the story you want me to tell, is the one that explains why I left you and dad in the middle of the night and never came back.

Well, I suppose that is the story I'm going to tell, only me running away is the end of that story and not really what is important.

I'm in California now - I guess you guessed that from the postmark? I'm in a little place out by Huntington Beach. It's an absolute hole, but it was so cheap! I got the place for less than $30,000 and I can walk to the beach!

I surf every day. That's kind of my life now. I suppose that must seem quite surprising. Though I can hear dad saying that

I spent my whole life wasting time, so perhaps it's not such a surprise after all?

I'm happy here. I have a dog, Ralph. He's a chocolate-coloured Labrador, just like I always wanted. He comes to the beach with me, but he's afraid of the water! Can you believe it - I think I got the only dog in California that doesn't like the ocean and I spend my whole life on it!

London seems like a different life. I don't think about it unless I have to.

I hope that you and dad are ok. I know that sounds like it's an empty thing to say, but I mean it.

I guess you guys are in the same place? If not, I hope that this will get forwarded on to you.

I'm sorry.

Yours,

J

7

EVIE

(ON BEHALF OF HARVEY HAWKINS)

Harvey loved what he did. He was a great detective and the police force was like an extended family to him, and to me. Almost all of our friends were people who worked for, or with the police. I'd like to think that it wasn't quite his whole world, but outside of me and the children, it was his only hobby!

Sometimes, when a case was really tough, then I think we might have come in second place to the work. But it's only because he cared so much.

He really believed in justice. I suppose that sounds daft to you young people, but it was what got him into the job and what kept him going for 47 years.

47 years. Can you believe that? I met him when he was just a few years into the job. I can replay every second of the moment our lives touched. 15th May 1954 it was. I was living in a tiny prefab on the Isle of Dogs in East London. My daddy was a warehouseman on the West India dock. He'd come back after the war to find our house had been blown to rubble, but they built us this flimsy thing to keep us warm and dry until

we moved into a council flat in 1955. I say 'we', but I only lived their 5 minutes, so fast was my courting with Harvey.

Anyway, I know it was the 15th May we met because that was the day Britannia, the Queen's yacht, came sailing down the River Thames and we welcomed her home after 6 months away doing fancy things in the Commonwealth. Millions of people were out on the streets. It was like a holiday really.

Well, things got very exciting as the boat came past and my girlfriends from the warehouse typing pool where I was working started screaming and waving like lunatics, thinking that Prince Philip might wave back no doubt. I got caught up in the moment and before I knew it, some cheeky bugger had grabbed my handbag and was making off with it. It spoiled my morning to be honest. There was nothing much in there aside from a few pennies and a lipstick, along with my now pointless identity card, but it was a nice bag. It was my only decent one actually.

And it was that pointless identity card which brought Harvey knocking nervously on our door on Stewart Street to return my handbag. He'd apparently seen the thief tipping out the contents in some alleyway or another and clobbered him for it.

He was my hero from the very first day we met. He had such a good heart - I could see it even then on that doorstep of a horrible already-falling-down house, not 10 years after the war that took so many good people from us all. He was my hope, before I knew that I was so desperately in need of it.

We had a wonderful life together. It wasn't flash or fancy. There were moments where we both felt like time and the world were moving faster than we could cope with, but we had each other and that was enough to get us through.

You know he brought me flowers every Friday. He was always shy about it; didn't like to make a fuss. Sometimes he wouldn't even give me them directly, I'd just come home and find a new bunch of flowers in a vase on the kitchen Every Friday for 45 years. And then he missed one. And ⟨ was when I knew our time together was nearly over and my heat broke. Ever-so quietly. Ever-so slowly. I'm not sure I even realised at first what was happening, but by the time Harvey was gone, I had crumbled from the inside and there was almost nothing left worth rebuilding.

8

DAN

Astrophel, if you're listening to these tapes I guess I've either found my backbone, or I've finally joined my sweet Mary in Heaven and I have left you with a burden I was too afraid to share with you in life. And for that I am truly sorry. I tried to be a good man all my life, but I know that I wasn't a brave one.

Taking you in was the one courageous thing I did and I do not regret it for a second. You were the triumph that crowned the life Mary and I built together. I just wish we had had more time together. And I wish that there had not been such dark shadows and secrets hanging over us.

I think, I hope, at least, that for a while, you have been spared some of the worry. I don't know if this was the right thing to do, but it was an attempt at kindness. Please do not hate us for that. By the time we fully understood what had happened, we didn't know how to disentangle ourselves from the net of lies that had already been cast.

I barely know where to begin my dear Asty. I suppose I should start with the truth, because there has been little enough of that in your life.

Your name is, and always has been Astrophel - the star-lover. Your parents were called Auden and Jessica Everston. They are now dead. They were not dead when Mary and I took you in. That was the first of many deceptions.

You had a brother. His name was Jericho. I believe him to be dead. He is the reason I took you in; took you away from the Everstons.

My love, you were 14 years old when Mary and I took you away from London and brought you here. We lived for many, many years as a happy family. We shielded you as much as possible from the illness that took Mary - the worst year of my life, and yet you remember absolutely nothing of it. The pain of loss was one I was becoming well-versed in already, because of you.

We took you away in 1994. It's now 2013. When you look in the mirror you see the same 14-year-old girl who hid in the back of my van with Mary as we drove for five and a half terrifying hours down to the cottage in Devon we had been renovating for our retirement. The cottage you have called home now for nearly 19 years.

None of this makes sense, I know. I wish now, as I hear myself say these words, that I had told them to your face, that I could have helped you understand and that I could have held you and comforted you as we smashed down the walls of the cage that has held you captive for too long.

There is a microchip in your head. On the anniversary of the day we took you, every year for the last 19 years, it has been resetting your memories so that you forget almost everything that has happened. And every year Mary and I, and now just me, we have had to start almost from scratch and find a way of explaining to you why you have woken up in a room you don't recognise, with people you don't know, in a place you have never visited.

Some years are harder than others. Some years it seems like bits of memory escape the purge. But in truth, each year I have felt the loss of my dear Astrophel, only to have to find the energy to go and find her again. And now it seems it is I who am lost, and I can but hope that you will be able to find yourself and hopefully somehow, hold on to a little bit of the life we built with you.

Last year Auden Everston died. Within weeks of this the chip in your head stopped receiving transmissions. I know this because I have a neural enhancement scanner that a friend of mine brought years ago when neural implants became fashionable but were still temperamental. I've scanned you every night for the last 18 years and it had transmitted a steady signal until a few weeks ago.

I understood what the chip did, but I never really understood why they did this to you; after everything else, it seemed cruel. But I'm just a gardener Astrophel. A retired one at that. When the signal stopped I figured that we'd either be free, or we'd be in more danger than ever. I honestly didn't know what to expect.

I still talk to Mary, all these years later. I know she would have told me to buck up and prepare for what was coming. We both knew that it would all come out in the end. I just wished we had found out more than we did.

So here it is kid. Everything I know. The truth, the lies, the dead-ends and the unanswered questions.

In a few weeks it will be what we came to call your birthday - the day we took you. The day they reset you every year. The day we never got to celebrate once in 18 years. Well, this time there won't be a reset, but I don't think that I'll be around to see it. I'm dying my little star-lover. And every last ounce of energy I have is going to go into ensuring you have everything you need to find out who you are and what happened to your brother.

I fear I now know what André Malraux meant when he said that a "man is not what he thinks he is, he is what he hides." The weight of this secret has held me down my love. I want the truth of it to set you free.

I loved you. We both did. I'm sorry that we didn't do more. I wonder if every parent doesn't have the same thought in the end; did I do enough? Are they ready for the world? I know that you will be Astrophel. You are a wonder. You filled our lives with love.

9

ASTROPHEL

Dan left the tapes wrapped up, along with a load of notes, newspaper clippings and photographs, looking to all the world like a birthday present. He then checked himself into a hospice and died.

Listening to his voice on that first tape broke my heart. The life of a quasi-14-year-old-girl is built upon the markedly unsteady foundations of figuring out who you are and attempting to be ok with the innumerable failings and flaws you find. That first tape smashed the picture I had carefully been curating. It was a tsunami sent to flatten a sandcastle and I was dragged out to sea to flounder for the grains of sand that still held truth whilst trying not to drown.

It may surprise you that I didn't immediately sit down in front of Dan's ancient stereo system, complete with CD, vinyl and cassette-playing facilities, don his enormous over-ear headphones and listen to every single second of those tapes.

The first recording certainly shocked me; it slowed me down, left me feeling a strange cocktail of numb, hyper-sensitive panic, but the words written down seemed somehow easier to deal with. They seemed less personal, less likely to plunge a dagger into my heart, less likely to confuse the living-shit out of me, the way his voice did.

Nothing seemed connected at first. There were lists, names, places, things crossed out, things highlighted, things highlighted and crossed out. Handwritten notes. Typed notes. Always on a typewriter though. Dan was a lot of wonderful things, but he was also intensely paranoid about surveillance. He wasn't anti-tech as such, but the one computer we had bounced off several VPNs and used a browser which promised to make you a ghost online. He never typed anything that saved to a machine.

It explains the tapes I guess.

Old school. And untraceable.

There was an obituary for my birth father. This Auden Everston. Auden Albert Spenser Everston - I suppose that helps me understand where the hell 'Astrophel' comes from! I wasn't ready to read any more than his name and to confirm that he was indeed dead. 1942-2012. A solid, but far from spectacular effort.

Instead, I was drawn to something which seemed so utterly out of place. An A4 binder filled with neatly curated, hole-punched pages that were a printout of a blogpost and all of its comments. The original post was made in 1999, but comments had kept the thread alive for nearly 20 years.

The story had nothing to do with me, my family, Dan or Mary, and yet the furious scribbles, arrows, and annotations told me that this story meant something. I just had to figure out what.

10

THE ANONYMOUS ANGEL

Blog Post: The Anonymous Angel
Date: 16th June 1999
Author: Ivan Washington

I wanted to find some way to share my story with someone. I wrote to the newspapers and they laughed at me. I told a friend and they told me I needed a holiday. I speak the words out loud and I know how foolish they sound, but I believe that I met an angel. I believe I met an angel and they saved my life. I believe that I met an angel and they healed me.

I know that this sounds crazy. I'm not a person who takes liberties with the truth. I believe in truth and facts. If someone else was writing these words and I was reading them, I would think they were crazy, only I'm not crazy. Of course, that is exactly what someone who is crazy would say.

All I know is that I believe I met an angel. In the most unexpected of places, in the most unlikely form, at a time where I had no reason to hope for a miracle. And that is what I got. A miracle. An old-fashioned, inexplicable miracle on a biblical level. And I don't even believe in those things.

I post this here because I needed to share these words, not because I expect a response of any sort, other than agreement that I am probably some crackpot lunatic with an internet connection, proving to the world why the world wide web was such a bad idea.

Only I'm not that. I promise.

I met an angel. He spoke with me. He touched me. And I was saved.

11

DAPHNE

It took Teddy a while longer to realise that he was in love with me, but he got there in the end. We made a great team, in every sense of the word. Once we understood each other, the job became easier. I learnt when I could take the lead and when Teddy would be more effective. He understood when to take on driving duty and let me run into a tricky situation and when that was only going to mean requiring an extra ambulance for me (which to be fair to me, only happened twice!).

After that night with the croup-boy, we grabbed some chips from a late-night food truck and we talked. It wasn't 'the talk'; I didn't tell him about my family, or my dreams, or the fungal toenail I'd been trying to self-treat for 18 months, but it was honest and real. I told him that he made me nervous, and he apologised for coming across as a bit of a dick. He told me that he really loved this job and he got frustrated when he didn't think his partners took it as seriously as he did.

He told me years later that he actually got a written warning from the station chief for the way he reprimanded the mother of croup-boy after I'd left. If he hadn't told me this on the night he proposed, I think I might have got down on one knee myself!

I know that people often think it's crazy that we live and work together. They say to me 'don't you need a break from him?' Or 'what do you talk about?' But it isn't really like they imagine. I think they reckon we sit about in an ambulance most of the day chatting and drinking coffee out of a thermos, occasionally turning on the sirens to go and shock someone back to life or cut someone out of a mangled car, only to then return to our still-warm coffee.

It definitely is not like that. Even on a slow day - of which there were around about zero in the 35 years or so I did the job. We get called out for all sorts. It's not like they make it seem on TV - you spend a load of time going to calls that turn out to be a complete waste of time: a heavy nosebleed, some moron who took too much Viagra medication and is freaking out; we've been asked to deliver puppies because the vet was closed; some absolute pig of a man demanded that we go and pick up his kid from a disco because he couldn't find his car keys. We had one quite early on where this guy had called in, saying that he was having breathing difficulty (always a bit of a red flag, as you can imagine); when we got to him it turned out that he was trying on some weird homemade leather mask to 'impress a friend' that was coming over later, but he hadn't cut the nose holes in the right place. When we arrived, he'd got straws poking out of this mask at a funny angle, so that he could breathe through them! He looked like a mouse from a Tim Burton horror story!

The time-wasters really are awful. They made Teddy so angry. He must've nearly lost his job a dozen times for going ape-shit with these people. But in truth, I didn't always mind them. In some ways they were better than the serious callouts. At least the ones where you lose people. The times where it's 50:50 and you know that on another day, maybe if it hadn't been raining, or if you'd had another hour of sleep, or you didn't have a headache, or the traffic lights had been more green than red so that you could weave through the cars quicker, that you might have saved a life - those cases were the worst. They left me feeling sick in my stomach. They're the ones you don't forget.

You see some really shitty things too. People dying, people who have been hurt on purpose, freak accidents that will change the person's life forever. Teddy said that I was a 'trauma magnet' because we seemed to get way more of the dangerous jobs than the other crews, but I don't think that this was true. I think he told me that to help me understand that it was okay to find it hard, because it was hard.

The victories keep you going. The babies you deliver, the lives you save; they make it all worthwhile.

Anyway, so when people asked how we coped with living and working together I tell them: at work Teddy is the other half of our ambulance crew - we talk about the job and not a lot else most of the day. When we go home there's no 'how was your day?' crap. We know what happened; we know if we need to talk about it, and if we don't, we can carry on safe in the knowledge that we've banked what happened and can come back to it if we need to. So when we're at home, we're at peace, away from the job for a little while.

You don't need to take the job home.

But sometimes it follows you. And when that happens, you don't have a choice.

12

JOSÉ

It's difficult to ask someone to look back objectively on their life and ask if they were a good person. I don't think we much enjoy seeing the moments where we did bad or shameful things, when there were other choices we might've made. But I am not too proud to do this. I came from a sad home, often filled with people who were not good. I learnt to defend Mamá from her own bad choices when I had to, and she came to rely on this far too much, making worse and worse decisions until I felt like I went from being a doorman at a nightclub to a personal bodyguard the rest of the time.

Kevin Costner made it seem way more glamorous than the reality. I remember watching that film with some chica whose name I can no longer remember and whose face mostly looks like Whitney Houston, thinking that it looked amazing. It was just a short hop from the security work I was doing at that point; I knew guys who had made the jump that weren't ex-military. And then I thought of Mamá - she was no Whitney, but she needed me; I couldn't go and be some live-in lifesaver when she was so desperately...desperate.

Anyway, I've jumped ahead. Sorry.

What I wanted to say was that John, the guy whose nose I broke, he never came back to the bar again. His mum wouldn't let him - Phil told me she said he was ugly enough as it was and getting a wife was hard work and he wasn't exactly going to be able to win someone over with his brains or personality. So that was that; once his nose recovered John's mum enrolled him in hairdresser college. I let him cut my hair once. I guess I was trying to apologise. He deliberately buggered it up - basically looked like a sodding bowl cut. Still, it grew out and his nose still looks as crooked as a dog's hind leg, so I let him have that one.

I have learnt the art of forgiveness. I just apply it selectively sometimes.

Phil recovered pretty quickly from the accidental beating I gave him and we ended up working the door of *Lucky 13*, the hell-hole of a bar, in a dark alley between Soho and Chinatown, I had been frequenting far too often. As I said, Phil became a mate. In fact, he became a brother really. He was about 10 years older than me. He'd made a lot of the mistakes I was making and for whatever reason, he wanted to try and help me.

He saw that I was angry and he helped me channel that. We signed up to this mental martial arts place in Chinatown run by a guy who claimed to be a Shaolin monk. The guy was nuts and Phil gave up after a couple of months, but I stuck with it. I don't know why; I told myself it was bullshit, but I also kept going back anyway.

I pretty much had an asthma attack after every session, but it felt good to be in control. In the end though, the dude running the place turned out not to be a Mr Miyagi type - he got busted for threatening some of the other local business owners and demanding protection money. And I was no Daniel LaRusso. I'd seen enough of the world to know that learning how to kick like a crane wasn't going to be enough and I needed someone to show me what that was. Phil was helping, but he was a cheerleader - I needed a Sherpa.

So I stopped trying to be the Karate Kid and thought I'd give Rocky Balboa a go instead.

13

MIA

(RECORDED IN 2004, 10 YEARS AFTER THE INCIDENT)

Did you know that the Ancient Egyptians believed your heart would determine your fate in the afterlife? They thought that when you died your soul would wake up and be led by the god Anubis to the Hall of Truth. When you were there, Anubis would weigh your heart on golden scales in front of Osiris. On one side of the scales was your heart, on the other side, a white feather belonging to the god Ma'at. If your heart was lighter than the feather, you would be allowed to proceed to the Field of Reeds, their version of Heaven. If it was heavier, the heart was thrown to Amut the gobbler - a crocodile-headed god that ate your heart. When the heart was gone, your soul simply ceased to exist.

It's a beautiful, frightening story.

I have spent many nights unable to sleep, wondering if Amut would eat my heart; wondering if ceasing to exist would hurt; wondering which of my hearts they would put upon the scales.

I think that soon, I will find out the answer.

That sounds morbid. Sorry.

I have just spent a really long time thinking about these

things. I was born with a ventricular septal defect - a hole in my heart. It was picked up quite quickly I believe and wasn't thought to be a massive problem as I didn't seem unwell. I lived a pretty normal life. I was a happy kid. I loved my home. I loved school. I LOVED science. OK, maybe not that normal then, but it was a good life.

And then I got sick.

14

JACK

Dear Mum,

For so long I have wanted to undo the disappointment that I know you felt every time you looked at me. Dad could barely bring himself to be in the same room as me and I was made to feel ashamed of a failure that wasn't even real. At least not in the beginning.

It was easy enough to create the lie - nobody in their right mind would think that a kid with a tremor in their hands could become a doctor anyway. So when it looked like I dropped out of medical school I simply managed to prove you all right. But it wasn't true. At least not in the way that it seemed.

I was a really good student Mum; I could have been a great doctor. But yes, the tremor got in the way a bit when it came to the practical stuff. I suppose it was a good job we were slicing up cadavers in those first couple of years! I would have made a real mess! I actually chopped a guy's ear off once; I was aiming for his chest, but I just couldn't calm myself down enough. It might have been almost amusing, but it fell on my partner's shoe and he started to freak out and then vomited. That set off a bit of a chain reaction and in the end they had to cut the session short because the room stank so much!

Anyway Mum, what I'm trying to say, is that I didn't drop out. I was chosen to do something else. And for a while it was awesome! This guy approached me one evening in the Student Union bar. He was very handsome. Clearly older than me. And not drunk. Therefore he had 3 advantages over me before the conversation even began.

He told me that he had been speaking to some of my supervisors and apparently I had been scoring extremely highly in all of my exams. This was true. And I was flattered to hear this beautiful man tell me I was brilliant. *But,* he said, *I gather that surgery is not going so well?* I stood there, dumb, embarrassed and frankly a bit pissed off. I thought this guy had maybe seen me around campus and taken an interest in me. But now I just felt like a loser. *I can help with that,* he whispered in my ear. And from then on, I was goddamn putty in his hands. But his hands were being held by someone far scarier, and that made me something even worse. But by the time I figured that out, I was already well and truly screwed.

This isn't sounding great. This isn't how I wanted to tell you what happened. It's why I never did. Every time I try to tell it, it comes out wrong. But enough time has gone by now. I am as free as I will ever be to tell you who I am.

I miss you Mum. I really do.

I was 34 yesterday. I had a little party out on the beach. It was great; chilled; happy. But I missed you, and even Dad. I wanted you to be there. But I know that it's probably too late for that now.

I'm sorry.

I'll try again another time.

J

15

EVIE

(ON BEHALF OF HARVEY HAWKINS)

If you spend enough time with someone, you begin to know them in ways that you can't quite describe. He was never much of a talker; he said I did enough of that for the both of us, but I knew what was on his mind. We didn't need to always be sitting, chatting and the like for me to see when he was happy and when he was hurting. He was a steady man I suppose, so maybe there wasn't much to decipher sometimes, but I could see how much he loved our girls and that meant more than words.

The night that our Bessie fell asleep at just over four months old and decided to go to heaven, rather than wake up, well it nearly destroyed him. I was heartbroken of course, but Harvey was torn up in a different way. He blamed himself for it, without ever knowing what he might have done wrong. He was the one to put her down that night and so he held it in his heart, like a tumour that festered and grew black, that he was the reason Bessie went away. *Cot death*, the coroner said. There's no comfort or answers to be found in that.

When Wendy came along a few years later, he didn't barely want to touch her for the first couple of years. Anyone watching would've said he was a cold father, but I knew. I knew that he was terrified of losing her. Once she was big enough to trot after him, well it was like years fell off of him and them two were like peas in a pod. They'd go digging and planting goodness knows what down at the allotment, for hours on end. When they came home they were both covered in mud, giggling like a couple of silly old maids. I did so love seeing them coming down the road with the sun setting behind them; I used to think that that was Bessie watching over them both, warming them and loving them from afar. My three angels I would think. I remember running out of the house one day with Harvey's new camera so that I could catch the three of them. I don't think I took one other photo in all my life, but that was the one that was by my bed, always. And that was the one that I had copied and put in with Harvey when we buried him. It's still by my bedside. And now I just long to join them. I see myself running out of that house, which doesn't exist no more, and I will run towards them and scoop them up and when I look up at the setting sun, Bessie will be there and she'll fly down with her little angel wings to let me hold her and we will be the family we was always meant to be. And that will be forever.

I wondered for a long while what was keeping me rooted here and then you called. I suppose this is the thing Harvey needed me to tell before I went.

16

DAPHNE

You get a lot of 'frequent flyers' in this job; that's people who call out an ambulance on a regular basis. You don't get blacklisted unless you're taken to court and even then you'd need to be calling out maybe a couple of times a week for a year. But there are certainly people you get to know at the slightly less extreme end of the spectrum - usually people who are really lonely and vulnerable. It's tough to weigh up the cost of a call-out against the fact that you might be the only contact these people have in a week, and yes, you are not in the job to help an old guy find his cat (who by the way, deliberately put it in its carry cage under a blanket in the garage), but you are there to save lives, and maybe that's what you've done by responding. Maybe not. I don't know.

Some of those frequent flyers are less straight-forward. Sometimes they're people troubled by violence or danger and they really do need help - it's just not always the sort that we can offer.

A LocMatch on a call-out is short for 'location match' which is a place identified as having a history, often where the police need to arrive in advance of an ambulance crew. When you've been working an area a while you get to know these without the call-handler telling you and you make the necessary adjustments.

Teddy and I, having been married a few years, decided that we wanted a change of scenery. We moved all the way from Shoreditch to Southwark; about a 15-minute tube ride, but crucially, we were now south of the River Thames - how fancy were we!

We started working out of Waterloo Ambulance Station, serving a new area, new hospitals and new people. It felt like a real adventure. And we were loving it.

Until we weren't.

It's not ideal for a new crew to be receiving jobs from a new call handler - neither know the area quite as well as they'd like and this is how mistakes happen.

Teddy and I were sent to a job in a block of luxury apartments near Elephant and Castle. Apparently it was a minor assault and the tenant had possible concussion, and might need observation in hospital.

Nothing out of the ordinary. Unless you knew it was a LocMatch. Which we didn't.

We arrived and were buzzed into the building. Just as we were waiting for the lift up to the 15th floor, Teddy grabbed at his stomach. He had a look on his face which I understood to mean that he was going to need to find a bathroom, fast. I held back the urge to tell him that I had warned him that a prawn cocktail sandwich left over the heating vent all afternoon was asking for trouble, but instead I nobly pointed out that there was a public toilet over the road.

'Wait for me?' He whispered. Not daring to speak too loud in case it invited a bowel movement he couldn't control.

'I'll be fine, Ted. Think I can handle a posh geezer with a bump on his head.' He ran off, unable to argue.

He never ate prawns again for the rest of his life.
He never forgave himself for the rest of his life.

17

JOSÉ

The one thing Phil gave me that no one else could, was purpose. He knew what it was like to grow up in a home like mine, because that was his life too. But he was not going to be defined by it. And yet when it came to it, I got to be Julia Roberts in Pretty Woman and he was the friend whose name nobody remembers, stuck turning tricks for scumbags and no money.

Forgiving other people, it turns out, is easy; forgiving yourself for the sacrifices other people make on your behalf - that is hard.

He helped me do things by the book - we both registered officially with Westminster Council to be 'proper' doormen with a license and everything. All the while I was boxing and beginning to get good. The problem was, if I didn't win fast, my lungs gave out and I would get knocked down, not by my opponent, but by my god-damn asthma. I wasn't going to make it to heavyweight champion of the world after all, but it made me strong and it was all part of Phil's plan for me.

I didn't have much education and to be honest, I didn't want to learn. But I had guts. I was happy enough to get in a ring with anyone twice my size; a Friday night outside of *Lucky 13* was more of a challenge. So I worked at being strong in body and mind. I wasn't afraid of anything or anyone, even if I did have to carry an inhaler in my pocket the whole time.

Phil was at every fight. He was my biggest (and only) supporter. He had a wife and kids at home, but he left them behind to come out and support me. Not because he didn't care - I don't think I know many guys that gush as much about their kids as he does. He did it to try and help me. He knew that I was six inches from the gutter and he was trying to help me roll away.

The thing I never understood about Phil was that he was happy. He was happy being a doorman in the evening and a postman three days a week. He didn't want more. He didn't need more.

I always wanted more.

But then 'more' came along and I did not like that much either!

18

MIA

(RECORDED IN 2004, 10 YEARS AFTER THE INCIDENT)

The human heart is a little larger than an adult fist. If you live a decent life, it will beat more than 2.5 billion times. I shouldn't think I'll reach that number.

But that's ok.

I've done enough.

Too much maybe. Maybe. I look back and I think of the chain reaction I caused and I wonder - was it good? Was it worth it?

I just don't know.

I worked so, so hard as a kid. I was obsessed with science. I loved everything about it. I wanted to be a scientist before I even understood what that meant. I wanted to build things, to help people, to solve problems, to travel to the moon, to visit the bottom of the ocean, to cure cancer, to cure balding (probably a little motivated by my dad's receding hairline), study bacteria, study animals, cure sadness.

I wanted to do it all. And if I'd had more time, or made different choices, maybe I would've. But as I said, I worked my socks off and I did well. I graduated university early and I was ready to get a job in a lab, to begin my journey.

But that was when my heart broke. Literally.

I developed something called Eisenmenger Syndrome. It basically means that my blood wasn't flowing the right way because of the hole in my heart, which isn't great, but this got a bit worse and caused pulmonary hypertension and that left me in trouble; they found this out pretty late and I was on the cusp of the blood beginning to shunt in the opposite direction - also not great. Actually, pretty catastrophic - if it gets to that point, you're looking at a heart and maybe lung transplant and the survival rates for those are things they keep well out of a patient's eye-line when they sit you down and have these sorts of conversation.

I was literally lined-up and ready for the interview of my life, working in a lab for this up-and-coming cardiologist (of course I was going to work with hearts; it fed my own sick and twisted sense of irony, that I might help others fix their hearts whilst mine floundered) — she was the youngest deputy-chair of cardiac surgery that Imperial College London had ever had. And she had a reputation as being a complete ball-breaker, which I loved. But instead of going for the interview, I had to call her office and explain that my own stupid heart was falling apart and so I wouldn't be able to attend.

Ten minutes later she calls me back. Jessica Dryden called me personally! I think I felt like the girls at school when they started being all high-pitched and excited about David Cassidy, or Donny Osmond, or the guy in the leather jacket in Happy Days. I was slightly hysterical to be honest. This woman had already achieved almost everything I had dreamt of doing and she was only eight years older than me!

'Mia,' she says, using my first name! 'My secretary just explained your situation.'

Normally a sentence like this, with news like mine and knowledge like hers, would be followed by something like:

'I'm so sorry.' Or she could legitimately say: 'I wish there was something that we could do, but...'

Instead, she said: 'I think it was destiny that you called up today with this remarkable news.'

Remarkable was not a word I had considered for my entirely life-threatening condition, but she was excited, so I didn't interject. After all, in case I hadn't mentioned, this was Jessica Dryden!

'Mia, I have just finished a telephone call with a most extraordinary gentleman working in the field of robotics. His work is very secretive, but he sought me out because of the research I do and we have now, for over a month, been exchanging phone calls. In each call we have a theoretical conversation about the role that robotics might play in cardiology in the years ahead. We discussed wonderful things - things that even someone as brilliant as you, might not have considered.

'It was all rather charming, but to be honest I'm not sure why I indulged such fanciful behaviour and from a man who would rather work with machines than people! But today I understand why I did that. Today, I understand that there is such a thing as fate. Because today Mia, is the day that this gentleman says to me, 'everything we have spoken of is not conjecture, is not fantasy, it is now; in fact for me, it is already yesterday, for today, I can do things that I have not even dared speak of.' And so I demanded everything of him and he told me that he has built robots that can rebuild parts of damaged hearts, from inside a person! That he has machines which will give life to those who have lost all hope and that he wants me to be his partner in this great adventure. 'Today,' he tells me, 'is the day that will mark the start of a new hope for those who were hopeless.' And as we talked and talked Mia, as he painted pictures of what he can do, I imagined in my mind, your heart, exactly as you have explained it. I imagined a heart just like yours and I imagined how I might now save it, when yesterday I might have lost it.'

I was silent. The ability to speak had left me. What this woman, this hero of mine was saying, was madness. It was deranged, or cruel, or both and yet my damaged heart raced and I knew it was not because of the effort it was making to pump blood around my thickened, stiff arteries, it was because, inexplicably, I believed her.

And because of this, I agreed to meet her, and because of this, she agreed to meet the charming gentleman on the other end of the phone. And because of this, Jessica Dryden met Auden Everston. And because of this...because of this, I do not sleep anymore.

19

JACK

Dear Mum,

Leaving you was hard, leaving Dad, less so. But it was necessary. I tried telling Billy so many times and then finally I did tell Billy. I told him everything I'm going to tell you, and he left. He told me that I was disgusting. He told me that I was a walking lie. He told me that I deserved to die alone. I could not have agreed more.

I wonder if he ever came over again after I left? Of course he didn't. Why would he? Dad never made him feel welcome. He was just another example of my failure to be the right son. The son he wanted. Someone he could tell his golf buddies that he was proud of. But what was there to be proud of? He ended up with a son who was a med-school dropout and a crippled queer to boot. What larks he must have had telling that story!

Well, the truth is worse, I suppose. Billy thought so and Billy was never wrong. But I wronged him. And you. And others.

This dude who started talking to me that night in the student bar, told me to call his office in the morning if I was interested in accelerating my career. He said that this was an opportunity unlike any other I would ever get. He was very persuasive. And did I mention how handsome he was? So, I called his office and a fancy-sounding secretary put me through to the Head of Research & Development at EverTech. The flattery continued, but this time it was interwoven with wild promises of fame and glory.

I admit that I have always be a vain son-of-a-bitch, but as I have thought about that conversation over the years, I genuinely wonder if he was some kind of psychic; I felt like he was a siren and I was a Grecian sailor being lured onto the rocks. Everything he said was pitch-perfect; tailored to my exact needs. I felt enslaved by the promise of hope that he offered and my god, every damn thing he said was the truth. The problem with the truth of course, is that it's all about perspective.

I was a dumb kid with a crush, being seduced into a world that was going to devour me as if I were an hors d'oeuvre at a burger-eating contest. I knew then that something wasn't right. I was not worth the fuss that was being made, but when you're young and destiny appears to come knocking at the door, why the hell would you turn him away? Especially if he's wearing an Armani suit!

So, I dropped out of medical school and that was more or less all I was allowed to tell you. But every day, instead of trotting off to HMV on Oxford Street (I still can't quite believe that this is the job you thought I'd settled on by the way!), I was heading south of the river to the EverTech offices. They were nothing like you'd imagine for a high-end, highly secretive technology company. I think the building used to be a school. It was red brick, big white surrounds on the corners and windows. It was classic. And it was the perfect disguise for what went on inside, far, far below the surface, away from prying eyes and inspection.

Day 1, I was taken by my charming seducer to meet Auden Everston. This guy is an insane tech genius. There's literally no one like him on the planet. He is without a doubt the smartest guy I have ever met; you know that you will only ever be able to cower in his intellectual shadow within about five seconds of meeting him. That is why you do what he tells you to do. That is why I did what he told me to do.

That, and the fact that the very first thing he said to me was not 'Hello' or 'Welcome to EverTech' or anything so banal and mundane. He said *I am going to make you the greatest neurosurgeon who has ever walked upon this planet. And I am going to start that process by curing you of that ridiculous tremor.*

I didn't know if I should be excited or scared shitless.

I was both of course. And that was the entirely appropriate response.

I'm not quite up to telling the next part yet. It's not going to be easy to read and I am not sure that I will be able to find the words to make you understand.

I love you. I know that's not enough. I know you need answers. But at least it is true.

J

20

EVIE

(ON BEHALF OF HARVEY HAWKINS)

He knew about you. He didn't know where you were, but he believed that one day there'd be someone who came asking questions and that they would be good. They would be looking for the truth. He always said to me that there are two types of people that work a case - those that want answers and those that want the truth. He said the people that want answers always think they're the same thing, but those are the people most likely to be deceived. The truth, he said, wanted to be found, but there are often many other things that will work against you to ensure that doesn't happen. Sometimes on purpose, sometimes by mistake. And even after nearly 50 years of working cases, he still believed that the truth would win in the end. Maybe he was right. But the tough thing about the truth is that it isn't always the thing you want to know, nor the thing you would like it to be.

I don't know you. But I know that you were important to my Harvey. You're the missing person - the piece of the puzzle that he simply could not or would not find. You think that I will have answers for you, but the truth is that you are the answer I've been waiting for. I can tell you the things Harvey wanted you to know, then maybe you'll tell me the bits I don't know and when I go and meet Harvey, I can tell him how close he was. I can tell him that it was ok in the end because it all worked out.

He died because of you.

I'm not telling you that to make you feel badly about anything. I'm telling you that so that you know he was on your side. He knew that he should have given up the case and retired. Everyone told him that it was a dead end. Everyone knew that there was an iron wall, 100 feet tall, surrounding the answers he wanted and that he was never going to find a way in. But he didn't care. He wanted the truth. He was a stubborn old fool like that.

I'd seen him with the bit between his teeth before, but this was different. Maybe it was because it involved children. Maybe it was because he could smell the corruption. He knew someone was lying. He hated that. He was so kind, but he was naive. He thought that the world should think like he did - that there was good and bad and that good was good and bad was bad and bad should be stopped. But it isn't like that, is it? There's a lot of things in the middle and at the edges. Things that don't make sense. Things that seem bad, but might be good, and things that seem good, but turn out to be bad, and then all the other stuff that doesn't make any sense at all.

He didn't want to know about that. He wanted to fix things. He spent his whole life trying to fix things. He spent his whole life trying to fix things because Bessie died for no good reason and that was unacceptable to him.

For a long time after he died I was so angry. Bessie died because that's what the world decided. Harvey died because he was too pig-headed to leave things alone. He wanted justice for you, or the boy in that car. He didn't even know you, but in the end I suspect you were the last thing he thought about; not me, not Wendy, not even Bessie. You. Your life, he said, was hidden behind a secret that was not his to reveal. He was overwhelmed by the tragedy he foresaw in your life; it consumed him, for years. Eventually those bastards at EverTech realised he was getting close to finding something important out and that is when my Harvey gets sick. Never been sick a day in his life, but just as he says to me that he thinks he's close to finding the truth, he gets sick and within a week, he's dead. And I'm alone, waiting for someone to explain to me why my husband refused to take retirement to pursue a case that he knew would end this way.

Now you're here asking questions and I have to live out the worst few years of my life all over again.

21

DAPHNE

Considering there had apparently been a disturbance, it was weirdly quiet. I guess that's the beauty of having money, I thought to myself; you can afford to argue more quietly. I knocked on the door and was immediately greeted by a man in his late 40s wearing a nice pair of pyjamas and a dressing gown. He was holding a bag of frozen peas on the back of his head.

He welcomed me in to a dimly lit, modern space. It was sparsely furnished with marble-looking floors. There was a kitchenette to one side and a living room area with a seriously plush rug under a strange-looking coffee table which had a huge roaring tiger underneath it instead of legs. One wall was all glass and you could see far beyond the river. I reckon I could easily of spotted our old flat from that window.

I suppose it seems rather odd of me to recall all of these details. I certainly don't remember noticing them when I walked in that night. But I have been back to that place many, many times since, finding new things to see on each visit. I wonder how much of it I add in from my own fantasy of it. I know that tiger table was real. I'm not that creative!

Anyway, dressing-gown guy introduced himself as

Benjamin and I asked him to explain what had happened. He told me that it was all rather embarrassing; he had got into an argument with his lover. '*He* stormed out after a terrible argument and as he swung the door open to leave it hit me in the face and sent me falling backwards onto the floor. *He* didn't stop to see if I was ok.'

Benjamin emphasised the word 'he' both times he said it. He wanted me to know that his lover was another guy. He wanted me to be shocked by this. After all it was 1987; AIDS hysteria was reaching fever pitch, we were only a year away from Thatcher's Section 28 clause and the gay community were being attacked in the media and in real-life. Teddy and I saw this regularly. I'd lost count of the number of men we had stitched up following a 'gay-bashing'. If Benjamin wanted to shock someone, he'd chosen the wrong audience. I'd seen it all.

But that wasn't really what this was about.

I asked him to sit down so that I could take some obs. He was compliant at first. I checked his pupils, took his other readings. Everything seemed ok. I was about to tell him as such when he stood up quickly. 'I need you to take a look at something.' he said. He began to undo his dressing gown. *Not another flasher!* I remember thinking to myself.

He had turned his back to me, so I couldn't see what he was doing. His robe fell to the floor. I assumed the PJs were going to follow. I hoped Teddy was feeling better and that he would be on his way up. I figured I could take this guy down if I had to, but a witness would at least be helpful when it came to writing up the report later.

But Teddy wasn't on his way up yet. And Benjamin wasn't going to strip off any further.

'I don't have many visitors you know.' He said, still turned away from me.

I decided to pack my bag up as fast and quietly as possible so that I could get out. I felt a monologue coming on - we got these from time to time. I was beginning to realise that this might be a psych case that got mis-communicated. Not my forte and not something I should be dealing with alone.

'Especially not pretty company.' He continued. 'Too pretty really.'

He turned so fast, that at first I didn't see the huge knife in his hand. But as he swung it towards my face, I managed to roll backwards and out of his reach for a moment. My radio fell off of its clip and out of reach. If I wanted help, I needed that radio, but it now sat between no-dressing-gown-knife-guy and me. I heard Teddy quietly let me know that he was ok; in a little code we had invented for ourselves he let me know that he had managed not to shit his pants. I smiled. Why did we even have a code for that? Benjamin kicked the radio away.

He walked towards me.

'No need to make a fuss.' he said. 'Looks are a dangerous thing for a woman, don't you think? Much better to not give those nasty men something to look at.' He lunged at me again; I managed to put an armchair between us. But he wasn't done. He spun round and grabbed my hair as I was trying to move away.

I thought that he had wanted to cut my face, so instinctively I turned to face him and got as close as possible so that he couldn't get to it.

No-dressing-gown-knife-guy it turns out, was well known to the police and the ambulance service. He was indeed noted as a LocMatch and if the dispatcher hadn't taken the call whilst her mentor had been in the bathroom that night, we might have known what we were walking into.

He wasn't a gay man, he hadn't had an argument with a lover, he didn't have a particular issue with women, and his neighbours reported him to be a particularly pleasant and polite man. But he was in fact deeply troubled. He was also incredibly wealthy. So whatever he was or was not, was at least partially hidden by the amount of money he was able to throw at the problem. He might have had a personality disorder of some sort. I don't know. I don't care.

That's not true. I do care, but the specifics don't matter.

Well one specific did.

As I threw my face into his chest that night, he lowered the knife and aimed with full force at my stomach. The blade drove deep into my lower abdomen, down into my pelvis. For a moment I felt nothing. And then I felt fire, burning me from the inside out.

I saw everything as a series of vignettes as my blood left my body and I struggled to stay at one with the world.

Teddy came crashing into the apartment. He threw himself at no-dressing-gown-knife-guy. I don't know what he did to subdue him, but a moment later he was with me.

He was calling for support.

He held me.

He told me everything was going to be ok.

In return, I continued to bleed out on a very expensive and comfortable rug.

22

JOSÉ

For whatever reason, Saturday night was always more hectic than Friday. I think everyone's more happy, but more tired on a Friday. By the time you get to Saturday they've got more energy and that's when things can get messy. But to be honest, for a London bar, even in Soho, even in the early 90's, Lucky 13 was pretty chilled given what I'd heard from some of Phil's mates who worked at the bigger clubs or the new 'jungle' bars that were popping up everywhere. Lucky 13 was tame. I had been one of its most controversial punters! And I was a pussy cat really.

And then things changed.

We started getting a group of lads who came down all suited up in pinstripes and big jewellery, making too much noise and flashing too much cash. They wanted everyone to think they were gangsters. But they were just city boys who didn't have a clue. They reckon you start spending big money and smoke a cigar and you're the shit.

These guys came in every Saturday for a few weeks. They pissed off a lot of people and broke a few chairs, but they spent a lot of cash so the management tried not to mind too much.

Phil and I weren't stupid - we'd seen enough moron piss-heads to know when to watch from a distance rather than go in hard. There wasn't a lot of room to fight outside the bar, but that meant that if we were outnumbered, which we would have been, then things could get tricky.

They would always get a bit lairy at the end of the night and invariably one or both of us would have to politely ask them to leave. There was always plenty of chat, and one night the loudest, most obnoxious moron of the lot of them, walked up to me after I asked them to finish up and tapped my cheek a few times, as if to slap me very gently. 'Whatever you say sweetheart.' He said, looking round to his little crew for supportive laughter, which of course he got.

Six months ago, I would have punched him so hard in the face that I would have shed tears in a mixture of agony and ecstasy, but Phil had taught me a great deal about patience and self-preservation. So I let it go. For about 15 minutes.

Because a quarter of an hour later I stepped back outside to mind the front door having split up a couple of ladies who had inadvertently discovered they were seeing the same guy. Can you believe it, the guy had given one of them a pair of his tiger-print y-fronts as a souvenir and they fell out of her bag when she was getting out her fags. The other chica recognised them and all hell broke loose. Who fights over a guy who wears tiger-print pants! Anyway, I step outside and the wannabe gangster who had mock-slapped my face was getting way too friendly with one of our regulars who clearly was not interested.

Turns out slapping was his thing; when she tried to call out for help, he sent an absolute stinger across her face, and then another for good measure, with the back of his hand. She almost fell to the floor with the force.

Whatever patience Phil had taught me, ran out. I jogged over as quietly as I could, tapped the geezer on the shoulder and as he turned, did exactly what I should have done in the first place - I broke my hand on his face to ensure that he would not forget how rude he had just been. It was totally worth it.

In case you're keeping a tally, I have forgiven myself for this.

23

MIA

(RECORDED IN 2004, 10 YEARS AFTER THE INCIDENT)

It filled my father with joy when he saw me reading the great works of literature. He loved it most when I read Kafka; he identified with the confusion of Kafka being a German-speaking Jew living in Prague. My father wrote about identity more than anything else - he found me, his own daughter, a most fascinating subject - British-born daughter of a Catholic Czech (also from Prague) and an African-American Methodist, most definitely not from Prague. And despite my desire to spend as much time with numbers as possible, I did love to read, and I did so from my wonderfully eclectic heritage. But as is so often the case, my love of reading led me back to my love of science. And the book I read over and over again was actually a play - Karel Čapek's *Rossum's Universal Robots*. Čapek was the first human to use the word robot and all because when he was scrambling around for a name for his humanoid creations, his brother told him he should call them 'robota' which means 'forced worker'. It was the first time that robots were written about and immediately they are shown to overthrow humanity. At the end of the play, they are left to take over the world. Perhaps they would do a better job than us. A low benchmark perhaps?

So often literature predicts the future without intention. Čapek, like so many writers, knew how to look into the heart of mankind and pluck out the threads of truth that bond us all together. Those threads, once knitted tightly into yarn, create a great veil that dulls our brilliance; it is the veil of self-destruction.

Sorry. I got distracted.

I mentioned Čapek because he is who I thought of when I awoke from the secret surgery that made me part machine. I wondered if I would find that I had lost any part of myself or indeed that I had become something different, or new. The scientist in me knew that this was ridiculous, but the heart is more than just an organ; it is an icon of our humanity.

I felt underwhelmingly the same, only there was a kind of stillness within myself that I had not remembered, or had not known I was missing.

Between Mr Everston and Jessica, I had been given a life I had not expected to have. Everston had built a perfect, working replica of my heart made of titanium and silicone. This in itself was remarkable; that he would have the audacity to suggest that this would be a viable option for human transplant was practically obscene. That I said yes, well that I said yes, is almost embarrassing; I knew that it was science fiction - an artificial heart is the holy grail of cardiology. The hope was that they could be used as a bridging device whilst you awaited a heart transplant. You might live a few days if you were lucky. And here I was, with a heart that he told me would outlive the rest of me by a thousand years.

It was powered by my own body; *like hydropower, but with blood*, he said. I should have been on the cover of every medical journal in the world; I was a miracle; this was a feat decades ahead of its time. Everston and Jessica toasted me with champagne whilst I recovered in a hospital bed built especially for the surgery in Jessica's laboratory, rather than a hospital. But there were no news stories, no articles, awards, fanfare, nothing. This was a silent, secret victory. I was a secret. I was a secret who must remain silent. I was Frankenstein's monster, without the ability to run away.

I did not want to run away. I was in love with them both. They had given me life; they were my second parents. And they exploited my love for all it was worth.

What is worse, is that I begged them to do it.

24

JACK

Dear Mum,

I'm not going to mess around this time. I'm slightly pissed and to be honest that was the only way I was ever going to get these words down without spiralling out of control.

Not exactly setting a calming scene I guess. Sorry. I just really want someone who might forgive me to read these words. I reckon if Ralph could read he'd be my best shot. But you're next in line. You would be first, but to be honest I'm fucking terrified of what you're going to think. The dog has to love me - I feed him. You have to love me because you're my mum. But honestly, that might not be enough.

Day 2 at EverTech and I'm hauled in front of a panel of brilliant scientists. Three of them. They were tightly scripted, telling me a story that felt like it came out of a comic book, though they looked more like the Three Little Pigs than The League of Extraordinary Gentlemen. Between them they had mapped the brain with the kind of precision that was certainly beyond any textbook I had seen. But more than this, they had begun to understand how to manipulate it. They had built a microchip that when implanted directly into the brain, could send signals and commands, to work with, or even override it. This, they told me grandly, was how they would stop my tremor. And this was how they would make me great.

Eventually, they said, the microchip would be miniaturised to such a degree that it would be injected through the nasal cavity, where it would weave its way through the cribriform plate and lodge directly into the underside of the brain. But that tech was a little way off. So instead, they would drill a hole in my skull and lodge it in the old-fashioned way.

Yippee! I said, at no point whatsoever.

I told you I fell off my bike and hit my head on a jagged rock. You didn't ask questions. You just assumed I was an idiot for riding a bike at night. You were right at least, about being an idiot.

The surgery itself didn't scare me. The possibility of losing the tremor was a hell of a carrot to dangle in front of me, but I knew that if this worked I would be indebted. That worried me. What should have worried me more, was that an organisation who were clearly doing some seriously shady shit, was installing a tiny computer in my head which might do a lot more than stop my hand from shaking.

But I worried about that later. That was dumb.

When I woke up, they had called you and pretended to be the hospital looking after me. They told you that because of the surgery I couldn't have visitors; too great a risk of infection. By the time I came home I was scared, but my hand didn't shake anymore. Faking that it did, was one of the most perverse things I think I've ever done. But they told me that you could never know. They only told me that afterwards by the way. Would that have changed anything? I wish I could say that it would've.

That was the beginning. They had baited me, let me hook myself on and now I was ready to be fed to the sharks. But I loved every single second of it. Honestly. Apart from lying to you, I was making a stack of cash, my tremor was gone and now they were using electrical impulses from the chip to help me study and learn harder and better than I ever had before. They were feeding me information like it was candy and I was lapping it up. It wasn't until the day it all went too far that I understood who I was in this unfolding drama; I thought I was the hero in a real-life sci-fi, but in fact I was something far less profound; I was the prize-winning turkey in *A Christmas Carol*. Only I wasn't going to be fed to a starving family - there is at least some nobility in that - I was going to be dog food. Maybe I'm that talking horse in *Animal Farm*? He outlives his use and gets turned into glue. Maybe that's a better fit. Anyway, I'm not there yet. I'm still living inside the illusion at this point.

The Three Little Pigs take measurements and readings every day and every day they nod and smile quietly to each other. No wolf today. The house still stands. I try not to think about the fact that the house is my brain. I really hope they used bricks; there's no place for straw or sticks in this story.

For two years I felt invincible. I was a god. Untouchable. Brilliant. Evolving. In this tiny fragment of time, I had learnt to perform the kind of surgery that someone with 10 times the experience could only have dreamt of. I had access to equipment that didn't exist anywhere else in the world. What I didn't know; what I never remembered to ask, was why me? That was also dumb. There's a pattern emerging.

They liked to test me. They put hypothetical challenges in front of me all the time. What if...What if you're performing posterior loss decompression on a patient with undiagnosed osteogenesis imperfecta and the skull begins to shatter? What if a patient begins speaking in a language they have never studied during a craniotomy? What if you had performed encephalomyosynangiosis on a young patient presenting with Moyamoya disease only to find that you had caused brain compression?

I smashed these questions out of the park.

And then they asked me the questions they had been holding back.

What if we asked you to perform a brain transplant from a living donor to a recipient?

And the follow-up question, before there was an answer:

What if you were to do this in tandem with a cardiologist and transplant the brain and heart with spinal cord intact?

And one more for luck:

What if you were to perform this transplant from a living donor into a synthetic recipient; what would you require of the future host?

These were not normal questions. These were not medical questions. Not today. These were questions for Luigi Galvani, or gothic novel writers. Or maybe Isaac Asimov. He would've liked these questions I guess.

I did not like these questions.

I don't think there is any way in which I can tell you the next part of this story whereby you'll understand how I let it all happen. Why didn't I run away? Why didn't I report them? Why...why...why?

And I don't have an answer that is good enough. It wasn't good enough for Billy; it shouldn't be good enough for you.

I was scared. That's a bullshit answer. I was, but that isn't what kept me there.

I wasn't allowed to leave. Also a bullshit answer. I knew that I was being observed at all times. I had seen the same couple of guys walking not too subtly in the shadows wherever I went. And I knew that they weren't just bad at their job - I was supposed to see them. And I knew that the chip in my head could tell them everything they needed to know. I knew that if they wanted to, they could make me stay. They could make me hurt; it wouldn't take much to change up what the chip was meant to do.

But none of that was really stopping me. The truth is I stayed because I was curious. I wanted to know if this could be done. If I could do it. If I could build Frankenstein's monster for real. And save the world.

Yeah, they threw that into the mix too. *When you do this Jack, you will be starting something that will end up saving millions of lives. When you do this, no one will forget that it was Dr Jack Lewis who changed the course of human history.*

Ugh! It makes me sick thinking about how fucking gullible I was. I lapped it up. Jesus, Mum, I begged for it. I loved hearing it. Because them saying these things meant I could stay in their little bubble and that is what I so desperately wanted.

25

EVIE

(ON BEHALF OF HARVEY HAWKINS)

When something wonderful happens that we didn't foresee or plan and it endures, we call it destiny or fate. When something terrible happens and we can't see how it might have been avoided, we talk about being doomed. I don't really believe in either of those things, but Harvey did. He thought that it was fate that he should be working on the day my handbag was taken and that I would keep an out-of-date identity card in the zipper of the bag. I think I was just lazy or disorganised. He said that being assigned this case felt the same way. It was supposed to be some other chap, Sloane I think his name was, who should have taken the case, but he broke his leg real bad when a sewer cover gave way as he walked over it. Ain't never heard of such a thing happening to anyone, that's why he thought getting this case, and it being what it was, was some sort of miracle. He was a daft old sod really. You and your family brought him nothing but misery and worry and yet he was desperate to help you. And he didn't even know you.

He never met your brother either.

I did.

He is the reason I am speaking to you.

He is the reason I am still here on this earth.

He is the reason I know that I will see my Harvey again.

He is a miracle in a world where we no longer deserve such things. And only God could have created something that good.

I know that he was maybe not quite normal, not quite...as we are, when I met him. But that is not the measure of a person - what they're made of is of no consequence, of no importance to me. It's what is within them. What was there, that was always there.

Harvey was a good man, with a good heart. People don't seem to think that's important anymore. But it's the only thing that matters. He was never going to be a police commissioner or any such thing, but that wasn't who he was. He was kind and honest and gentle. That's what Jerry was too. You could see that the second you met him. He was alive with love; it didn't matter what else he was made of.

I met him after Harvey was gone.

26

DAPHNE

I was lucky to be alive by the time I got to the hospital. When I have occasionally put that thought into words over the years, Teddy huffs and says that it was obviously nothing to do with his excellent medical attention or extremely impressive driving which got us to A&E at St Thomas' at what must have been frightening speed.

Of course it was all because of him. He saved my life. But it doesn't do to let his head get too big.

But in saving a life, his was changed. Ours was changed.

I was out of action for a long time. There was some serious surgery to piece me back together. 'Penetrating pelvic injury' they said to start with - keep it technical, keep it vague. Then as I drifted in and out of consciousness I heard them say things like peritonitis, laparotomy, CT scan, punctured colon. None of it sounded great, but I woke up eventually. I was alive. And it hurt.

That was good. Apparently.

The doctors, some of whom had faces I recognised, looked dour as they began to explain the injuries. But they left the punchline until a few days later. Until they thought I would be strong enough to take it.

Pregnant.

But not anymore.

Probably not ever again.

Damaged ovary on one side, scarring on the fallopian tubes and possibly the uterus. Scarring everywhere.

We hadn't really been trying, but I had suspected that it might have happened. I had been going to take a test. No need now.

So there I was. In a hospital bed, as a patient. A victim of a brutal, pointless assault. A different future to the one I had planned in front of me. And all I could think about was Teddy.

He was crushed by what had happened. He couldn't look me in the eye. And he didn't yet know about the baby. I decided then that he did not need to know. What good could come of that? But the reality of not being able to have a family was this vast expanse between us and somehow we would have to find a way to cross it to find each other in a different place to the one we were now in.

I was 29 years old. I was lucky to be alive. I had a husband who loved me. A job that scared the shit out of me, but which was magic. I would recover. I would have a long life. I had friends who would fuss over me for as long as I needed them to.

I had never felt more alone.

27

JOSÉ

That night outside *Lucky 13* did something to me. Not only that night, but what happened afterwards too.

Ana-Maria, who was the regular (though I had not known her name until that night) had come back a few days later and left a message for me at the bar. I called her back a bit too quickly to be playing it cool and we met at a quiet bar well away from *Lucky 13*.

She had a really terrible black eye; she kept touching it and apologising for how she looked. I thought she was beautiful, but I didn't say anything - I don't know why. Why do we ever not do things we want to? I guess because I was scared.

She told me that the police weren't interested in what had happened. No evidence that it wasn't an accident. They had spoken with the 'gentleman' concerned - apparently he'd contacted them to report a drunk woman who had been verbally and physically abusive. Ana-Maria fit the description. He wasn't going to press charges! There was no mention of the bouncer who had lamped him.

After Ana-Maria left that evening I was angry. She was a good person. She was just about to open up a tiny tapas place in Borough Market. She was full of wonderful ideas and creativity. I could smell the empanadas as she spoke. She was intoxicating. And kind. And the world didn't seem to give a shit.

I was done working the door. I was done dealing with shit-heads like the fake gangster. I knew that much. But what I did next, I wasn't sure. I knew a few guys who were heading out to see action with the Army in Kuwait and Iraq. I would have joined them if I could. But I couldn't - I still ultimately had the lungs of a baby pig.

I wanted to fight and to serve; it seemed like the right combination for me. I wanted justice to be a thing that existed in the world. I wanted to help do that. I wasn't going to be the Karate Kid, I didn't think I could take the repeated blows to the head that Rocky did, I didn't have the resources to be Batman, but maybe Beverley Hills Cop?

I imagined a life where I could walk into Mamá's house wearing a uniform that meant something and force the low-life that was currently leeching off of us to get the hell away from her. I imagined a world where I would have the authority to help Ana-Maria prosecute the dill-hole who had tried to hurt her, or where I might use my connections to find my Papá, just so I could tell him that despite his failures, I had become something.

But before I got that far, a god-damn cat nearly killed me.

28

MIA

(RECORDED IN 2004, 10 YEARS AFTER THE INCIDENT)

Once I recovered, Jessica offered me the job I had been going to apply for. I jumped at the opportunity to remain near her.

As I became her new, clueless but adoring puppy, she was busy with Everston.

They had what can only be described as a whirlwind romance almost worthy of a cheap, celebrity magazine. They went to expensive restaurants, he flew her to beautiful places, they laughed and joked with interesting people and they thrived on the excitement and intensity of it, the way a parasite feasts from its host to become unstoppable.

They were married within a year. I was almost invited to the wedding, but instead I was promoted within the lab to a more senior role. They charged me with something they knew would keep me busy in ways that would nullify any threat I might pose.

Perhaps I overplay my own importance in all of this; perhaps they didn't even notice me. At least not at first. They wanted me near because I was an experiment that needed checking up on. But I also did good work. I'm not so humble not to know that I was running rings around most of the other researchers after six months. I was conducting work of real value and merit. I was useful and I had purpose. Jessica liked that. Everston was far away in his own lab. He did not validate me and I did not look for his validation.

Time passed. So quickly. My metal heart worked flawlessly. I was fitter and stronger than I had ever been. I could run and swim and dance. The scar on my chest was fading and one day I thought, I may just let somebody see it. And that would be a good day. I was ready to love someone other than my creators now. *I must learn to be more,* I told myself.

And then I did something that was so much more. So much more than anyone had thought possible.

Part of my work has involved bringing particularly complex or inexplicable cases, and by cases, I of course mean people, into the lab. This is pretty unusual, but often they don't question it for a moment, so desperate are they to find an answer to their problem. We had a room setup for this very thing; we made it look like whatever was going to be most comforting to the participant; a bedroom, a kitchen, even an office. Once we transformed it into a garden, complete with pond and working water-feature because the participant had managed to convince us that the sound of water was having a positive impact on her condition. It wasn't.

The room had one-way glass on one wall so that we could observe the participant without getting in their way; all they had to do was play make-believe and pretend there weren't half a dozen doctors and lab assistants on the other side of the oasis we created for them.

In this particular instance, the case was a young boy called Drew. He had a kind of arrhythmia which no one seemed able to explain. His heartbeat was irregular, sometimes too fast, sometimes too slow; sometimes he would blackout, at other times he was almost euphoric. He was only 8 years old and his mother was scared. Of course she was. She was on her own, having lost her husband in the Falkland Islands conflict, Drew was all she had left and now his heart was playing games that she did not understand.

We wanted to observe Drew in action to see what might be triggering this fluctuating heartbeat. He had told us that his bedroom was a safe place, so his bedroom is what we made. But of course, none of this feels very real if you're hooked up to a load of big machines with wires and monitors, so I have to hand it to Everston for yet another contribution to our cause; he had designed an ECG machine that was powered by batteries, meaning that Drew could be monitored doing his thing without any unpleasant distractions.

But Drew was so painfully shy. He was terrified by the whole thing and when he got into his bedroom he just sat on the bed, not moving. The idea was that he would play in the room for a little while and then we would attach the ECG electrodes once he was relaxed. But relaxed wasn't coming round the corner any time soon.

I was apparently the least threatening of the lab assistants, so was sent in to talk to him. Within 30 seconds he was crying. I don't think it was anything I said, in so much as all I managed to say was 'Hi!'

He managed to calm down a little and began asking for a biscuit. Like lightning, I ran from this rather uncomfortable situation to grab him a snack from the staff lounge. I rummaged around the biscuit tin, trying to feel for something that felt slightly less stale than the rest and returned to him holding a couple of slightly tragic-looking chocolate bourbons.

When I offered him one, he only cried more. 'Biscuit!' He kept calling out, 'Biscuit!'

I was not especially good with children and this moment was on track to set my ovaries back a good decade, so mortified by it was I, but then one of our technicians came in, looking equally awkward and whispered in my ear.

My face lit up. 'Biscuit is your dog!' I exclaimed.

Immediately he stopped crying; he looked at me with forlorn eyes (which I suspect he might have learned from the aforementioned Biscuit) and nodded, then waited expectantly, invisible tail wagging in hope.

'OK,' I said, 'I don't see why we can't have Biscuit come and say hello. 'Is he nearby?'

'Car.' He managed to say in-between snuffles.

A few minutes later Biscuit the dog is wheeled in and the boy smiles. There was hope! I explained that now it was time for us to stick some dots on to him so that we could watch what his heart was up to whilst he played.

More tears.

Then an idea hit me! 'Would it be ok if Biscuit played along too?' I asked Drew. I had piqued his interest. He didn't reply, but he was certainly willing to hear me out. 'What if we stick some dots to Biscuit and then you can both play?'

'OK!' He said, way more enthusiastically than I had expected.

And that is what we did. One boy and one dog hooked up to our portable ECGs. We were in business!

I just had to sit back and watch the monitor now; looking for signs as to why Drew's arrhythmia started and stopped so abruptly.

They say curiosity killed the cat don't they? Well, the same is not true for dogs don't worry - Biscuit survived his little experiment, but my curiosity...my curiosity will be the thing that I shall miss least when I am gone. But on this day, it led me to something unexpected, perhaps something that might have been harmless, something that I could have left out of my report even, and yet I knew that it wasn't any of those things. If nothing else, it was fascinating and that word is the very reason I had been so obsessed with science as a child. There were mysteries in their millions, staring us in the face every day and I had wanted to solve them. Only a curious mind can solve a great problem, because without that, you don't bother looking. Without a curious mind I wouldn't have turned on Biscuit's heart monitor readings. I wouldn't have thought to myself, *wouldn't it be interesting to compare them to Drew's.* And then I wouldn't have noticed that when they were interacting with each other, they became almost identical. When they were apart, they dropped out of sync.

I watched this happen two, three, then four times. Each time, the same result. Both hearts moderated their cadence and found a frequency that they could share. As I watched the readings line-up, I looked up at the monitor, which was giving me a live feed of what Drew was doing in his fake bedroom. I watched him as Biscuit walked over and nuzzled his head under Drew's arm, forcing the boy to hug him. Drew buried his face into Biscuit's fur and smiled in the way that you can't force because it comes from a secret, happy place that science can't explain, and I understood what I was watching - love.

29

JACK

Dear Mum,

I may have slightly thrown up on the final couple of pages of the last letter. I don't know why I'm telling you that. I don't know why I'm even writing to you. I'll never have the courage to post a single page to you. What would be the point? It would make you sad. It would pile fuel onto the bonfire of disapproval and disappointment.

Do you know why I called my dog Ralph? It was because when he was settling in on the first night I had him, he started barking and I swear, the longer it went on, the more it sounded nothing like 'woof' and an awful lot like he was saying 'Ralph'. Thinking about that as I couldn't get to sleep make me smile. And then I started laughing. It was a slightly crazed, sleep-deprived sort of laugh, but it was the first time I could remember laughing in a very long time. I tipped into crying, howling really. But just for a few moments, I felt normal and happy and free. In the morning I named him

Ralph and his bark still sounds like he's calling out his own name; now and again it still makes me smile.

EverTech wasn't a place where you could smile; there was no one to joke with. People only used your first name if they wanted something. When Auden Everston sat me down over a private lunch in his office, I was 'Jack'. When I heard him talking about me to the Three Little Pigs, I was, at best, 'Lewis', but mostly I was just 'him'.

That lunch was a messed-up affair. He was testing me the whole time; feeling me out, ensuring I was on message and up to the task. And I did a stand-up job of convincing him that I was.

The next day, everything stepped up a gear. I was taken to a new lab. It had been cleared of almost all furniture and fixtures. Greyness covered everything. There were no windows, one door, cameras in each of the four corners, mounted high, looking down, ensuring nothing would be missed.

In the middle of the room was a table with a pair of gloves and a black helmet of some sort. The Three Little Pigs told me that this was the most advanced virtual reality experience in the world. The gloves and helmet would work together to give me a completely realistic experience of the procedure I was being prepped for. No detail was too small; after a few minutes they promised I would barely know I was in a simulation.

And it was impressive. It felt very real. But there was one crucial difference - I wasn't essentially killing anyone in the simulation. As soon as I had that thought, I understood why this was the path they had chosen for my training - no cadavers; nothing that smelt in anyway like death. And no robots or machines to distract. This was the perfect combination of *real without consequence* and it built me up with each successful run until I really did think I could perform this procedure.

I never did the simulation with the cardiologist though. Another blatant tactical decision. If I couldn't discuss the ethical merits of what we were doing until there was a body in front of me, that would be better.

As I write this, I see how unbelievable it sounds. How could I be so calm about doing something so bizarre? I basically lived every day in a parallel universe where impossible, weird and crazy became normal. New inventions and developments which would have made any surgeon in the NHS hot under the collar, became almost mundane. Innovation was dull. It was genius really. We were numbed to the impact of progress. We were almost programmed to dismiss it as obvious. We just did what we did. I say *we* in the loosest possible sense. I assumed that everyone else was under the same spell as I was, but I could well have been the only joker in the deck; I never really knew that for sure.

I practised the procedure 238 times. When I really understood it, the whole process was completed in a single 16-hour stint. For two years I lived and breathed this process. Then the day of reckoning arrived. And everything I had rehearsed with such precision went out the goddamn window.

A child.

A goddamn child.

They brought me a goddamn child to perform this fucked-up, bullshit procedure on.

I nearly lost my shit completely.

I literally didn't know what to do.

And then Jessica Everston, cardiologist extraordinaire; the wife of my boss, the hypothetical co-owner of the organisation comes in screaming. She's blinded by tears and rage in equal measure and as she grabs for the boy on the table, I swear to

God my heart stopped beating for a good 10 seconds as I realised what was happening.

I was stood in the middle of the single most fucked up thing I could never have imagined in all my life. This child was not some random donor, some stray from the streets who would cause no questions to be asked. This was their goddamn son. This kid was the son of the owners of EverTech and I understood now that I was to perform this surgery with his mother; she was the unseen partner who would preserve the heart as I coerced the brain to sustain it.

But her screams were wild. She was distraught in the way a woman with so much power would never wish to be seen. She was not in control of anything she was doing; this was survival - not of her, but of her cub. It was terrifying and beautiful all at once. She hissed at her husband, who without removing the surgical mask which covered his face, turned to her, as security guards tried to wrestle her into submission. *Don't pretend now that you didn't know who would end up on this table; it was your lab that did the research; it was you who found the anomaly. Don't pretend to be a mother now, when we have moved so far beyond such paltry and insignificant things.* She looked dumbly at him. I wasn't sure at first that she could even hear him. But then her eyes dimmed; the fire was out. *You are the centre point of this procedure. Without you, he dies.*

And that was it. He had said enough to break her. We carried out the procedure.

We carried out the procedure. Jesus, I even sound like one of them. I wonder sometimes if I lost my heart that day as well. I don't want it to sound clinical, but I had to go into autopilot; it was the only way to get through. Every time I noticed something real - that he had clearly been in some sort of accident; his body was mangled, badly - I blocked that thought and moved to the next step of the surgery. If I had thought about what we were doing - if I had thought about the ethics, or the pain we were inflicting - I might have been able to put down the implements and walk away. But then he would have died. Fully died. Not just a bit. That's what kept me going. There would be a rebirth. Maybe it would be better. That was what I hid behind.

When it was done I walked out of the facility, which had been transferred to a disused power station just up the river a little, and I puked my guts up. And then I found some nasty little cafe that was still open, or had just opened - I had no idea what time it was - and I sat with a mug of untouched coffee until I think I fell asleep with my eyes open.

Before I made it to my bed, they paged me. The subject is awake. There are tests to run. Come in now.

Mum, I never meant for any of this to happen. I was blinded and by the time the blinkers came off, I had done this thing which is beyond the boundaries of what any human should do to another. And now they wanted me to meet my creation.

I can't say any more today.

J

30

EVIE

(ON BEHALF OF HARVEY HAWKINS)

I lied last time we spoke. Well I didn't lie; I bent the truth. Harvey said that the only difference between a truth-bender and a liar was perspective. He said the irony was that a liar was more honest - they went all out and were clear with themselves about what they were doing. A truth-bender lies to themselves as well as someone else - they fool themselves into thinking that by hiding only a little of the truth they are honouring honesty. This is the biggest lie of all.

I lied when I said that Harvey and Jerry never met. They did. It's just that he was technically dead at the time.

You see there was almost no record of the car crash you were in happening. EverTech took care of that. When Harvey was called in, it was because of a sweet old chap called Mr Okorie. Mr Okorie had come to London from Togo when he was just a baby. His daddy had opened up a business on Southwark Bridge Street. He had worked out of tiny corner office on the ground floor for 35 years, helping young African families relocate to the UK when they were trying to escape persecution or corruption. Mr Okorie had taken over from his father after he retired. He had kept the same little office; he said it was important that his clients knew that he took family and legacy seriously, and that they knew he wasn't wasting money on a nice office when he could be using it to help find them flights or lawyers. Anyway, Mr Okorie phones the police and tells them when he has come in to work this morning, his office is in ruins. *It looked like a wrecking ball had taken a swing at my walls*, he says. *The landlord hasn't reported any issues*, he is told after being put on hold for a long while. *My landlord hasn't seen the damage then*, he says. *Sorry, but you don't own the building, so this is not going to be a priority. But it is my office. I can't work*, he says. *Shouldn't think that matters much. Excuse me?* He says. *Thank you for your call, sir.*

The case went into the Lift-Off pile, Harvey told me. It stands for Leave It For Tomorrow, Or For Forever! They were the calls that no one ever got round to dealing with because they didn't have any reason to help. Harvey didn't ever get anywhere far in the Police force because he used to go looking for these cases. He went and dealt with the crap no one else wanted to. I loved him for that. It didn't put much food on the table, but I knew that he was helping people that didn't get much help. Mr Okorie came to his funeral you know. People remember people like my Harvey.

He met Mr Okorie at the office. It was pretty obvious that a car or a van had hit the building at some speed, but somebody had cleared it up in a hurry. Someone must've seen something. He went back to the station and looked through the records for yesterday's assignments - nothing doing. So he then rang through to the call-handling office and that's when he knew this wasn't going to be a normal day at the office.

A lady had called in to 999 at 22:06. She reported that a black car, 'something fancy-looking' had smashed into the building on the corner of Sumner Street and Southwark Bridge Street. There was already a black van on the scene and security guards; she wanted an ambulance to come. 'They look like the Gestapo' she said. She couldn't see the license plate for the crashed car, but gave the registration of the van. Harvey looked it up and traced it back to a leasing company. At first the manager was very unhelpful. He blocked every question Harvey had, but in the end he talked; in fact, he sung like a bird begging for freedom. You see Harvey knew that the only people who don't answer your questions are the ones who have something to hide; the challenge with this is that you need to find something they are less willing to lose than the secret you're trying to extract from them. In this case it was that the manager was secretly paying himself a handsome top-up to his salary through a fictitious employee that he had created. Harvey only discovered this because he had tried speaking to each of the employees when the manager had been out of the office, only to discover that none of them knew this other person.

Anyway, Harvey let the manager know what he knew and the chap honestly thought that by revealing his client's identity he wouldn't get in trouble for this massive fraud. Bless him, as Harvey walked out, I don't think he could quite believe that someone from the Fraud Squad walked in!

No doubt if you've been digging around for long enough you probably know what I'm going to tell you - the van was leased to EverTech, which if I have understood all of Harvey's notes correctly, is the company your parents owned together?

Harvey and I were never terribly technologically-minded. The whole world wide web business really rather passed us by, so when he started looking into EverTech he really didn't understand what on earth they were up to. He just knew something was off. He told me that it would probably have been easier to get an audience with the queen than it was with Auden Everston. He was offered other people - the Head of Public Relations, the Communications Executive, even his

PA, but never with the man himself. And it was whilst he was waiting, battling against a tsunami of shadow games that Harvey saw a story in one of the papers that blew the whole thing up. He kept the article you know. All these years later I still have it.

31

CUTTING FROM THE GUARDIAN

**The Guardian
Date: 23/11/1994**

Autonomous Car Kills Creators Son

In a turn of events more fitting for last year's Sci-Fi hit *Demolition Man,* secretive technology firm EverTech have reported tragic news that the company's founder, Auden Everston has lost his son in an accident involving an extraordinary piece of equipment - a self-driving car.

The Ever-Tech founder reported to his board members that the accident had happened sometime in mid-September after his son had activated the vehicle which was being tested at the Everston property in Central London. The company have not released details, but a spokesperson did read a statement from Everston. 'This was a tragic accident. It is a terrible loss personally and for my family, but also a frustrating setback for the company.' The spokesperson refused to take questions, but confirmed that the child was the only son of

Auden and Jessica Everston. Jessica, who was a brilliant cardiologist before joining Everston's company, was not available for comment.

32

DAPHNE

I did of course recover from my injuries. There was a hell of a lot of scar tissue and expert after expert agreed that there was no hope of a pregnancy. My ovaries and uterus had been compromised by either the wound or the subsequent surgery - no one could quite tell me.

Of course whilst I was recovering, Teddy was assigned a new partner. A chap called Ross, who he seemed to get on pretty well with. When eventually it came to me returning to work, I initially spent a few months doing emergency dispatch handling. I enjoyed it in some ways - connecting the dots between those in need of help and those who could provide assistance, but bizarrely, against every reasonable thought in my head, I missed being out in the rig.

But then there was Teddy. He was still a mess, all these months later. We talked about it; we even had some counselling together - I needed him to know that it wasn't his fault. I broke protocol and it was just bloody bad luck. He was terrified about the thought of me returning to the job, but he knew that he was going to lose that fight.

We decided though, that for the sake of everyone's sanity,

we would no longer crew together. I think we were both sad that this was the right decision, but we also knew that Teddy would be worried the whole time and I would get frustrated at not being able to do the job properly.

So, in the summer of 1988 I got a new partner - Julie Watkins. We were a solid team. Jules wasn't much fun, but she knew her stuff and we did good work together. There wasn't much chit-chat, but actually that probably suited us both. We worked together for 3 years at which point I think we had not only had enough of each other, but also of every drunk on a Saturday night calling us dykes or lesbos. It was bloody exhausting to be honest - nothing would have surprised me more that if Jules had turned out to be interesting enough to have a sex life of any kind, but anyway, we got to 1991 and just the most wonderful opportunity presented itself: Waterloo Ambulance Station would be the first place in the UK to launch the Motorcycle Response Unit (MRU). This, I was sure, was the answer to my prayers!

I took all of the tests, the advance rider courses, passed it all with flying colours, convinced Teddy that this was a good thing, that it would give me something exciting to work on. I think he was more intent on having me settle down at home with a cat-that's-not-a-baby-but-will-have-to-do, but I wasn't ready to let that unrelenting churning chasm of sucky-misery take over just yet, so this was going to fill the void.

And it did. It was exhilarating. I felt free. The gaping hole in my womb was filled. Teddy and I were able to heal each other and find some peace. At least at home.

On my bike I was reckless. I was dangerous. But I saved lives and I didn't care. Teddy couldn't see me. It was like a drug, but one that I was paid to take. I wriggled through the crowded south London streets to shock hearts back to life while my own floundered.

Another 3 years flew by. Undoubtedly cracks were

beginning to appear in the flimsy facade I had created around myself. Teddy and I argued more every month. The pain in my stomach left by the scar tissue that formed after my surgeries never quite felt right. I had been in trouble a few times with the station chief. I had turned my radio off once or twice, riding just out of area and setting myself up on the riverbank. I didn't do anything. I wasn't drinking, or doing anything illegal. I wasn't bringing the service into disrepute exactly. I just sat on my bike and watched the river. I watched the boats and the people. I watched the families walking by, the tourists taking their photos. I watched life. It passed me by and I tried to find a way of being ok with that. Then on other occasions I'd gone too far the other way. I found myself taking risks at callouts that were completely unnecessary. I performed a procedure that demanded a second paramedic to be present and nearly got suspended. If I hadn't saved the guy's life, no doubt I would've been.

It was all unravelling really subtly, so much so that I didn't quite notice. And then we arrived at 17th September 1994 - the second day to entirely alter my life in ways I could not begin to imagine.

33

JOSÉ

I'd been getting to know Ana-Maria for a little while and was spending some nights at her minute studio flat across the river, but I had started to feel unwell and I didn't think I was quite ready for her to bear witness to my man-flu, so I decided to head back to Mamá's house for some rest.

I'd taken about 30 puffs of my inhaler on the way over and was feeling pretty awful. I walked in and nearly screamed as the biggest god-damned cat I had ever seen in my life was sat on the sofa in the front room, exactly where I had intended to throw myself in my self-pitying misery!

'Don't mind him, honey,' said Mamá from the kitchen. That's just Mickey.'

'Where the hell did Mickey come from?'

'He's Jason's.'

'Who the hell is Jason?' I asked, hissing at the ridiculously named Mickey the cat, sending it trembling into the other room.

I never heard the answer.

It turns out that I am highly allergic to cats. My asthma,

which was already bad, went into full-on crisis and I could barely make a sound as I felt like I was being strangled from the inside. I managed to bang on the coffee table loud enough for Mamá to investigate. I passed out after that, but I assume either she, or Mickey the cat, called an ambulance, because I woke up in a hospital.

They did some scans and tests - I had something called 'airway remodelling' which meant my lung tubes had become thicker. They said all the asthma attacks I'd been having, plus the smoke in the bar, probably combined to screw me over. I was now a 'severe asthma sufferer.'

Kiss goodbye to Beverley Hills Cop.

No flying. No crime-fighting. No fighting at all.

What next?

I came out of hospital a few days later. Ana-Maria made a nice amount of fuss over me. I liked that. No one had really ever done that before.

I didn't humiliate myself by asking Mamá to choose between Mickey the Killer-Cat and Jason or me. I knew where I stood in her pecking order. So I grabbed a bag (once I knew the cat was out) and I moved onto Phil's sofa.

Two weeks later Phil told me about a job his uncle had heard about. He was a groundsman or something at this place and they were looking to beef up their security. Private Sector! No military history needed and best of all, no medicals. It sounded shady as hell, but it was undoubtedly the best offer I was going to get.

Within a month I was finally dressed like a bodyguard, working mental hours for a tech company that made some seriously crazy shit.

It was one of those situations where you knew there was something not quite right, but the money was good, the other people were decent enough and the company looked slick as anything. I figured it couldn't be too bad. Even met the bossman a few times and he was proper posh, very polite and friendly. A real gentle gentleman - pride of Britain sort. Knew my name and everything. I was impressed. But I suppose if Anakin Skywalker can become Darth Vader, you never can really know what someone is capable of doing.

34

MIA

(RECORDED IN 2004, 10 YEARS AFTER THE INCIDENT)

For days after Drew, Biscuit and his mum left, I could think of little else.

Had I over-dramatised what I was looking at? Was I making connections that didn't exist? Was I seeking out answers that took me back to my own feelings of isolation and loneliness? Would Freud say I was projecting? Possibly. But I looked over that data a hundred times and each time I came to the same conclusion - this boy and his animal were invisibly sharing a connection; somehow they were transferring information to each other in ways that couldn't be seen. And that data bonded them and connected them in their hearts.

The ECG had not helped me find a cause for Drew's arrythmia. This meant I had a reason to ask him to come back in. This time we would conduct an EEG to map his brain activity at the same time as the ECG. We had already begun to understand the correlation between the two in an individual, but I had a new question I wanted to answer and to my shame it was not, 'What is triggering Drew's arrythmia?'

The setup was similar; Drew and Biscuit came in, we hooked them up to two monitoring devices this time and I left them to interact, now with a series of activities for Drew to complete.

He did some exercise, watched a video of someone doing quite incredible, but really dangerous tricks on a skateboard, he read out loud and he sat quietly. I watched as the results were as expected - brain wave activity and heart rate had a correlation; when one was raised, the other followed. Nothing new there. But after each activity, I asked Drew to go and interact with Biscuit, who was to do nothing but sit about and wait for Drew (luckily he seemed to be an intensely lazy dog, so there wasn't much of a problem there!). And each time they interacted, not only did their hearts find synchronicity, but there were also flickers of brain activity which suggested that each was aware of the connection. I could see that Drew's EEG picked up on Biscuit's ECG readings and vice versa.

This mean that not only did the heart send out a signal, but that the brain of another being could somehow receive and respond.

Drew died 4 months later.

I had failed to find a cause for his arrythmia.

And I moved on and repeated these experiments dozens of times, only using people - couples and siblings. Each time I found even stronger results. Each time I thought of Drew and I thanked him and I asked him to forgive me. I hope that he has not. He helped me uncover something strange and wonderful and I let him die. And he would not be the only one. I hope that I will be suitably chastised in anything that is ever written about my work. But I am invisible - why would anyone write anything about my work?

Where we could have found something beautiful, we built something awful which would unravel the lives of many good people. And when the time came and I was offered redemption, I rejected it. I wanted to pay, to re-balance the scales. I did not believe I would make it past Amut the heart-gobbler, but I wanted it to look less of a foregone conclusion.

But there is still a little way to go. So far the blood on my hands is circumstantial; Drew would have died no matter what I had done. I know that now. I did not know that then. This truth offers me no comfort.

35

JACK

Mum,

In the end, I guess you know that I ran away. I ran away from that, like I have done a million other things. But I promise you that I did at least try to fix things first. I was just one guy; their first creation, used to build their next, but I did try.

A few hours later I was in a soulless room, sat behind a desk with the Three Little Pigs and Auden and Jessica Everston. They brought in the...boy. I didn't really know what to call him. Strictly speaking I suppose the word that comes closest is cyborg, but that is a grotesque word that doesn't explain the humanity of what we did.

He was beautiful - flawless. He looked nothing like the boy who was brought in on a stretcher; the proportions were the same, but nothing else endured at least not on the outside. The casing, the body, was unbelievably life-like. There was no way that you could know that this was not a fully-fledged human being and yet he was machine all the way until you reached the brain, spinal cord and heart we had implanted.

I had watched as the machine merged with the human tissue - it was the most astonishing thing I had ever witnessed. The simulations had not prepared me for the beauty of what Everston had achieved. The robotics were inexplicable. Microscopic machines grafted synthetic stem cells from the titanium and graphene skeleton to the boy's nervous and circulatory systems making him almost impervious to external trauma. When we had completed the transplant, the metal skull and ribcage enclosed our work and then I watched as another machine printed a layer of skin over the top. When it was done, the butchered remains of the boy who came in were strewn across the operating table and in their place, a pristine Pinocchio whose wish had come true.

Now it was up to me to establish what was left of the boy we had destroyed, so that Everston could wish upon a star and make his own twisted dreams come true.

When they brought him in he was in a wheelchair. He looked drugged, or blank; it was the least human he would ever look to me. There was nothing behind the exterior. My job, I was told in no uncertain terms, was to help coax out just the right level of humanity. If I over-achieved, there were measures in place to reign in whatever was unleashed.

I noticed that the two women who had brought the boy in were not nurses, or if they were, they were moonlighting as security. Each was armed with something that looked like a gun, but which clearly fired something other than bullets. I had no desire to find out exactly what they could do.

I started with an experimental test being used in dementia clinics to establish the level of cognitive impairment; I may have kept the boy *alive* in some way, but no simulation could tell me what was going to carry over from one body to another.

What is your name?
No response.

Where do you live?

No response.

What is the date?

No response.

Can you tell me something that has happened in the news recently?

No response.

How many fingers am I holding up?

No response.

I was sweating. I could feel the unblinking eyes of Auden Everston burning a hole in my temple. I was exposed - my failure was a chasm opening up at my feet, ready to devour me.

Then, finally, something.

Where am I?

He sounded far away, a voice from within the machine. Whose voice it was, we didn't yet know.

One of the Three Little Pigs opened up a laptop and started hammering buttons with his fat, sweaty fingers.

Brain stabilisation protocols have been initiated. Cranial chip launched and…3,2,1, implant engaged. Stabilisation impulses are running.

The boy looked at me for the first time.

My name is Jericho Everston. I live at Kensington Palace Gardens in London. Today is likely to be the 18th or 19th of September 1994. Earlier this year the Channel Tunnel opened, Tony Blair became leader of the Labour Party and the first women were ordained as priests in the Church of England. You held up 3 fingers.

Nobody dared breath for at least ten seconds and then Jessica Everston began sobbing quietly. Auden Everston turned to the laptop-wielding pig and gave a slight nod.

Recalibration initiated.

Then it was back to me.

Ask him the questions again, Everston commanded quietly.

What is your name?
I can't remember.
Where do you live?
I think I live here.
What is the date?
I can't remember.

Can you tell me something that has happened in the news recently?

I'm not sure. I think there might have been an accident.

Everston turned sharply to the Little Pig in charge of the laptop. This was not an authorised answer apparently.

How many fingers am I holding up?
Two.

Everston got up and walked towards the boy. He turned and nodded to the laptop pig who nodded back, before furiously thumping the keys in front of him.

Your name is Jerry. You are correct in surmising that you live here at this facility. Today is the 18th September 1994; it is in fact your birthday. You were born today and you will achieve great things. Tell me Jerry, do you know who I am?

There was a silence that lasted forever. I felt the air turn thick and sour as we waited. Jerry was frozen. I knew he was not a robot, but I still wondered if they could or would reboot him if this went wrong. Hell, I was technically still entirely human and I had wondered if they'd do the same to me!

I do not know who you are, but I would guess that you are the man in charge of this place.

And what makes you say that?

You were sat in the middle of the row of chairs behind the desk and you were the first person to stand and walk towards me. Unless you are trying to claim authority which is not yours, I would say this suggested that you are in charge.

Everston laughed. It was a genuine laugh of joy and

wonder and yet from his vocal cords it sounded nightmarish, sinister, cold.

You're quite right Jerry; I am indeed the man in charge. He turned back to the table behind which I sat and pointed to Jessica. *Do you know who that is?*

No. He answered, far more quickly this time.

She tried to wipe it away before it travelled down her pale cheek, but I saw the tear that escaped Jessica's eye. I could not begin to understand what she was thinking as she looked at this machine within which parts of her son existed. The parts which clearly Everston wanted to suppress as much as possible.

But if that were the case, then why the hell did we do what we did?

I had thought perhaps that this surgery was all about paving the way for people suffering from degenerative diseases to survive in a new body, or perhaps on more cynical days, for the rich and famous to switch out an ageing body for a new, firm and perky one. But this, this made no sense. Why take a boy and insert the essence of him into a new body only to crush the memories of who he was?

I didn't have to wait too much longer to find out, but the truth did not set me free.

I'm tired now. I will finish my story tomorrow.

I love you.

J

36

DAPHNE

So here it is - 17th September 1994. I get a call-out to a Road-Traffic Accident on the corner of Southwark Street and Sumner Street just 5 minutes on the bike. No details, just that there are possible casualties. It was after 10pm, but there had been another accident earlier in the night blocking some of the main routes. An ambulance would be dispatched too, but it would struggle to get there fast.

So off I go.

I'm 2 minutes out and I'm told to stand down. No reason given. This is odd. I ask the handler if the report was wrong. She tells me that there was a follow-up call saying that there had been a mistake. *Same number?* I asked. Same number, different voice.

I was intrigued. And I was 30 seconds away. I was always going to take a look.

How different life would have been if I hadn't.

There was a cordon up already blocking off the turn into Sumner Street and the riverside of Southwark Street for 20 yards either side of the turning. A black van partially blocked my view. As I went past I saw the crash. A black saloon had smashed straight into the building on the corner of Sumner and Southwark. It must have been moving at a serious speed. Another van, unmarked, with a blue light flashing at the top, was parked up just behind it. It wasn't Police. No sign of Fire-Rescue. And it wasn't me. There were a number of men in suits standing almost like guards or soldiers around the crash. No one seemed to be doing anything.

I fired off the bike's siren and made a showy entrance to the scene. There was something off about this and I was paranoid enough given all that I had encountered in the job, to want to make sure at least someone else saw me go into the crash site.

As I jumped off the bike one of the soldier-suits approached me. 'We do not require emergency service support ma'am.' He said in a robotic voice.

But I was walking towards the car and even from the angle I was approaching, I could see that there were people in the car. Soldier-suit went to grab my arm as he repeated his message. 'You get your god-damn hands off of me now, or perhaps I'll call into my station to get police support down here.' He looked suitably uncertain and let go of my arm.

I approached the car. There were a few small flames around the impact site, but the car itself was mangled, not flaming. The doors had buckled in the impact and both driver and passenger doors on the right side had blown off.

I drew level with the back seats of the car and looked in. I was not expecting to find two children. Nearest to me a girl, barely in her teens. Unconscious. Bruising to her head and chest was already becoming visible. Some bleeding to the head as well, but nothing that I couldn't deal with.

There was a boy on the other side. Well, he had been on the other side. He was strewn at a sickening and unnatural angle across the far side and centre of the car. His body looked utterly broken. He probably died on impact. He was younger than the girl. He was not wearing a seatbelt. Later I would cry for him. But I would pray for this girl. Pray that what I did for her was the right thing.

Before I did anything else I looked in the front. What I saw was inexplicable. The driver had no head! I had seen a lot of terrible things, but this was unprecedented. This just didn't happen in real life. I looked (because I suppose I thought it was my job) around for the head. It was sitting calmly in the passenger footwell, facing backwards like it didn't have a care in the world. And that is when I realised it wasn't real! It wasn't real!!!! Oh my God! I looked back at the body and I saw that where a neck spouting warm, life-giving blood should have been, there was circuitry. This thing was a machine. It looked like a person. Well, actually it looked a lot like a cheap mannequin. It wasn't that believable up close. But, I thought, no one was supposed to get up close. That was what the security was about. What the hell had I ridden into?

I didn't have time to dwell on the fact that I was in the middle of a sci-fi freak-show. I went back to the girl. She was breathing. Surely a robot couldn't breathe? I had to assume she was real. I touched her. Her skin was clammy. Her face looked too frightened to be fake.

I began taking obs. And then there was a huge explosion.

It blew me onto my backside. I took a deep breath. It wasn't the car. It was further down Sumner Street. The soldier-suits all ran towards the explosion. I got back onto my knees and tried to feel for the girl's pulse.

A hand gently grabbed my shoulder. I assumed it was the ambulance crew.

It wasn't.

It was a man in shabby clothes with a white, close-shaven beard. Late 50's, early 60's. He looked terrified.

We often get members of the public approaching us as we try to do our job. Sometimes they want to help, mostly they want to know what's going on. I once had a lady begin to try and sell me double-glazing whilst I was attempting to resuscitate an elderly lady on the high street! I politely declined all of the offers. But this guy didn't look like he wanted to sell me anything.

'Is he alive?' He asked.

'Excuse me sir, but this is a live crash scene; I need you to step away.'

'I'm sorry, but that's not possible. I need to know - is he alive. The boy?'

There was no way he could have known who was in the back of the car from where he approached.

'Please sir!' I had a very well-rehearsed gentle-but-forceful-enough-to-know-I'll-kick-your-ass-if-you-don't sod-off voice. But he wasn't listening.

He's just seen the girl.

'Oh my God! What have they done?' He said quietly - not to me. Barely to himself. I don't think he even knew that he was speaking.

He looked at me then. His eyes were desperate. The way a husband turns to you when you stop giving chest compressions to his wife, or a mother, just before you load her child into the back of the ambulance. Utter, selfless desperation. It's a beautiful thing really; at least it would be, if it weren't almost always in vain.

'Please miss, you have to listen to me. This accident wasn't an accident. That girl, she shouldn't have been here, but that boy, he was destined to be in this accident tonight.'

He sounded like a madman, but the intensity of his eyes forced me to listen.

'The boy, he's nine years old. He's about 4 foot 2, dark messy hair. His name is Jerry. This is his sister Astrophel.'

The girl seemed to stir at hearing her name.

'We have to get them out of here. The boy is in danger. And if Astrophel is here, then she's in danger too.'

I turned to the girl. She was trying to move. She hadn't seen her brother yet. 'Do you know this man sweetheart?' I asked her, trying to keep all of her attention looking out of the car.

'Mr A, what's...going on?'

'There's been an accident Asty, nasty one. You're going to have a few bruises, so no sweeping for you for a little while.'

'Okay.' She said dumbly.

'Was just passing by and I saw you. Thought I might take you home so you can get some rest.'

'Okay.' She repeated. 'Wait, what about...'

Then she saw him. Her brother.

She didn't scream.

She just looked. She reached out a hand and stroked his hair. She couldn't see his face.

'Is he...'

'I don't know honey; I need to check on him.' I lied.

'So miss, can I take her? I've got a van just there.' He said pointing to a white van over the road. There was a plump woman sitting in the passenger seat. 'That's my wife. She's going to help me.'

For a moment I considered handing over this girl to complete strangers and their van. For a moment I clearly lost all sense of reality. 'I'm sorry sir, but this can't possibly...' I was never sure if I was going to finish the sentence the way I had intended to, but the choice was taken out of my hands. The soldier-suit who had tried to stop me was suddenly standing over us. His shadow casting a darkness that brought silence and obedience.

'Sir, you are going to take this girl with you.'

I couldn't believe what I was hearing. I stood up to protest, but soldier-suit pushed me back down.

'Ma'am, everything he just told you is true. Something awful is happening here right now. I can't stop it. The boy...I, I can't stop what's happening. But this girl, she wasn't supposed to be here. No one knows she's here. You can help her. Please help her.'

I did not understand what the hell was going on but the absolute calmness of his voice couldn't quite hide how much effort it was taking him to not just grab the girl and throw her into the back of this other man's van himself.

'Do you know him?' I asked the old guy.

'No. No I don't, but I know who he works for. Please, let me take the boy as well.'

'You can't.' He said coldly. 'Without him, this doesn't work.'

They stood watching each other for a moment.

'It's a life for a life. It's all we've got.' Said soldier-suit quietly.

And then it was done. It was agreed in silence that solider-suit would keep the other soldier-suits away and I would help the old man get the girl over the road to the van.

We could do it. Hell, I wanted to do it. I could see that something bat-shit crazy was going on and if this kid was in danger I wanted to help her. But she was not in a good way.

'Can you take her to a hospital?' I asked. 'Guy's is just a few minutes down the road.' He shook his head. Of course he couldn't. So I said something stupid. 'Ok, well I'm coming with you.' He was going to protest, but I didn't let him. 'Are you a doctor?' I asked.

'No.' he said quietly.

'Is she?' I asked again, pointing at the women who was getting out of the van to meet us.

'No.' he said again.

'Then I'm coming with you.'

'What about the bike?' He asked.

Turns out the old guy had a ramp in the van for getting machinery in and out. I rode the bike round the corner to a spot they could meet me away from the accident. I rolled the bike into the van, we strapped it in and away we went.

Two kidnappers and a paramedic. There's a shit joke in there somewhere.

37

JOSÉ

I stayed at EverTech long after I knew I should leave. And then I got to the point where I was too frightened to do anything but stay. And then the worst day happened, and I lost the ability to choose.

A lot of the work was bloody boring. You stand around watching and listening. The watching was not as fun as I expected. The first time you see a robot is pretty cool, but you quickly realise that they're not really able to do that much, at least not without someone pressing a lot of buttons. It's not like I was expecting C-3PO, but a lot of what I saw wasn't even Johnny 5! They were clumsy and seemed to spend more time falling over than anything else.

Turns out though that this is only what they wanted us to think. The truth was right there in front of me every day and I had no idea until it was already too late. I say that like I could have done something about it, which is a joke. These people were beyond geniuses and powerful in ways I couldn't even begin to imagine.

I had some weird assignments in my first year or so. One

time the team I was in were asked to form a huge perimeter around a fort out in the water between Portsmouth and the Isle of Wight. It looked like some massive, abandoned barrel. All night we heard muted gunshots and explosions, metal being smashed together, all coming from the fort. Some of the guys who were based closer said there were boats bringing rich and famous people to the fort after dark and they were all watching some sort of robot Battle Royale through a glass roof. It sounded amazing, but pretty bloody creepy too. But no one was getting hurt - if rich people want to spend their time watching robots kicking 7 shades of shit out of each other and were happy to pay me to make sure the paparazzi never saw them, who was I to care?

But then someone did get hurt.

It was 17th September 1994. It was the worst day.

I had been assigned another strange job but a seemingly easy one. Be stationed discreetly with a team of 6 on the corner of Sumner and Southwark Street at 22:00. Wait there. There would be an incident. All pre-planned. Nothing to worry about. There will be a collision. It was expected. It was a test. Our job was to do absolutely nothing other than surround the incident, discourage the public from engaging with the incident in any way. Wait for a tech-team to show up. They would be recovering the tech from the site and taking it to a secondary lab nearby.

Piece of cake.

'The incident' turned out to be a black Mercedes-Benz 500E careering into a building at 50 mph, about 10 metres away from where I stood. I'll admit that it caught me by surprise and it took me (and the rest of the team) a minute or so to pull ourselves together.

We were ordered to fan out around the car. I was on the Southwark Street side, facing the main traffic. As I looked around, pretending to all the world that I was a boss and that me standing there with a load of other guys in black suits was completely normal and also very cool, I saw that there was a little old lady in a phone box over the road. At first it didn't register, but then I saw that she kept looking at me and the car and pointing. Shit! She's called 999. I went over to the phone box, but she was already done. I asked if she'd just called the Police, but she scrambled away from me and I didn't think chasing after some crusty old abuela was going to help this situation stay any more discreet.

I went into the phone box and called 999 myself. I told them that someone had just called about a car crash, but that actually everything was fine. I told them it was my car and there was no need for any emergency services to attend. I had it all under control. The girl I spoke to, took it and I thought we were in the clear.

3 minutes later a nurse on a bike shows up! It wasn't a Kawasaki Ninja, but it made a lot of noise and had a flashing blue light, drawing even more unwanted attention. She walks straight towards the car, which by the way, I was a bit disappointed about, as it didn't burst into a raging fireball like it would've in the movies! I grabbed her arm as gently as I could when I saw she was deliberately ignoring me. 'Please ma'am,' I said, 'we don't need an ambulance. This is all under control.' But she ignored me. In fact, she gave me some back-chat, but I let her go. I wasn't a bouncer anymore and I wasn't supposed to be making this worse.

She kept walking. She'd seen what I had not. Hadn't I? Did I choose not to see it? I don't know. But I looked in the direction she was walking and I then couldn't un-see it. There was a kid in the back of the car!

This was messed up. This was messed up on a level I hadn't ever imagined. I went back over the instructions for tonight. They knew this crash was happening. They wanted this crash to happen. They wanted this crash to happen, with a kid in the back seat. What were you supposed to do with that? I needed to get this woman away; I needed to think, but before I could even begin to think of a way out of this, there was a massive explosion at the other end of Sumner Street. My team automatically ran towards the action. I guess there was a chance this was part of the drill. I went to follow, but by the time I got to the other side of the car, I turned back and hid myself on the opposite side to the paramedic lady. I listened to her breathing. She was shocked. I could tell that from here. I peered up and looked through the front passenger window which had been shattered.

That's when it sort of started to make sense (in so much as it didn't make any sense at all, but what I saw was what, if I were a bit smarter, I should have expected to see - a headless driver).

Before this job I would have assumed that what I saw was only possible if I had actually walked onto the set of a Schwarzenegger film. For a moment I wondered, I hoped even, that was it. This was all a terrible misunderstanding and the director was going to come running over to me to tell me I'd ruined the shot.

But that wasn't it. If you looked closely, it didn't even look that real. James Cameron would have fired the prosthetics guys if this was the sort of crap they put together. But in the outfit, in the driver seat, it looked like a person. It looked exactly as it should have looked - a high-end chauffeur service carrying a rich kid.

I looked in the back and I'm not going to lie. I saw a second kid, totally bent in all the wrong directions and I spilt my guts all over the floor.

Two kids. This one was definitely dead. I had just watched

a car driven by a robot smash into a building and kill one, maybe two kids. And I knew that this was all planned. Someone was paying people to setup a car crash that killed kids.

'Alpha Team, this is base.' My radio buzzed to life for the first time since we checked in. The team leader replied. Then more from base: 'Alpha Team there is one asset and a package in the vehicle. Please confirm that both are good picks.'

I could see my team leader coming into view. 'Base this is Alpha 1. We had a disturbance. No visual confirmation yet, but I have Alpha 6 at the source.' He pointed at me. 'Alpha 6 please confirm one asset, one package, both good picks.'

An asset meant a robot of some sort. A package was a person. A 'good pick' meant that the thing being referred to was immobilised and safe to approach. In all the jobs I'd done, I had never been asked if a human being was a good pick.

Then it struck me. They only thought there was one person in the car. One of those kids wasn't supposed to be there. Maybe I could help one of these kids. But which one? Which one did they want? I looked again at the horror story playing out in the back of the car. The boy hadn't been wearing a seatbelt, that much was obvious. The girl had. I didn't know what that meant. They wanted the package immobilised, but a crash at that speed, surely seatbelt or not, you'd be unable to get up and run.

Every swear word I had ever learnt in English and Spanish ran through my head. What was I supposed to do?

I walked round to the back of the car. The team leader was going to require an answer. I made it look like I was inspecting something.

I heard the paramedic talking to someone. I looked through the space that had previously held a windshield: a guy. Old-ish. They were talking as if the other kid, the girl, was alive. He wanted to take her.

He knew this was going to happen. He knew it wasn't an accident too.

I heard him speak quietly; saw him kneeling down and talking to the girl: 'There's been an accident Asty, a nasty one indeed. I reckon you'll have a few bruises.' he said.

I turned back to figure out what was going on at the other end of the street. Shit! They were coming back. 'Alpha 6, please confirm the status of the package.' I fiddled with my earpiece in a really obvious way so that they would see it.

I made my decision.

The boy wasn't moving. He couldn't be alive looking like that. This old guy knew something. And he wanted the girl.

'Alpha 1, I can confirm asset and package are good picks.'

It was now or never. I turned off my radio. 'Sir,' I said walking as big as I could from round the back of the car. They both started - that would help. They'd listen. 'Sir, you're gonna take this kid with you and get the hell out of here. Right now.' The paramedic lady tried to argue, but I could see her heart wasn't in it. 'Look chica, what he just said is true. I can't help them both. The boy, I...I can't stop what's happening, but this girl, they don't know about her. You can help her. Get her the hell out of here.'

'Do you know him?' She asked the old guy, looking at me.

'No.' He said, 'But I know who he works for.' There was so much venom in his words. He knew what until today I had only suspected - that EverTech was dangerous.

He begged me to let him take the boy as well, but I couldn't let him. It would be too risky. They'd never get away.

'Look,' I said, trying to keep my shit together. 'It's a life for a life, or everyone dies.'

They started to get the girl out of the car. I walked towards the returning team. I'd keep them distracted as long as possible. I walked over to them laughing and smiling, asking them what had happened. Why was it only me that took their job seriously? Started making jokes about Peterson's wife (Everyone did it. I'd never met her, but apparently she was not a handsome chica). I kept the banter going as long as possible.

When we got back to the crash site, there was one asset and one package. They were both good picks.

38

MIA

(RECORDED IN 2004, 10 YEARS AFTER THE INCIDENT)

I had begun mapping how far apart subjects could be to still register an effect on one another. It seemed as if the heart was generating a magnetic field that could reach several feet away from the body and that others could sense this. I wasn't sure what this meant. I just knew that it felt important.

I didn't have a lot of spare time; I liked it that way; it meant that I didn't have time to think about much, other than my work. If I made time for other things I began to ask myself questions I didn't know the answers to and then I spiralled.

What if this metal heart in my chest gives up?

What if it malfunctions?

What if I get sick and need to go to a hospital...what do I tell them?

What if this whole thing has been a lie and it doesn't work, or worse, they're using me as an experiment?

I know they're using me as an experiment - why else would they not tell anyone about the surgery?

And so it goes on. I can't stand myself when I enter that headspace. Therefore busy, is good.

So I went to the library and I read. I read everything I

could find about the heart, about energy, about heart energy, energy transfer, heart-rate alignment, communication, heart energy communication and alignment transfer! Anything that would help explain what I had seen.

What I found is that apparently this is nothing new at all. The concept of Qi has existed in Chinese philosophy for thousands of years; long before it could have been examined or understood. That an energy force exists within the body and can be transferred or moved, sometimes even from person to person was a foundational belief when it came to Qi and from what I could find (which was very little), it is still being practised in China today. The problem was, there is no science to back it up.

The poet-father and jazz-band mother genes in me wanted to believe that this is what I had discovered - scientific proof that we have energy that we can control and manipulate to heal and preserve ourselves and others; that everything in the world can be explained by this one thing that extends beyond countries, race, religion or gender and can do magical things. But my cold, metal, science-driven heart told me that what I had was a little boy who loved his dog.

Nonetheless, because I so wanted to be worthy of what they had done for me, I shared my findings with the Everstons in the way a cat brings a dead bird into the kitchen for its owner; as an offering which begs its recipient, who asked for no such sacrifice to be made, to accept it as a crime committed with love.

I knew that between them they would see something I had not; they would see that they might build something truly magnificent for the world.

And I suppose that is what they believed they were doing. But they were wrong.

39

JACK

Dear Mum,

This is it I guess. The endgame as they say.

Every day for the next two weeks I was assigned the brain surgeon equivalent of janitorial duty - I was sequestered to an office where I was fed a constant stream of EEG readings from Jerry. These were being transmitted wirelessly from nodes in his titanium skull to a computer in my room. Given the level of trauma and the extreme odds working against us, it was incredible and yet mundane, that Jerry's readings were so consistent and normal. His brain was at peace with the body that we had put him in. It was a feat of almost godlike achievement. But I felt very far from any sense of power or accomplishment.

I was not allowed to see the boy, speak to the boy, or know about anything to do with the boy. For the 'purity of the science' I was told, I will observe only the readings - this way I will not be influenced by what I saw. I was obedient because I had no choice but to be so.

Everything changed on the 16th day after the surgery. The calm, melodic flickering of his brain waves transformed into a raging tornado of activity and then for more than a minute, I assume that he had died - there were next to no readings at all. I sat, stunned into inaction. I held my breath, watching and waiting for something; a sign of hope. And then it came in the form of even, calm peaks and troughs, as steady as they had been before.

The whole episode had lasted three or four minutes.

I broke protocol and ran out into the heart of the facility in search of someone more senior - someone who could tell me that the boy was okay.

Like the slightly belligerent moron I can be sometimes, I headed, without entirely realising what I was doing, to Everston's office. When I realised that I was almost at his door, a surge of adrenaline pushed me past the two, maybe three PA's that guarded entry to his office. I walked straight into what looked like the closing scenes of an episode of *ER* (which I'd started watching a couple of weeks before, to help numb the boredom of waiting for news). There were doctors smiling and congratulating each other, a patient smiling on a sofa, Everston, sat in a huge leather office chair behind a mahogany desk, playing the role of hospital manager. The only thing at odds with this jubilant scene was the small, unmoving boy sat on a straight-backed wooden chair in the corner. He was not smiling. He was blank.

Everston looked at me in such a way as told me in no uncertain terms that if I did not get the hell out of his office right now he would happily ensure that someone pressed some buttons on a laptop which would see my brain fry itself like an egg done over-easy with a side of death in the most painful way imaginable.

As I turned to leave he called after me: *I expect a full report of your findings on my desk in 3 hours. If it is late, do not bother returning to work tomorrow.*

It was 10pm.

The report was on his desk by midnight.

It was just about the most confusing thing I had ever written.

I suggested that the subject must have experienced some sort of seizure - I would go as far as to say a generalised tonic-clonic seizure. I outlined my questions in as clinical and professional a way as possible, but essentially I didn't have a fucking clue how the boy had basically been brain dead for over a minute and then just resumed normal brain activity. What I had seen of him in Everston's office offered me no helpful clues either.

I was called in to a meeting with the Three Little Pigs and Everston the following morning.

I told him that I wanted to see his ECG readings for the same period. I needed to know what sort of strain his heart had been under.

We have someone else taking care of the heart. Your job is the brain.

Most of my other avenues of inquiry were similarly blocked.

I learnt almost nothing from that meeting, other than that they were pleased with their initial interactions with the subject. My job was to continue to monitor brain health and activity from a distance.

A month later, an almost identical event occurred. Jerry's readings were off-the-chart wild for two or three minutes and then he flat-lined. This time for a horrific 97 seconds. I didn't move. I watched. I studied every tiny flick, every high and low of the boy's EEG. Unlike the first time, for several minutes afterwards I noticed tremors of activity in the temporal lobe, then a flash on every sensor; it would then stabilise for a minute or so, then repeat. This happened for 19 minutes after the 'main event'. I wrote my report, sent it to Everston and continued to watch.

For seven weeks nothing happened.

Then Everston himself came knocking on my door.

It's time for you to see what it is you're watching.

I followed him to his office. There I found the boy seated opposite a very sad and tired looking man of about 80. They were surrounded by the ever-present, increasingly bloated, Three Little Pigs.

This is Mr Davis. He is 76 years old and he is suffering from advanced Alzheimer's Disease. He handed me two charts - one with EEG readings and one with CT scan imaging. Neither are conclusive on their own, but they certainly helped paint a picture. The hippocampus in Mr Davis' brain was significantly reduced even for a man his age. *You have already met Jerry. Jerry is going to help Mr Davis.*

I obviously looked confused. Everston enjoyed this.

I have taken the liberty of having the EEG feed sent to this laptop - please feel free to watch the screen as we proceed.

Mr Davis sat motionless on the chair in the middle of the room. Jerry stood, approached the old man and then placed his hand gently on his head. Mr Davis' eyes closed. His face seemed to soften. As I watched this strange scene, my eye was drawn to the readouts on the laptop Everston had supplied. The crazy generalised spikes were beginning, but as I looked at Jerry, there was absolutely no sign of distress. In fact, he looked...angelic. He was the epitome of peace. He too had closed his eyes and there was a very subtle, warm smile on his face.

And then it was over. Jerry removed his hand and stumbled backwards into his chair. His eyes closed and this is where his brainwaves dropped to almost imperceptible levels. I went to approach him but was blocked by Everston.

You are an observer Mr Lewis. Nothing more. Are the readings as before?

I looked carefully at the screen. *Yes. More or less identical to the previous two events.*

Everston nodded in approval.

Tomorrow you will meet Mr Davis again. I suspect you will notice a slight difference.

And with that I was ushered out of his office. There was nothing more to see. I did not understand what I had just witnessed. Once I did, I wanted nothing more than to take that boy and run far, far away from EverTech and everyone within its orbit.

I didn't sleep that night. Instead, I watched the boy's EEG. The tremors in the temporal lobe lasted for far longer this time. I desperately wanted a CT scan and to see what his heart was doing. I felt like I had both hands tied behind my back - this information was telling me something was wrong, but they didn't want me to know what.

What should I put in my report? The truth? Exaggeration perhaps? Would that get me in front of the boy? Overlook it? Let them think everything is okay and find a way to get to him without them knowing?

The chip in my brain had made me smarter, but I was no James Bond. Maybe I could lie to you, but I mostly achieved this by hiding away. It is my greatest regret: I didn't know how to do anything else. I wanted to be your son and instead I became a cloud under which you lived. I don't suppose my going away did much to change that, but no doubt now, after all this time, perhaps you feel that there are sunnier days?

I lost my nerve and I filed an accurate report. The following morning, I was brought back to Everston's office. Sat on a smart green, leather sofa opposite his desk was a man. At first I didn't recognise him as Mr Davis. This man was so alive - he was vibrant, chatty, smiling - everything that the Mr Davis of yesterday had not been.

Before I could say anything, Everston handed me EEG and CT scans. Any neurosurgeon who knew anything about the ageing of the brain and its quietly diminishing returns would have assumed that I was looking at the data for a person aged somewhere between 20-50 years old. But in the top corner: G Davis, 20/12/94. I looked up at the man who was still happily talking to Everston. These scans made sense. What did not make sense was that this was the same man whose degraded, sorry data made sense the day before.

I stood, utterly dumbfounded and listened.

Auden, old boy, I don't entirely know what it is you've done here, but I want in. And I want in, big. I will buy that thing you put in front of me yesterday - there is literally no limit to what I will pay. I assume you can control it, like the bots I saw at one of your robot battles? Of course you can!

Everston said nothing, but still the old man went on.

Come on old chap, don't play coy with me. I gave you your start; I seeded you when there wasn't a bank, or lender, or scientist who would take you seriously. Yes, you've given me something back, but I think you've got plenty more to spare. Let's not play games with each other - it's terribly dull and it looks like I've got a few more years to enjoy now. Give me a number. Literally anything you can come up with; I'm expecting 7 zeros, so don't be shy.

Everston deliberately turned his attention away from Davis and acknowledged me properly for the first time. *Well Jack, it's a miracle isn't it? Yesterday Mr Davis' cognitive functionality was poor. Significantly developed Alzheimer's I'm sure you'd agree. Today, what do you think?*

I didn't actually get to give my feedback - which is good, because I had nothing more constructive to say than 'Um...wow!'.

Don't fucking ignore me Auden. Don't talk about me as if I'm some piece of shit experiment to be marvelled over. I made you! Now I want what you've made. It's simple.

I'm sorry George but I don't have anything that is for sale.

You son of a bitch! You just carry on playing games; I'll call in every fucking penny that you owe me and let's see how many breakthroughs you make once you're bankrupt and having to build robots out of matchsticks in the goddamn gutter. Who would touch you after...

But he never got to finish the sentence. Everston, who was a tall, gangly man, moved with a speed which seemed unnatural. He had the draw of his desk open before I'd registered anything. He held up a gun and before Davis could react - bang - Davis' head flew back and tiny bits of his brain splattered my shirt and trousers.

That was a bad goddamn day Mum. A really bad day. Worst of all Everston wanted to keep talking as if nothing had happened.

You must have questions Jack, about how we did it?

I was too stunned to talk, so Everston filled in the blanks. And as I listened, as I began to understand what I had helped create, I was almost able to ignore the dead body that sat slumped to my left.

The boy has the power to heal. There was something special about his human heart and it has long been understood that the brain is far more complex and sophisticated that any computer we can yet build. That is why they were both transferred, along with the spinal column which unites them. The machine part was there to fulfil the job that the boy's heart was doing. He could communicate with other humans at an almost undetectable, almost atomic level and the nanobots which made up the pseudo-skeleton Everston had built, deployed through contact between the boy and the subject. The bots were primed to listen to the instructions that the boy's heart and brain sent them. They healed the subject. They healed the boy. The world could be rid of disease.

Simple.

Not replicable though.

Whatever it was about that boy's heart, they hadn't found it anywhere else and they couldn't fake it. Apparently they had tried. Fixing up the brain was easy. I was living proof of this. The heart, however, was different. Or at least the connection between the head and the heart.

I walked away from that encounter a different person. I was a person who had seen too much; I was a person who was afraid, and for the first time in I do not know how long, maybe ever, I was afraid for someone else. I was afraid for the boy, Jerry. I understood that he was a pawn in a game that was un-winnable. Everston was a smart guy. He knew from my reports that the encounters he was setting up between Jerry and these people who needed help, were hurting him. But he didn't care. Why would he? He had already sacrificed his son once; he was surely happy to continue doing so. I just didn't understand what his plan was. If there was something that unique about Jerry's heart and these processes were hurting him, why waste them on someone you then killed?

I was no detective, but I knew everything that I needed to. I was going to find the boy and I was going to speak to him. Maybe I could save him.

Perhaps this was the greatest decision I ever made. Meeting Jerry was like finding God in a sandstorm; he let me see when there had only been darkness, and yet I failed him. I think.

I can't tell you that part today mum. I don't think the words would make sense. When I think of Jerry now, I see a blinding white light, with all the colours in the universe dappling the edges of his brilliance. I see that light coming towards me, gently, with warmth. And then it fades. And I see I am as jaded and lost as I ever was. And I miss you more than

I could ever explain. Those are the nights when I take my board out into the ocean and hope to be overwhelmed by something against which you cannot fight. But every time, I hear Ralph howling into the wind and I lose my nerve. I wonder if he is scared to lose me, or if that is just my cowardice creating a new story. Either way. Those nights end with me and the dog wrapped in a towel, shivering on the beach, staring at a tattered picture of you, me and Dad sitting on some knackered, striped deckchairs on the beach in Brighton.

J

40

CUTTING FROM THE TIMES

**The Times
Date: 22/12/1994**

Billionaire Found Dead In Botched Robbery

Billionaire businessman George Davis, founder of the property development firm *GD Homes*, was found dead in his home last night after what Police have described as a failed burglary. Davis who lives alone following his recent divorce from his fourth wife, former Somali model Hani Taban Amin, was apparently shot before the robbers were apprehended by on-site security guards. One guard, who spoke directly to our newspaper said 'Mr Davis was a great boss; really active too. For a man his age he was always on the go. He must've confronted the burglars. He always was very brave.'

Davis, who at one time found himself on the wanted lists of a number of UK police departments, rose to his fortune following a string of shrewd investments, allowing him to break clear of his seemingly shady past and into the mainstream business world. He is cited as having helped develop one of the most sophisticated assembly line setups of the 1960s, allowing him to build and package cheap, imitation watches and jewellery at a pace his competitors could not match. He dominated the markets in the UK, mainland Europe and western Asia.

Davis, who even in his later years still courted controversy, seemingly in the hope of a good headline, had become less prominent on the London party scene amid rumour that he had developed early-onset dementia. His lawyer, Harry Phantoon gave this comment: 'George Davis was a kind, successful businessman of the highest order. That anyone would attack and kill such a man is a travesty and a sad indication of the decline of moral fibre in this country. I have no doubt that George will have fought for his life and he will take comfort in knowing that his beloved cats, Alfonso and Petal, have survived the attack and will be suitably re-homed'

Mr Davis is survived by all 4 of his former wives and, if unconfirmed reports are to be believed, 18 children. An inquest is open and we await further details from the police about how the investigation into his death will proceed.

41

DAPHNE

I rode with them all the way down to a little cottage, which in another life might have been somewhere Teddy and I could have lived out our retirement very happily. But this isn't about us. This is about the girl.

I decided to stay with the old guy and his wife for a couple of days. I needed to make sure she was ok and that they weren't actually psychopaths. Not that I was sure I was the best judge of such things given my previous experiences.

When I started out on the bike with the MRU, Teddy had insisted on buying me a mobile phone. I guess it was pretty cool, but I didn't really know how to use it, or need it in fact, given that I had a radio for all the callouts, but he had insisted. Well, I found out that using SMS messaging was a good way of avoiding a difficult conversation, so I sent a very cack-handed one to Teddy saying that I needed a bit of space and so was going to take a few days off and stay in a B&B somewhere.

He didn't reply. Maybe he didn't know how.

Physically, the girl was in good shape. She'd had a seatbelt on and that seemed to prevent the impact from reaching out to harm her. She was sitting up talking and even smiling within a day or so. The smile was paper-thin though and every time she thought we looked away, you could tell that she was seeing her brother in that car.

On the third day something seriously weird happened. She was sitting there, quietly watching some TV, the three adults in the room watching her like a hawk and suddenly she slumped forward.

I rushed over to catch her and help her fall more gently to the floor. I lay her on the carpet. Her eyes had shut, but she was still breathing and her pulse was normal. She opened her eyes a few moments later and looked startled. She backed away as quickly as she could, seemingly unaware of where she was. She was going to scream, then she caught sight of the old guy.

'Mr A? What's...what's going on? Where am I? Where's Jerry?'

And that was it - the strangest thing I ever saw. This kid had literally just lost a whole bunch of memories. She had no recollection of anything that had happened over the last three or four days. She had no idea who I was; she didn't remember getting in a car; she had no idea where we were or why; she missed her parents and her brother.

But despite all of that, she did not ask to leave. Something somewhere was telling her that this was okay.

I was confused, but selfishly I knew that I had life that needed returning to. So I left.

I never asked the old guy's name. I didn't want to know.

The girl, Astrophel however, haunted my dreams. I prayed to a God I didn't quite have enough faith to believe in, and then I prayed to him even harder when I found that I did.

42

JOSÉ

Two vans showed up that night. One was a tech team. They dragged the robot chauffeur out of the car and literally threw him in the back of their van, decapitated head and all. They drove off pretty quickly back out onto Southwark Street in the vague direction of EverTech headquarters. The second van was a black 'Private Ambulance', but EverTech employees got out of the back - I recognised the crest on their overalls. These folk were not techies.

They approached the smashed-up Mercedes cautiously and when they saw just one male child in the back, nobody freaked out. I'd made the right call. I was beyond relieved!

They seemed to take a bloody long time getting him out of the car. They didn't treat him the way I figured you might if you reckon you're dealing with a dead body, but I suppose I'm maybe not as sentimental about these things as I could be.

Anyway, they get him out and put his body on a stretcher. Jesus Christ he was more mangled than I realised! It was an absolute shit-show and it freaked me out. But I kept on watching. I couldn't stop myself. They hooked him up to some machines; even put a mask over his face. Did they really think he was alive? Or was it just for show? But if it was, who the hell was the show for? No one was around to see this.

The explosion had clearly stressed people out. We were told that we would be supervising the vehicle to its destination. I was assigned to walk alongside the van with three others; the other two were in the back with the boy and the EverTech bods.

I wondered how the hell we were supposed to walk alongside a van without being really bloody obvious that we were doing something strange. But we began walking and I immediately realised that we were walking in the opposite direction to the one I expected. We crawled down Sumner Street towards the River Thames. We looked like a funeral procession, mournfully walking alongside some pimped-out mega-hearse! We'd be at the river in moments. I didn't understand where we were going.

We stopped outside a huge building, black against the muddy-blue night sky. Across the water I saw St Paul's Cathedral. I realised we were standing next to an old power station; Bankside. Hadn't been used for years. You know it as the Tate Modern now. When the delivery entrance shutters rattled up and we walked the van into the silent turbine halls, all I could wonder was whether this concrete monstrosity was going to be the place I died.

It was absolutely terrifying. And not at all what I was expecting.

If it had been some dank, wet, abandoned wreck, it would have been disturbing, but at least it would have been what it should have been. Instead, I walked into a well-lit, polished building, buzzing with people. It looked like some sort of hospital, but I couldn't see any patients and it wasn't clear if these people in EverTech scrubs were doctors, nurses, or techies.

The van stopped in the middle of the turbine hall. A

dozen or so people appeared from nowhere and mobbed the back doors, almost clawing at the stretcher. They all wanted to be the ones to touch it and get it wheeling across the floor. I was ordered to follow silently behind the stretcher and accompany it to Laboratory A.

I walked dumbly down too-bright, freshly painted corridors to a glass-walled room. Laboratory A.

I would go no further, but should wait here in the hallway for further instructions.

I could see everything. It was like watching a TV show without the sound turned on.

They put the kid in the middle of the room. Machines were rolled in to almost surround him. To the side, people, doctors I guessed, were washing their hands and putting gowns and masks on. I caught a glimpse of one before he covered his face. It was the boss. As in the big boss. The guy who was a hardcore robotics genius. This guy was Einstein reincarnated for sure, but even I knew he wasn't a doctor.

More people came into the room. One of them rolled in a little trolley with this horrific looking device. It looked like some sort of circular saw.

Well turns out it didn't just look like one! Shit. When they fired that thing up, I could hear it. Didn't hear a damn thing else that was said in that place, but I could hear that saw spinning.

The guy holding it got the nod from the boss man and I saw him begin to lower it towards the kid's chest.

That's when my chest fired up in sympathy. I could feel every fibre in my lungs tighten and my chest contracting. I was wheezing, fighting for breath in seconds. This was going to be an absolute bastard of an asthma attack. The last thing I saw before I passed out was the boss man's face. Cold as god-damn ice.

43

MIA

(RECORDED IN 2004, 10 YEARS AFTER THE INCIDENT)

In the months leading up to the incident, the lab took on a different energy. The teams who ordinarily would work together, sharing findings, observing and commenting on research and results became more divided. There was a quiet suspicion cast over the building; everyone was a threat, but the enemy was unknown. My team were reassigned; no more observations, back to microscopes and petri dishes. In many ways I didn't mind. The work I had been doing was unsettling; it brought me too close to people that had lives which extended beyond this building and I was not ready at that point to consider such a place.

Jessica was at the lab far less often. I would see her almost running from her office, which was just visible from the small lab I was now working in. I would look out of the window a minute or so later and see her delicately climbing into the back of a black Mercedes, destined, I knew, for yet another rendezvous with Everston.

Six weeks before everything changed, an announcement came: we had been purchased by EverTech. Our work, our research and our very souls, were now all owned by Auden

Everston. Jessica, who seemed more like a willing disciple than a life-partner, was to be Vice-President of the organisation. It was evident immediately that this had left her almost entirely powerless.

Half the technicians were made redundant that week. The other half were cowed and silent in their protest. I was retained. Of course I was. I was their dirty secret. Just how dirty, I still did not realise. But the work changed again, and so did the faces that I was working with.

I was handed a report - 'Read this. Verify the findings. Report back in 36 hours. You have access to any lab, but you work solo.' I was told by a newly appointed manager, who I was certain knew absolutely nothing about cardiology but a lot about how to ensure people did the jobs they were told to do. The report was bound in the EverTech colours - blue and gold, logo front and centre and was unlike any report I had ever read before. Where there should have been science, there was mythology, where statistics and facts should have driven conclusions, outcomes were set and I was to find the numbers that would make it possible to proceed. This was a rambling manifesto and I was to be the puppet to make it real. I felt as if Karl Marx had handed me the keys to the factory, but instead of the good order and equality I might have delivered, he wanted revolution, fire and death, so that he could prove to the Bourgeoise that they were doomed because he had told them that it would be so.

I had never started a fire, but I now had a box of matches in my hand and the whole wide world had turned to tinder.

44

REPORT: PROJECT H

EverTech Report | Project H
5th March 1994
Author: Confidential
Recipient: Mia Svobodova

Executive Summary

When the story of Hephaestus and his creation, Talos, was first told, the Greeks had no real understanding of the beauty of their concept. I dare say that Mary Shelley, thousands of years later, had even less of a clue that her patchwork man would in fact be a blueprint for medical miracles sought by a secret elite in the Twentieth Century.

The creation of life from nothing, or indeed the recreation of life from death, would be the most radical realisation of mankind's potential. It would put us on a par with any god that dared to challenge us. To create life and use this life to save or end life, would indeed surpass anything that nature has so far produced.

Project Hephaestus will be the singularly most spectacular demonstration of human ingenuity witnessed anywhere throughout our history.

For a number of years EverTech has quietly brought the greatest scientific minds into its fold and with suitable resource, these trailblazing men and women have created miracles. The work being done in our facilities is twenty, thirty, maybe even fifty years ahead of the rest of the world. Our robotics are able to offer the most extraordinary precision, strength and agility, with both in-built and human-controlled intelligence.

In recent years our human integration prototypes have met with extraordinary success. We have transplanted limbs onto eleven subjects, using a hybrid skin that contains both synthetic and organic compounds, which has been so successful that several patients have actually been able to retrain their minds into forgetting that an amputation had ever occurred. The limb works synchronously with the rest of the body thanks to our patented Brain Enhancement & Stabilisation Training chips.

These tiny computers are of course our best-selling product. The base model, approved internationally, has transformed the mental health crisis. A more sophisticated product, which allows for other, more generous modifications is now available through what has become known as the Silent Network - a hand-picked assortment of resellers, placed within the most elite echelons of society, who have no known or traceable affiliation with EverTech. BEST chips, which are powered by the brain's own electro-magnetic field, have allowed us unprecedented access to the inner workings of the brain. Through the data they have harvested we are now able to program them to enhance the rate of human learning, inhibit or remove negative memories or even unhelpful emotions.

Neuro-enhanced humans are the future of successful society. Those humans will be utilising EverTech technology. But Neuro-enhancement is only the beginning.

We have recently discovered an unexpected connection between the brain and the heart. Research suggests that the heart itself is in fact an independent brain-like entity, capable of sending as well as receiving commands and responses to the brain and producing a significant magnetic field which can radiate several feet outside of the human body.

This development has a number of significant points of interest for EverTech investors. The brain has thus far proven itself too complex to replicate in technological form; the promise of quantum computing does little to make us believe that a viable solution of similar proportions and power will be synthetically constructed. The heart, however, is easier to replicate.

There are currently 3 test subjects fitted with fully automated EverTech hearts. We will conduct the following tests:

1. Monitor neurological communication between the artificial heart and the brain of the subjects
2. Replicate the magnetic field of the human heart and monitor reception with other subjects

Should both tests prove to demonstrate replicability with fully human subjects, further testing will be conducted to begin the realisation of Project H (Classified).

45

MIA

(RECORDED IN 2004, 10 YEARS AFTER THE INCIDENT)

They wanted me to conduct tests on myself. This is why I was of use. They wanted to know if my heart worked in the same way as Drew's. They wanted to know if my heart could talk to my brain and if my heart would reach out and be sensed by the unconscious part of another person.

If it did, then there would be more tests. There would be a further unveiling of Project H. I would become the ultimate test subject for something bordering on insanity and so far over the line of illegal and immoral it was difficult to contemplate.

But of course, I ran the tests.

My heart and brain communicated on a neurological level in a fairly standard way, however, the 'heart-brain' alluded to in the report was not visibly active. The science around this was new to our lab and to me; the fact that it was even a possibility in complex living matter was extraordinary, that it might have been carried across when my tin-heart was hooked up to the rest of me, was frankly laughable.

Then I tried to measure my own magnetic field. I found nothing.

My heart had no magnetic field. It did not transmit unconscious, barely traceable messages to the equally unconscious minds of those around me.

It was a sobering, quite miserable moment.

Whilst I was grateful that I clearly was of no use as a test subject for whatever weird pseudo-science Everston was playing God with, the fact that my artificial heart was merely a functional alternative to my faulty, but beautifully real original, made me feel somehow less...real. I transmitted nothing to the world beyond what you could see or hear. I was doing something less than Drew and even Biscuit the dog.

I submitted my findings to the new lab manager. Within an hour Auden Everston was on the phone to me. Was I sure? Had I run the tests properly? Had I repeated them? Had I accounted for electrical interference? His questions went on and on and with each negative response his voice became more desperate.

'Then it is not enough.' he said.

'I'm sorry Sir, what is not enough?' I asked.

'To replace something with a replica more perfect than the original. It is not enough, because it is the very essence of the flaws of the original within which its secrets are hidden.'

That was the end of the call.

That was the last time I spoke to Auden Everston.

46

DAPHNE

The third of the three strangest things that ever happened to me was very different to the others. Partly because it was happy. Partly because it was nothing to do with my work. Partly because it was something that endured. So little of what we experience in life endures. People enter and leave your life. Sometimes we're happy, sometimes sad. Mostly we're tired, but sometimes too excited to be. But this final experience brought me wonder. And I kept it and held it in my heart every single day since the moment it was bestowed upon me.

It all happened in a supermarket.

I know - the least profound place on earth.

I was searching desperately for 'whole cloves' to jam into the ham I was inevitably going to overcook that Christmas, because, well, because that is always how my ham turned out. When I got to the spice section there were none left. I thought about crying - shopping has always been one of my least favourite things to do, but the shopping just before Christmas I found particularly troubling. I think it's because I knew that the pressure to host my mother-in-law and Teddy's siblings and their families was an endurance event the likes of which no number of cardiac arrests can prepare you for. I didn't particularly care for the idea of being the 'perfect wife' but I did think it was a bit unfair that the universe was conspiring against me. I just wanted to make a decent ham!

I small poke in my lower back made me jump. I turned around and was confronted by a child. Quite a small one. I think it was a boy, but I'm not completely sure. It was wearing a beanie, jeans and a plain white T-shirt. It was maybe seven or eight years old. It smiled at me and held out a thin jar for me to take.

'Thank you.' I said automatically. Then I looked at the jar and saw that it was in fact 'whole cloves.' I looked back at the child. 'How did you know?'

He just smiled.

'What's your name?' I asked, dropping into friendly-paramedic mode.

'I can't tell you.'

'Oh yes, of course. I understand. I'm Daphne.'

'Hello Daphne. It's very nice to meet you.'

'It's very nice to meet you too. Thank you for finding the cloves for me.'

'That's okay.'

He, I'm going to say 'he', was so sweet. He had huge, blue eyes. It was like looking at a human-puppy. I think his tail might have been wagging if he'd had one. 'Are you lost?' I asked, suddenly worried that no one was lingering in the background to claim him. 'Do you need me to help you find your mummy.'

'No thank you Daphne. But would you mind very much if I held your hand?'

Well, I didn't really know what to do to be honest. He was so gentle. I wondered if this was his way of telling me he really was lost. 'Of course not.' I said. 'Where would you like to go?'

As his hand took mine I felt something almost

indescribable. I felt warmth radiate across my whole body. I felt like I was becoming lighter, that my feet were lifting off of the floor. I felt joy fill my heart. My eyes had closed. I was smiling and yet I could feel huge, warm tears welling up in my eyes. Memories, happy and sad flooded my mind. I saw my life with Teddy; I saw my secrets, I saw laughing, I saw myself crying in the hospital bathroom after they told me what had happened to me. I saw Teddy carrying me across the threshold of our wonderful shit-hole of a flat after we got married. I saw the face of the first patient I lost on a call-out, I saw croup-boy and his mum, I saw the girl in the car crash, I saw myself helping her to the van, I saw Teddy rush to the door to hold me, the evening I returned from that adventure.

Every moment was wreathed in a gentle light that softened the sadness and heightened the love buried within each moment.

Then I felt the little boy in the supermarket put his other hand on my stomach.

Heat roared through my clothes and I felt it deep within my body. I looked down at the boy. For a second he looked like he was surrounded by light. And then it was over. All of the warmth, the visions, the light, it was gone. I looked around awkwardly. It was as if nothing had happened. No one was staring, I hadn't fallen to the floor and started speaking in tongues. The world was exactly as it should have been.

'What just happened?' I asked him.

'Everything is going to be alright now Daphne.' He said to me. 'You have done wonderful things. You have saved many lives. You have brought so much love into the world.'

'What, what are you talking about?' I asked, stunned by the gentle authority of his little voice. I felt my cheeks flushing red; I didn't understand what was happening. I wondered if this was some sort of awful joke.

'Daphne, you have a good heart. It is said that if you set

your heart on doing good and you do it, over and over again, you will be filled with joy. You will now have this joy. It will grow inside you and fill your life up with love.'

I was dumbstruck. I understood everything that he was saying to me; I heard the words, understood the subtext of what he meant, but what he said was impossible. What he said were adult words that couldn't possibly have been meant as they were spoken.

'Thank you for the love you gave to the world Daphne. I am very tired now. I'm going to rest.'

He let go of my hand and walked slowly away.

He stopped to turn. 'She's going to be okay by the way; the girl you put in a van.'

I stood for, I don't know how long, in that supermarket. I stared at my hand; I rubbed my stomach. I could feel the imprint of his touch, of wonder and joy, coursing quietly through me.

Eventually I went home. Without any shopping.

Teddy was waiting for me.

I held him like my life depended upon it for a long while.

A few weeks later, seven years after I was told that I could no longer have children, I walked into our bedroom on a cold Thursday night and told Teddy that there had been a miracle.

47

JOSÉ

I never found out any more about what happened that night. I woke up from what was a major asthma attack in a private hospital across town. I was told that my employer had been deeply concerned for my wellbeing and that they were taking care of my medical bills.

When I left the hospital a few days later, I got back home (I had recently moved in with Ana-Maria) to a message. I had to go see the Head of Human Resources at EverTech HQ.

I walked out of that meeting having been reminded about 30 times that I had signed a very strict Non-Disclosure Agreement that lasted forever, which, I was reminded another 40 or so times, meant that even after I died, the agreement stood. So no writing anything down. I was also, by the way, out of a job. I was too much of a liability. Couldn't have a security team-member who was as vulnerable as I was. They paid me off. They paid me to be quiet. A whole year's salary to walk away.

And I did walk away. I walked back to Ana-Maria and told her we had enough money to really make a go of her Tapas place and that I would help. I wasn't good for much else. The doctors made it pretty clear that I was screwed (not the medical terms, but they were more complicated). I wasn't going to be running around watching kids get smashed up by psycho robot-lovers anyway. They did me a favour. I couldn't have stayed.

But here I am, definitely still alive, breaking that agreement and I didn't even mean to. But somehow that night was destined to change my life. I couldn't tell you about what happened next if you didn't know that. And I'm not scared of them anymore. It's all gone now anyway. I don't think there's anyone left to come and chase me. I read that the boss man died a few weeks ago. I'm not sorry.

So look, I'm not going to lie, the months after I left EverTech, they were okay. I mean it was not great worrying the whole time that I was going to have some massive attack and lose my shit in front of Ana-Maria, and despite the genes, tapas wasn't exactly where I thought I'd end up, but it was okay. I made my peace with it. I learnt how to do some basic accountancy. I learnt what a business plan was. I learnt a different way of handling customers to the one I had been accustomed to!

And we were doing alright. My pay-off had made the whole thing easier. And all I had to do was pretend I hadn't seen a kid get smashed up in a deliberate car crash and then have some sick bastard saw into his chest.

There were a lot of nights I didn't sleep. I'd wake up having a panic attack and then I'd need to go through a whole damn process to get my breathing under control. I got myself hospitalised 2 or 3 times in the first six months, but it was okay.

I wasn't forgetting, but I was learning to fake it, even to myself. I told myself I'd helped the girl, that that made up for it. She was alright. That's what I held onto.

Anyway, nearly a year or so goes by and we're picking up a

decent reputation. This kid walks in on his own and he sits down at one of the small tables at the back. He looks like he'd been sleeping on the streets for a long time. Ana-Maria and I look at each other, wondering what to do. We'd had a few homeless types walk in once or twice and try to scrounge a meal by just sitting at a table, but never a kid.

Ana-Maria grabs a bowl of patatas bravas that had been destined for a different table and thrusts it into my hands and basically shoves me towards the boy. She loves a lost cause that one - probably how we ended up together!

I walk over gently so as not to startle him and put the food down in front of him. Before I've even let go of the bowl, he's reached out and put his hand over mine. It was like being electrocuted, but without the pain - I was sort of stunned into stillness. He looked up at me and I was met by the bluest eyes I'd ever seen in my life. They didn't seem real.

'Thank you.' he said. His voice was quiet but clear. He wasn't embarrassed or uncertain at all. He didn't let go of my hand. It felt like we were locked in this moment for an eternity and I couldn't stop looking at him. I felt like I knew him, but I didn't know any kids other than Ana-Maria's little niece, Valeria.

'Would you sit with me?' It was an absurd question when you think about it. In what world was that a socially acceptable question to ask - a strange, homeless child walks into a restaurant and asks the waiter to sit down with him! But I did. Without hesitation.

'What's your name?' I asked as I slid into the chair opposite him.

'I'm sorry, I can't tell you.' he said. His hand was still on mine. One part of my brain knew it was strange, the other part didn't care.

'Okay, well I'm José and that one over there is Ana-Maria.' I said pointing to her. She was smiling, her head cocked sideways; she was almost laughing, not at me. I asked her afterwards and she said she felt happy, but like crying at the same time. She said it was like watching a beautiful painting that she never wanted to stop looking at.

'This is our place.' I continued.

'It's lovely.' he said.

We sat in silence for a few moments.

'José, I did not come here by accident. I am here because of you.'

I literally did not know what to say to that. So I didn't. I waited. I felt somehow that this was the right thing to do.

'I have spent a long time trying to find you. I wasn't sure at first if I ever would. You were not easy to uncover.'

'I...I haven't been hiding.'

'I do not think this is true. You have been hiding your whole life.'

His words hit me like a blow to the chest and yet I felt somehow at peace. His hand was still on mine. He did not say anything else for what felt like an eternity.

His hand was still on mine.

'José, I am here because I know you, and yet we have never really met. I know that you have a good heart. I know that you have hidden that from anyone who has been close to you. I am here because you will not hide that any longer. You have wasted many years pretending. This place where you find yourself right now is not the place that you thought you would ever be, but I have found you and that makes it the perfect place.' He paused again. He finally drew his hand from mine and immediately I missed it. 'I have come here to give you a gift.'

He jumped off his chair. For a moment he looked unsteady. He hadn't eaten any of the patatas bravas I had put down in front of him. He looked fragile and yet every movement was filled with purpose. He walked to my chair and with a strength which was entirely unnatural, he pulled the chair back from the table and spun it ninety degrees so that I was once again facing him.

He put his hand out and placed it gently on my chest. Immediately the warmth I had felt on my hand, radiated once more into my body. I felt my shoulders drop, as if someone had given me a hundred happy pills and I was going to float upon a cloud. I wanted to keep looking into his eyes; they seemed sad almost, but happy. I'm sure there's a word for that... but it was as if the warmth that now flooded my veins, was a potion to send me to sleep. It was the lullaby my mother had never sung and I felt like a baby who wanted to be held.

I knew I was smiling. I must've looked odd. But I didn't care. I was happy in a way I did not know was possible.

'José, you have a good heart, and now you will have good lungs too.'

His words jolted me from the euphoria. Did he just say that my lungs were going to be fixed? What the...? But another wave of calm derailed any confusion.

I felt him move his hand away. I opened my eyes. He was looking at me with the same expression on his face. I looked to Ana-Maria. Tears were rolling down her cheeks. The few other people in the restaurant didn't seem to think anything worth looking at was happening.

The kid reached for my hand once more. As I gave it to him, he pulled me to my feet. And then he hugged me. He rested his head on my stomach for a moment. And then he was moving away.

'Wait!' I called out. 'Where are you going? Won't you at least stay and eat with us?'

'José, thank you for letting me find you. My final gift to you is an answer to a question you have asked yourself many times: She was okay.'

I didn't ask 'who?' I knew exactly who he meant. I smiled.

ONE GOOD HEART

But then he was nearly out the door. 'What about the boy?' I yelled.

'Do not worry about him. There was nothing you could do for him.'

And then he was gone.

My heart was racing. I was breathing fast. I should have been having an attack. But I wasn't.

Ana-Maria came to me as I sat back down in my chair. She knew too well what should have happened next. She watched me for a moment, barely daring to take a breath herself. Then as I calmed down. I took the deepest of breaths, as if I wanted to suck up all the air in the all the world, all the air my lungs had never let me have before.

She smiled. Her lips, still wet with tears, kissed mine.

'Who was that?' I whispered.

'Un ángel disfrazado.'

An angel in disguise.

48

MIA

(RECORDED IN 2004, 10 YEARS AFTER THE INCIDENT)

'This is it!' I had never heard him sound so joyful, boyish almost, in the freedom of the expression.

I never spoke to Auden Everston again after that strange phone call, but I was in his presence one final time. The day of the incident. The day of 17th September, 1994. It was a Saturday. I was supposed to be going to see Take That at Wembley Arena. But instead, Jessica called me. She sounded strange, as if the words were being forced from her mouth against her will. Each one was almost spat down the phone; if they could have stung me through the receiver, they would've. 'You must come to the second lab tonight. There will be a procedure that requires careful observation. You are the best we have.'

I didn't know we had a second lab. I didn't know we performed 'procedures', especially not on a Saturday, or at night.

'I will have an EverTech driver pick you up at 8pm.'

And so she did. This is how I ended up at the Tate Modern. Of course, it wasn't the Tate Modern then. It was what looked like an abandoned power station. This was the second lab I had never heard of. This is where I watched Auden Everston exclaim 'This is it!' As an EverTech van drove into the turbine hall.

I watched dozens of people crowd the back doors of the vehicle, but they all made way for him. He parted them with a silent command that comes with only the most absolute power; the sort of power that weighs the heart on a scale against a feather; the sort of power which arbitrates and delivers the most final sentencing. I was standing in the Hall of Truth, in the presence of Osiris, who was also Amut. He would give life and destroy it with a solitary gesture and we were there only to witness the totality of his authority.

I don't know why I was surprised when I saw a loaded stretched pulled from the back of the van; after all, Jessica was a renowned cardiologist and she had talked of procedures, and I of all people knew that the Everstons' work was at the very edge of the realm of science, law and morality.

I only saw him for a moment, the boy on the stretcher, but he seemed familiar. He was rushed past me and I was to now go to my station - a viewing room attached to the 'procedure room' to monitor the readings being recorded on the machines I would find there. No one told me what it was I would see, only that there was a heartbeat that was of the utmost importance. 'The heart that you will hear and the readings that it gives, are the most important thing in our universe right now. Nothing else matters. If that heart fails, everything fails. If you see anything that looks wrong, you press the intercom button and you tell the team in the room.'

Pretty clear instructions. No room for doubt. Except that I found myself flooded with it. Nothing about what I was doing or seeing was right. Do I press the intercom to tell them that? Shall I buzz in and say 'Excuse me guys, sorry to disturb you, but what the fuck is actually going on here, because to me, this looks like some seriously messed up shit, and that is coming from a girl with a secret, self-charging metal heart that no one knows about?'

I didn't do that. I didn't do that because as I began to watch the soundless video feed that showed me the procedure room, I saw the boy transferred to a hospital cot; there was already another boy on a bed. Was this a transplant then? There hadn't been a lot of child transplants, but it wasn't secret work either. I didn't have time to consider that because this is when Jessica appeared on my screen. She burst into the room, looking like a mad, rabid tigress, thrashing her way past the theatre nurses to the boy on the table. A security guard ran in after her, tried to grab her, but I saw Auden Everston hold up a hand. It was enough to call off the dogs.

There was no audio feed on my monitor, but I could see that Jessica was screaming. She put her hand on the boy, then turned to face her husband. She grabbed something from the instrument trolley, a knife I suppose; she held it out in front of her. She went to stab at him. She missed and he slapped her.

Immediately she became a cowering puppy. She was still, silent, sobbing uncontrollably. He gestured to her and then the boy: 'Stay and help, or go!' I inserted for myself.

She stayed.

She kissed the boy's head.

She wept relentlessly.

Through the monitor and the foot of concrete that separated us, I felt the swirling vortex of fury that she insulated herself with as she took the scalpel in hand once more. This time though, she marked a point for incision.

Everston nodded his approval.

Machines rolled in all around them.

I was sure I could hear Jessica wailing over the sound of the oscillating saw.

I could block out the truth no longer. I recognised this boy because I had met him. The day Jessica had an unmissable meeting with a private funding opportunity. This boy, her boy, her son, had been sent home from school with a temperature.

'You can watch him can't you Mia?' She told me. 'He won't be any trouble.'

He wasn't. He was...perfect. He was the sweetest, most gentle child I had ever met. Talking with him as he rested quietly on my sofa as I attempted to work from home, was like being lulled into a happy dream of the ocean lapping at the shore. He was a sick child and yet when he spoke, I had felt safe and comforted, as if the world had been rebuilt to hold me in its arms and carry me into peacefulness.

And he was now lying on a hospital cot, looking to all the world as if he were dead.

Jerry.

I'm so sorry.

49

MIA

(RECORDED IN 2004, 10 YEARS AFTER THE INCIDENT)

What we did that day was both a miracle and an abomination. I am haunted by the sinister beauty of what was created. What I witnessed was closer to magic than to any science I knew and the end result was something that was designed to transform the world.

How it was possible, I never fully understood, but if Everston had wooed Jessica with the impossible salvation of my life through an artificial heart, then with this feat, he must have enslaved her very soul, for how she continued to live with him after he did what he did to their own child, I will never understand.

I met him again, their son, Jerry, a month after the procedure. I was to conduct my heart-brain interaction experiments on him.

He both was, and was not the boy I had met back in a world which was so very much easier to understand than this one. He did not look like Jerry, but there was still that intangible serenity about everything he did. He looked at me with a face that seemed to ask a question, like a puppy who tilts his head as he tries to fathom your new command. He sensed in me something familiar and yet he could not place me. I was forgettable I told myself, not wanting to consider any alternative reason for being unknown to a person who had touched my heart so deeply. To be forgotten by those that move you is to have a piece of yourself erased, as if you were the illustrator's mistake, a slip of the pencil that adds nothing to the composition.

I ran the tests.

Because of what I had witnessed that night in mid-September, I was not shocked. I had begun to piece together some of what they were doing. I knew by now that Everston worked almost exclusively in the realms of the impossible. But I also knew that what I was witnessing was nothing more than a hint at the truth of what they had done and this made me afraid.

When we concluded the tests, Jerry waved goodbye as he was escorted away. 'Bye Mia.' he said. As if he knew me? Maybe. But I did not know him; I did not know what they had made him.

I left my job that day. I walked away from the lab, from EverTech, from Jessica, Everston, Jerry, the work that had consumed almost every day of my life for more than 15 years. I left because they sent me Jerry's file to record my findings on. I had never seen anything like it; most of it was redacted, or pages had been hurriedly removed. Within the folder was my report: *The Heart's Electro-Magnetic Field & Its Relationship With Brain-Wave Activity*. Not a catchy title, but there was my name, stuffed within these other more anonymous pages. I knew then that I was not safe; that if anything were to go wrong, this file would lead to me. Sure, they'd know I wasn't the architect, but there was my name, posted on this pitiful piece of research that set into motion something no less remarkable than the story of Lazarus.

But Everston was no Jesus, and if 15 years of working with

hearts teaches you anything, it is that there is no coming back from death.

So I ran. I ran knowing that if he wanted to, Everston could press a few buttons on a keyboard and no doubt stop the miracle that he had placed inside my body. I had two thoughts about this: 1, a young woman suddenly dropping down dead would probably lead to an autopsy and when it did, there would surely be a very clear and obvious trail back to Everston, which no doubt he would rather avoid, and 2, if I were dead, I would at least not be around when the shit hit the razor-sharp, child-butchering fan.

I hedged my bets and here I am 10 years later. But not for much longer. You see I saw an angel and it offered me something better than immortality: forgiveness. Forgiveness and a miracle. It was more than I ever hoped for. And I insisted that it would not be free of charge. It costs so very much to allow someone to eradicate guilt; I have seen with my own eyes that it is the very worst kind of sickness, that can literally scar a heart, leaving it desperate and malnourished. So I begged the angel to allow me to do something, anything, that might make it happy. I did the only thing it asked of me. And now this is done, I am ready to leave this world behind.

50

JACK

Dear Mum,

In the end I found a way to be alone with Jerry. I was nervous at first. Since that first day of testing, I had barely heard him speak; I had no idea what level of control or monitoring was in place and so just being sat in front of him was a huge risk. But at that point I was possibly more afraid of doing nothing, than of being caught. Also, I had drunk about half a pint of gin. That helped.

I sat across a table from him wondering what to say. How to start. Where to go next if it went well. He broke the silence.

I would like to help you Jack. I can see that you are suffering and I would like to help you.

Are you programmed to say that?

I am not. Though there is an impulse within me that desires to help you. I do not think this is artificial.

How would you know?

I can feel the parts of me which pre-existed this body. I am aware of who I am, though there are many things at work to suppress this.

Do you know who I am?

Yes. You are Jack Lewis. You, along with Jessica Everston performed the not inconsiderable feat of transplanting my brain, heart and spinal column into this body. You were a medical student who had a tremor. There is currently an EverTech microchip lodged in your brain, as there is in mine. The chip in your brain has enhanced your intellectual capacity and nullified the tremor.

What does the chip in your head do?

Nothing.

Nothing?

I have disengaged it.

How?

This is how I would like to help you Jack.

You want to turn off my chip?

I wish to set you free.

My mind went into overdrive. I realised that he was right. The thought of no longer being beholden to Everston was the thing I longed for more than anything else. But I had come to this meeting to help him; how could I let him help me when I had done this to him?

You did not do this to me Jack.

Can you read my mind?

In a way, I suppose I can. I can feel the electrical impulses all over your body and I can sense the anxiety and uncertainty flooding your nervous system as we speak. I understand that you manipulated our meeting because you were hoping to make amends for a wrong you feel you have committed, but you have been as much a victim as I have. You were collected and rewired. You were manipulated to be something that they needed and you have found a way to lift the veil they so keenly wish to hold over your eyes. You are afraid. Afraid for your life and for your soul.

You feel that saving me would right a wrong. But I cannot be saved Jack. I have been forced into a place from which there is only one ending. This is not the case for you. I can help you walk a new path.

How old are you? In the real world I mean; how old were you? You looked like a little boy and yet you speak like...like someone more wise than I will ever be. Is that your voice, or is this something they have done to you?

I was nine years old when you met me on the stretcher in the operating theatre. I don't think I was a very normal nine-year-old, even before this.

He smiled. It was the first moment that I saw the absolute, unerring, enduring humanity behind the frame we had buried him in.

It was beautiful. It radiated lightness.

I loved him as if he were my dearest, fragile little brother. I wanted so much to protect him.

He knew he was getting weaker with every attempt to save someone. He foresaw an ending that was inglorious and ill-befitting someone who could do such extraordinary things. He knew that he would die in this bunker, far away from the light, far away from the real life I had helped steal from him.

If you help me, you'll disable the chip in my head?

He nodded.

And the tremor will come back?

He nodded again.

But you could fix that?

And again.

Please don't.

He stood up and walked around the desk that separated us, wrapped his arms around me and held me.

I would very much like for you to help me Jerry, but there is one condition: I am going to get you out of this place first. When I have done that, then you can help me.

Okay.

I'd like to tell you Mum, that I came up with some epic plan for sneaking Jerry out. But reality is so often a more mundane and sorry affair.

EverTech, like a lot of technology companies, was growing at an insane rate. They wanted the world to know that they were the next titans of industry, but didn't want to share 90% of the work they were doing with the world. They had a few big headlines; stories thrown to the press to keep interest up, but in truth these things were nothing compared to the truth of what was going on. Nonetheless, Everston was a vain man; he wanted to be adored. This, I suppose, was his Achilles heel. Only it wasn't - no one ever challenged him, doubted him, no one ever knocked him off of his pedestal, or gave him a bad write-up. No one. Ever. But, like many crazy-smart people, he was clearly paranoid as fuck. So, to make sure he was everyone's favourite secret megalomaniac, we used to do this thing where he invited schoolchildren in for the day to look around the EverTech Museum - a seriously sycophantic compilation of Everston's greatness. All I did was look at the logs for who was booked in, ordered a uniform for that particular school in Jerry's size and as they were leaving, got him to slide into the back of the group. I clocked out just before this, met him as he was lagging behind the group and off we went.

Well, that was the plan.

It didn't quite work.

What actually happened, was that long before we got to the top floor, a couple of security guards caught up to us as we were getting into the lift. Nobody made a fuss. I understood what was happening and neither Jerry or I was about to fight our way out of the EverTech bunker.

My hands were bound behind me using zip ties. On Jerry they placed some strange metal crown over his head. I had never seen this before, but it seemed to make him immediately passive. There was a faint blue light coming from the inside rim that touched his head; it made his skin grey. It was the only time I noticed how too-perfect his skin was; it was the only time I ever saw him as less than human. I imagined what they could do to him; I imagined him stomping mechanically around the EverTech campus, collecting trash and cleaning dishes in the canteen. I was ashamed of my thoughts in that moment. I was quick to reduce him, Jerry, who could save lives with the touch of his hand, to something other and alien, because I thought my own weak, fleshy exterior to be worth more.

I could not have been more wrong. I knew that already. I knew that if a choice was to be made of who was expendable and who was not, that I would not fare well. I knew that this would be true in a terrible and dark place like EverTech, but I knew that it would also be true out there, far away in the real world. That when light shone upon us both, there was only going to be one creature found wanting and lacking. And that was not going to be Jerry.

As I followed the guards, sullen, head down, I felt Jerry reach for one of my bound hands. He squeezed it gently, just for a moment. I turned. Before either guard had time to notice, I saw him smile, then wink at me. He was faking submission! The blue-light crown was useless now that his chip had been decommissioned. He released my hand and we were both shoved towards the now all too familiar entrance to Auden Everston's office.

Needless to say, I was scared shitless. Especially given the fact that I'd seen him blow out the brains of someone who had given him a fuck-tonne of cash. I had not done this and so didn't really fancy my chances.

When he did reach into his drawer, he didn't pull out a gun. He took out what looked like a remote control.

I'm sorry Mr Lewis, but you have shown yourself to be significantly less intelligent than I believed we had developed you to be. I'm going to press this button in a moment. Doing so will be an incredibly painful experience for you, which I will enjoy watching. When the pain subsides you will remember almost nothing of what we have taught you. You will in fact return to being a rather pathetic, failed medical student with a progressive, degenerative tremor, who will undoubtedly amount to very little indeed. You will have helped create one of the most sophisticated machines in the history of mankind and yet will know nothing of it. You could pass it in the street and not recognise your own creation; a creation that could of course spare you from the fate you are once again destined to suffer from. I rather detest irony in normal circumstances, but in this instance there is something quite delicious about it.

He pressed the button and the pain was...non-existent! I didn't understand. And neither did he.

Before he could change tactics and find the gun I knew was hovering all too nearby, Jerry walked towards him, revealing that he was no longer under his spell. He took hold of Everston's hand.

You were my father once. But I do not know you now any more than you know me. And yet you are not a stranger, so I am sorry for what I have done.

Everston tore himself away from Jerry, breaking contact between them.

What have you done?! He roared. He was gripping his hand, rubbing it as if it hurt and yet he was in no pain.

I have sent a single nanobot to gently press against your spinal cord for the next 15 minutes. You will be entirely unable to move or speak. Jack will leave. I will leave. Nobody will try to stop us and you will not chase us. After 15 minutes the bot will release the nerves and travel to your bladder. You will expel it later today and you will be entirely unharmed.

You stupid son-of-a-bitch; you ungrateful bastard! I made you! I made you twice. I have made you like a god and this is how you repay me? You try and save some worthless dropout and walk away from a project which could save millions of lives.

It is not your intention to save millions of lives. It is your intention to create an elite ruling class of near immortals who will control everything and want for nothing. And whilst yes, you had a hand in my creation more than once, you do not define who I am. You are not the common thread that binds my old self with the new; you are the old clothes that I cast off so that I may be dressed in light and truth. You were my father and the architect of my body, but you are also the darkness that wishes me to be blind.

How exactly do you imagine you will just be allowed out of this facility?

I will escort them out.

I turned around to see Jessica Everston standing in the doorway to her husband's office. She looked terrible; as if she hadn't slept for a hundred years, and yet there was fire in her wretched, bloodshot eyes.

Get the hell out of here Jessica. This is nothing to do with you.

But she could not take her eyes off of this Jerry; the robot that housed her son's heart and brain. This robot that was so much more than that; so nearly her son; maybe entirely her son. I didn't know. I still don't know.

He was our son Auden. If he wants to go...

We've been over this Jessica. You knew. You knew in your heart what I was willing to do. You knew when you told me about his ECG readings what I would do. You could have kept it a secret, but your pride, your unrelenting obedience and desire to please me overthrew any maternal instincts you might claim to have. So please don't pretend that now, stood in front of this thing we have created, that you would choose it over me and the work we have done. You...

But we didn't hear any more of what he had to say. Either the nanobot had reached its destination, or he was having a stroke. I can't say that I was bothered either way. But he fell silently to the floor and Jessica immediately ushered us out, closing the office door gently behind us.

Once we were across the street, away from the office, she turned to face us. She knelt down in front of Jerry and put her hand gently on his flawless, synthetic face. She never said a word, but tears streamed down her cheeks and her hand began to tremble. She stood to talk to me, but kept her hand on Jerry's face. *By tomorrow morning I'll make sure there's half a million pounds in your bank account. I want you to go far away Mr Lewis. Far away from this place, from this work and from Jerry. He has his own path to tread and I suspect your lives are unlikely to intersect again in the future.*

Like a dumb bastard I just stood there until it got uncomfortable. She walked away. Back to the EverTech building. She didn't say goodbye; she didn't look at Jerry; she didn't turn around and look longingly at what she was leaving behind. She just went back to work.

You knocked out the chip in my head didn't you? When you held my hand before?

Jerry nodded.

The tremor will come back now won't it.

Another nod.

And I'll stop being smart?

A shrug.

But I won't forget?

A shake of the head.

OK.

I can help; at least with the tremor.

I know. But I also know what it does to you, when you help someone, and I am not worth the cost.

The recipient of a gift does not determine the value or worthiness of the gift. I'm offering this because I want to.

But that wasn't what was happening before...in there?

No. Now I have freed myself, I can choose who to help.

But you won't be able to help everyone.

We can only do what we can do. And I can help you.

Please don't. Please don't help me. I helped do this to you. I don't want to be... But I didn't know what the end of that sentence was and I was crying. I honestly couldn't remember the last time I had done that.

OK. But I want you to know something. He took my hand.

No nanobots. No sneaky attack to help me.

No sneaky attack. Just words. You made some bad decisions. Everyone does that. And then you made a brave decision. Not everybody does that. You are not broken. You are not bad. But you are tired. Jessica was right; you should go somewhere far away and rest. What I can do could help your hand, but that will never be enough to make you happy again.

Will you be okay?

I will be fine.

How many people can you help before...

Before I can't? I think it will depend on what they need. I need to think first. I need to understand who I am. You can't help people if you don't know who you are.

I don't think any number of neuro-enhancements could ever have made me as smart as you.

I'm not smart; I have just spent a lot of time listening to the world.

Yeah? And what does the world have to say?

That pain makes a lot of noise. But happiness is like beautiful music, and if you can find it, you should dance like a crazy person, because there cannot always be music.

I don't think a day goes by that I don't think about that kid.

I am haunted by the terrible things I did to his body, but I also smile as I think of the insanity of what it is he could do and the wisdom that he carried in his heart. I hope with everything I have, that he is still out there in the world, doing something that makes him want to dance. When we walked away from each other that afternoon, that was the end. I never saw him again.

Jessica did as she promised and sent me the money. For a little while I tried to just lie low. I even tried to get a job in HMV! But Billy could see that I was struggling. He told me that I walked around like a rabbit being hunted. He went on and on at me for such a long time and in the end I told him. Everything. And that was the end of Jack and Billy. He was not quite so philosophical or forgiving as Jerry. Which frankly was a relief.

I needed to be hated. My self-loathing wasn't enough to force me into action. When he left...well when he left, you know what happens next. I left. I came out here, and I never told you anything.

For a long time, I told myself that it was to keep you safe. But the truth is something less noble. I didn't tell you what I was doing because I was ashamed. I am ashamed. I am your son. Your son who helped to kill a child. Your son who made a living machine that could literally save almost anybody on the planet who was suffering. Your son who could not now do either of those things because he has regressed into an anonymous, once-upon-a-time medical school dropout. With a tremor. And a dog.

I'm lonely mum. I miss you. I have such terrible dreams. But I worry one day that I might not. I worry that one day I might not feel bad enough to wake up with tears rolling down my face. And then what? Who am I then? I can never be your son again - just as Jerry can never be their son. I took that from him and I am taking that from myself. I am sorry that I have to hurt you, but it is better this way. My hatred has become like the ocean I ride; it may lap gently at the shore of my heart, or it might thunder violently against it, but always it is eroding it; tearing away at it, one grain of sand at a time. Eventually there will be nothing left. Maybe that will be peaceful.

I was forgiven, but I cannot forgive myself.

I can find enough love in my heart for you. But that is all.

J

51

MEDICAL REPORT
DAPHNE MORRIS

Sex: Female
Age: 37

In 1987 Mrs Morris was admitted for urgent trauma care following a penetrative pelvic injury. This resulted in significant scarring on the colon, ovaries, fallopian tubes and uterus, as well as the lower rectus abdominus muscle. Scans carried out at the time and post-surgery suggested that the chances of pregnancy were minimal. Ovary function had been significantly impaired and the scarring to the fallopian tubes means that eggs were unlikely to be able to pass to the uterus. The vast pelvic scarring meant carrying a child to term was statistically unlikely.

Scans taken in 1995 during and post-pregnancy show almost no scarring. The patient's body has done an impressive, indeed unprecedented job of breaking down the scar tissue. Laparoscopic tubal ligation reversal surgery was not considered an option due to the extent of scarring on the fallopian tubes, but there is now no evidence of blockage.

Mrs Morris has clearly demonstrated the benefits of an active lifestyle and positive outlook. The likelihood of conception was below 5%, but I am pleased to report that she and her partner now have a healthy baby boy.

52

MEDICAL REPORT
JOSÉ PEREZ

Sex: Male
Age: 42

Mr Perez is a fit and healthy male. He is Wing Commander with the 36 Squadron RAF Regiment, seeing active service in a number of active war zones including Iraq.

Medical history suggested severe asthma beginning in childhood and developing significantly in early adulthood. Scans from both NHS and private hospitals in south London revealed high levels of scarring and thickening of the smooth muscle on the inside walls of the airways, or 'airway remodelling'. Notes indicate frequent hospitalisation and various failed medical interventions. Mr Perez's medical records upon joining the RAF show no breathing difficulties whatsoever. A scan as part of standard medical protocols shows no signs of airway remodelling. Peak flow is exceptional and there have been no respiratory problems in nearly 20 years.

If Mr Perez had not insisted upon the severity of his asthma, I would suggest that there had been a mix-up of records. As such I suspect that there are missing medical records and that Mr Perez has omitted from his memory that he has undertaken extensive and extremely successful bronchial thermoplasty, which along with a significant, positive change in diet and exercise has assisted Mr Perez in undoing the damage done to his lungs in early adulthood.

53

MIA

RECORDED IN 2004, 10 YEARS AFTER THE INCIDENT

I don't know what possessed me to do it, but I posted about meeting Jerry on some blog site that I don't think exists anymore. I think I called it 'The Day I Met An Anonymous Angel' or something like that. I wrote it in-between the last two times we met. Both of these were after I had left EverTech. I think I wrote it because I needed to tell someone what had happened. But I knew that the whole truth would be even less believable than what I wrote. So, I wrote that I had been healed by an angel. This was at least 50% of the truth. The other 50% though is complicated and sad.

When I left EverTech I needed to go somewhere that would allow me to be unknown. There was no way that I could work as a researcher within the medical world; it was a small community and there would be too many questions. But I was afraid to leave the world of academia completely; I needed to be surrounded by the quiet and solitude that had so gently held me as I tried to navigate a way through the inevitable noises of life. And so I found peace as an assistant librarian at the Taylor Institution Library in Oxford. It was perfect really; to be surrounded by books is to be immersed in knowledge that is already growing old; it has substance, but is no longer a threat and in that place, there are few people less visible than those who sort and order simply so that others may find. I was nobody. But I was not fool enough to think that I was safe.

When Jerry walked into the Taylorian on a dark, wet evening in February; it was as if Auden Everston himself had flicked a switched and stopped my heart. I felt myself freeze in a way that suggested I had neither a fight nor flight response; I stood so still I wonder if I thought I might become invisible to him. But I did not.

He walked over to me, this child, small for his age when I had last seen him, no different now, 5 years after he had been brought solemnly into the operating theatre hidden in the abandoned power station. He was frozen in time, as I was frozen in space and yet somehow we met in the middle of the reading room. You would imagine that a child who looks no older than 9 or 10 years old, dressed shabbily in a dirty yellow anorak and a green Teenage Mutant Ninja Turtles rucksack would draw attention, but nobody seemed to flinch. Students too busy with essay crises and flirtation are, I suppose, an unlikely group to be drawn into the worries of others, but as he reached out for my hand, I took it, to pull him towards a quieter, more sheltered section of the library.

Surrounded by teetering stacks of as yet unsorted books, he kept hold of my hand and all I could wonder at was how warm it was. *Hello Mia.* He said, smiling softly at me with sorrowful eyes that pooled an almost unfathomable depth of feeling.

Jerry... I stumbled, taking a step back, away from his gentle grasp. *'How...?'* There wasn't really much more to say.

I have been finding my own way Mia, for nearly 5 years now. I wanted to see you.

What do you mean finding your own way? How have

Everston and Jessica, I mean your parents, let you out of their sight? How did you find me? Why on earth would you want to find me?

He smiled again, but there was more life in it this time; there was a little bit of naughtiness in it - I liked it; it made me happy. *I ran away I suppose. They couldn't stop me.*

But surely they're tracking you! I was selfishly worried for my own safety, for my own anonymity, knowing that this was pointless, knowing that they could ping the circuitry that was my heart, whenever they liked and be on top of me in moments.

Actually, they can't. I disabled the chip they implanted.

You...you disabled the chip? How? How is that even possible; the chip is inside your...

Head. Yes. Not very imaginative really and not terribly tricky to get access to or overwhelm with a quick power surge.

You mean you electrocuted your own head in order to short the tracker?' He nodded. I nearly passed out at the thought. He saw this and smiled. *'But they must be looking for you? They have so much money, they could employ an army to find you.*

They could. There have been many people sent to find me. Sometimes they do. But they do not take me back to them.

I felt a cold sweat break out under my arms. Was this kid some sort of miniature assassin? Was I a target? Did he think I was a threat?

Mia, please do not be afraid of me. I was so desperate to see you, but I cannot stay long and I don't want you spending the little time we have, worrying about EverTech employees bursting through the windows, pointing guns and overturning books.

He reached for my hands again. I let him take them. *There is nothing to fear. I came here to thank you.*

Thank me for what?

For being kind to a sick boy, when you had so much work to do.

You remember that? But that was...I mean you were...

Yes, in some ways I was different then, but I remember. I remember everything actually. And I wanted you to know that I am grateful for your kindness on that day I was sick, and on the day we met after the accident. I know that this was the day you left EverTech and I know that it was because of what happened to me. I know that you feel a great weight upon your shoulders, feeling somehow responsible because you were so very clever in finding a hidden message, buried quietly within our bodies and that they have used this beautiful thing you found and made something terrible. But Mia, you did something wonderful. You proved that there are unbelievably powerful ways for us to connect with the world. In the beauty of a boy loving his dog in such a way that all anyone could see it, you showed us that the world can feel this love too. You were the scientist who conducted their work with the heart of a poet.

I laughed at this. *My father is a poet.*

Then you carry him in your heart and in your actions.

My heart is...not like...is not as it should be.

Your heart may be made from metal, but that does not stop it beating with kindness and honour; that is not something that can be taken away.

For hours we sat, surrounded by some of the greatest learning known to mankind and Jerry told me a story that could never be written down. He told me everything that had happened to him; everything that he had done and what he would do. Silence surrounded us with a kind of tingling anticipation, desperate to draw our words out from the darkness. I held my hand over my heart almost the entire time he spoke; more than once I had to remind myself to breath. His words were both music and fire, a rhapsody of truth that left me both more and less afraid of the world.

I had shut the doors and dismissed the last of the students long ago; the deep, comforting shadow of night held his secrets to its chest but as the sky began to fill with light once more, I saw how tired this little boy looked. *Do you need to rest?*

No. There is no time for that; soon I must go. I wanted to do more than thank you. I want to help you; I will show you what is possible.

You have nothing to prove to me. I believe every word you have told me. And besides, what can you do for a girl with a metal heart!

He laughed at this. The way a young boy might when he finds something truly funny, like the first time you understand a pun, or when your teacher breaks wind in class. It seemed the most natural thing in the world and yet I knew that there must have been so few moments to laugh at in the years since we last me. *Okay Mia. Then let me help someone you love.*

Matka! I called out in hope, in the mother-tongue of my father, long gone from this world and beyond anyone's reach, but whose poetry haunted me, swarming my mind when it was ill at ease, soothing me with his beautiful words. He wrote so often about my mother that I thought everyone in the world must love each other in such a way. When I was finally released into reality, I realised that his poems had captured something far more rare. I tried to write a poem in his language once; I called it 'Matka', *Mother*; I wanted him to know that I loved her too.

Yes. Said Jerry, drawing me back into the world. *Yes Mia, that would be just fine.*

54

MIA

RECORDED IN 2004, 10 YEARS AFTER THE INCIDENT

I wanted to go back to that reckless post I had made all those years ago and write my final response to the thread which had been kept alive by conspiracy theorists and bored students for years. I wanted to write to tell them everything I knew about Jerry. But I couldn't. So instead, I shall tell you, whoever you are, that this could have been my final post and once it is spoken, I shall take my leave of this world, knowing that I did not light a fire under the belly of life, but that I did meet an angel, perhaps even had a hand in spreading his love across the world and that was enough.

The Last Post:
An Anonymous Angel by Ivan Washington,
aka Mia.

I wasn't lying when I told you that I had seen an angel. I really did. I saw him, I met with him; he wanted nothing more than to heal the wounds that I had allowed to fester in my heart. And he did. He freed me with his love. But he wanted to do more. He wanted to share his gift, so I took him to my mother. She had been diagnosed with pancreatic cancer and her treatment was not making a dent. The doctors had given up. They were ready to move her to a hospice. But I knew that she was not ready to die. The angel sat with her for an hour. He held her hand and talked with her in his gentle, melodic voice. I didn't listen to what was said; that is not my story. My story is that my mother rose from her bed the next day, as if she were a woman half her age. She walked across her room and picked up the trombone that we had left in the room, a memory of happier times, and she played it. She played it with the kind of soul that left tears rushing down the wrinkled riverbed of her face. The angel had saved her. And now he is gone. And I know that in all my life I shall never know a greater joy than when he took my hand and said 'Your heart is beautiful and your mother is healed. Every day will bring joy to you both, long after you choose to leave this place.' I know that I did not deserve such a blessing and yet this is what I have received. I don't suppose I will ever convince you that this is true, but know that there are miracles in the world after all. Know that in the darkest of days there is hope and you don't even need to be looking for it to have it find you.

Of course, if I had written this, it would only be part of the truth. He really did heal my mother. I watched him do it. I understood what it was Everston and Jessica thought they were creating and I saw that it was beautiful; it was literally a miracle. But I saw too that it came at an extraordinary cost. When Jerry tried to stand up and leave my mother, he tripped and fell to the floor. His eyes looked vacant and he didn't respond to me talking to him at first. When he spoke, it was little more than a whisper. *They thought that they would put me in this body and I would live like an immortal, sustained by the wonder of innovation. But a cage is a prison no matter how intelligent; no matter its desire to sustain, it will rot you from the inside out. They never understood what they were truly asking when they tore me from myself. My failure to survive will be their penance. I cannot do very much more before the time will come that my heart will refuse to do battle. When that time comes I wish to be left in peace.*

And I understood in that moment everything that he was telling me. I understood that he had come to me so that I could also find peace. He knew that I would see that his parents had tried to create a living machine whose heart was human, but better and stronger, than anything that had ever been before. They thought that technology would enhance him and make him a god. A god built by gods. Through them suffering might end and the winners would be those that could pay for the privilege. But he was not meant to be a human inside a machine and his humanity was being broken by each intervention. His heart would fail. And when it did he wanted me by his side to ensure that he was never found. Never examined. Never interrogated. Never known. Except to those who he had chosen to touch. They would know that for a little while an angel really did walk the earth. And that angel was a nine-year-old boy named Jerry.

And so, I was tasked with something terrible. It was my job to kill an angel. To destroy the shell within which he was entombed and to kill the mythology that would surely grow around him. So I didn't post another blog. Instead, I buried an angel where no one will ever find him. It didn't break my heart. My heart cannot, it seems, be broken. But in the end I turned back to my roots and the work of my father's favourite writer, Kafka. My father quoted Kafka at me in almost every conversation we ever had. His favourite thing to say was this:

"There are 3 things Kafka wrote which, if you understand them, will mean that you have accomplished everything there is to accomplish in life.

- Number 1: *Anyone who keeps the ability to see beauty never grows old.*
- Number 2: *Don't bend; don't water it down; don't try to make it logical; don't edit your own soul according to the fashion. Rather, follow your most intense obsessions mercilessly.*
- Number 3: *I am free and that is why I am lost.*"

Jerry had shown me that the first of these quotes was true. He was to be forever young until the moment he ceased to be, and he saw beauty and goodness in every breath that he took.

The Everstons had shown me that Kafka, if followed to the letter, could be dangerous. They were devoted to their own brilliance and progress for the sake of progress with no regard for anything. In the end they murdered their own son in order to make scientific history. That resurrected son ran away from them and quietly became an underground legend, the likes of which we may never see again.

And in the final quote I found the most frightening of truths. I was free now. I was free because I knew the truth about what had happened to Jerry, and I was free because whilst the threat of my destruction at the hands of Auden Everston remained very real, I simply did not care. But with this morbid acceptance of the random assignation of fate, I felt myself untethered to all of the things I had held dear. I had fallen out of love with the woman I had held up on a pedestal from before we had ever met, the music of my mother's making now belonged to someone else and I no longer marvelled at science because I had met an angel. I was entirely happy, but found no meaning at all in trying to carry on. Jerry was the pinnacle of what good could be and he was gone. His parents were, as far as I knew, very much still alive. This is not a world in which I wish to live.

I hope that the truth I have told will do some good. My

liberation came from another great Czech writer. Karel Čapek once wrote that 'You just can't make a bayonet charge underwater' and as long as Everston was quietly, subversively bending the world, bending technology and more importantly, bending the will of others to do terrible things with no checks, I was powerless to stop him. So I will instead stop what he gave me. And that will bring me peace.

55

EVIE

(ON BEHALF OF HARVEY HAWKINS)

It wasn't until he tracked down a paramedic who was on patrol that night, that he even knew you existed. But the poor girl couldn't remember your name. 'Apostrophe' she said; well she wasn't too far off really was she? But Harvey said that when he went to find evidence that you existed, there wasn't a pickle; nothing! He assumed you were a relative, he thought most likely a daughter, but that article and the fact that there was no birth certificate, no hospital records, nothing, meant he was no closer to tracking you down and yet he knew that you were the key to unlocking it all.

When the lady paramedic, Daphne, I think her name was, told Harvey what she knew, she could remember you calling the man that wanted to take you away from the crash site 'Mr A.' Wasn't much of a lead, but that was what he had, along with a description of what he looked like.

As it turns out, a firm like EverTech doesn't employ too many middle-aged men with a surname beginning with A. What he wasn't expecting was for the most likely suspect to be a groundsman. Then again dearie, he wasn't really a groundsman, was he?

Oh, I don't want to wade through this muck again, but I can see from your face that you know what I'm talking about. Harvey didn't know what you knew, but I can see it in your face; it's all coming together now for you.

So many lies. I feel bad for you, I really do, but I don't have much time left in this world and I can't waste it filling up my heart with other people's regret.

Harvey would of found your gardener, but that's when Jerry showed up.

He weren't really a churchgoer, my Harvey; seen too much hypocrisy in those that preached one thing and did another; instead, he would leave that to me and go for a little stroll around the park just round the corner. But he came home that afternoon and he said to me that he felt like he had been in the presence of God. And yet when he described this tiny little boy, I thought he might've gone mad. But then as he told me what Jerry had said to him, I could see from his face and the softness of his voice, which he had always reserved for our babies only, that something like a miracle had happened to him.

Jerry didn't tell him who he was at first, but Harvey knew. They talked about nothing very much at first; nice day, nice weather, wasn't it good to be outside? Harvey thought he was speaking with the most polite kid he'd ever met. But he wasn't really a little boy was he?

You're looking for someone. he said.
Maybe. Says Harvey.
A girl.
My Harvey says nothing.
She was my sister.
How's that then? Harvey asks.
I was next to her when the car crashed.
That can't be little fella. I have it on good authority, that the only person to survive that accident, was the little girl.

In many ways Detective Hawkins, that is true. But as far as it can be true, I have a sister and she is it.

How is that possible?

That is a long story.

My Evie is at church for a while yet; I've got some time.

Detective Hawkins, I would like to tell you that story because I think it would help to bring some peace, but I cannot; it is not ready yet to be told. What I must ask of you, is that you do not try and find my sister. She is in danger, but she is in less danger than she would be if you discover her.

You know son, a policeman doesn't take too kindly to such suggestions. It sounds too much like you're hiding secrets that shouldn't be hidden.

I am.

Then you should tell me. I want to help.

I know.

Well?

Detective Hawkins, you have lost things you love. Harvey said he felt his heart quicken, because Jerry reached out and held his hand in a way that made him think immediately of our Bessie. *I know that your bones felt hollow after that loss and that nothing has quite filled them up again.*

Harvey said that he felt a warmth spread from his toes, up his legs. He was smiling and had tears in his eyes all at once. Jerry had both his hands and he said to me afterwards that as he looked at that boy, he had never felt so loved.

I would like to help you Detective Hawkins.

But he pulled his hands away. *No son, no. I understand what you could do; I don't know how or why you would, but no. I want my pain; I don't want to forget what it feels like to be blindsided by a memory that hurts so much it could knock you over. That pain is part of me. I need it.*

I understand. I carry pain to remind me of things that are important too.

Thank you...

Jerry.

Jerry. Will you stay; tell me a bit more about what has happened to you?

I'm sorry Detective Hawkins, but there are other people that I need to visit, to try and make amends.

What could you possibly have to apologise for?

Well, that's a long story too. Let's just say that more than 2,000 years ago, someone far wiser than me understood that undeservedly we will atone for the sins of our fathers.

That sounds like something Evie's vicar would say. I don't believe that. I don't believe that that can be true.

Things that are true, don't require you to believe them, they just are.

How old are you, son?

I'm not really sure. Nine, I think.

Are you some sort of genius?

No.

Do you...do you have magical powers?

Do you believe in magical powers?

No.

In this moment Detective Hawkins, I am just a boy who wants to protect his sister.

What about you? Are you safe?

I am as I should be.

And that was that. Harvey never saw him again, but when he showed up at our house after he had passed, I knew immediately who I was looking at.

He never told me anything about you, or EverTech or nothing like that, but he came to tell me that my Harvey had a good heart and that he was sorry that he had not tried harder to take away his hurt.

But I told Jerry there and then that my Harvey knew that the price of doing the right thing wasn't always a reward. He'd been knocked down enough times to know better. But he kept on getting back up right to the very end; right until they made it impossible. I suppose in the end it was for nothing. I saw that that bastard Everston died. Ain't nobody spilling tears for him here; I just wish it had happened sooner.

In the end dearie all I want to know is whether or not it was worth losing the love of my life. Were you worth the price?

56

ASTROPHEL

Evie's question cut to the heart of everything I had been wondering. How could I possibly be worth all of the heartache and loss that had been caused? How was any of this anything to do with me at all?

When I met her to record that interview, I really knew nothing. Now, I know more, but she has joined Harvey wherever it is that people like them go and I cannot answer her. I smiled, walking away, pretending that I thought it was a rhetorical question. I knew that it wasn't; that she wanted an answer. But whatever I told her then, or now, would not have been good enough.

I guess I lied when I said this story wasn't about me. To be fair to myself, there genuinely was a time when I thought it was not. I thought this was all about Jerry; that I had a brother ripped away from me and who was special and who is gone.

It took me a long while to piece together what has happened to my family. I started with Jerry because I could not contemplate starting with myself. I knew that there were going to be things that I discovered which were going to make me unhappy. I never, for a moment expected that the truth would be so terrible, but my energy was on Jerry.

I had the faintest shadow of a recollection of him. I could see a smile on a hazy face; we were outside somewhere, in a garden or a park. There were flowers everywhere. There was laughter; some of it came from me. A dandelion exploded in my face and the hazy face runs away giggling. That is my memory of my brother. I cannot tell you how I know it is him, other than I have no memory of any other child. There is almost no one else that it could be.

I can feel in my heart that this is a happy memory, but when I go looking for more, there doesn't seem to be anything else. It's as if I have opened the pantry door looking for food, and all that is left are the mouth-watering smells of something incredible that has already been devoured. I am hungry to know more about my brother, and yes, even about myself. Jerry was the easier mystery. So many people had beautiful memories of him; I felt them all glowing when they said his name. I could feel the warmth he had put inside them flowing out of them as they remembered. It was like a part of him reaching out to hold me and let me know that he might have visited me too if only he could have found me.

57

DAN

When you were first with us I was already an old man. I had never thought that children would be a part of my life and despite actively seeking you out on the night I took you away, I was not at all excited by the prospect of having you around.

I know that you don't remember, but we first met, when I was tending to the gardens of the EverTech offices. I was pulling weeds up and you came stumbling over to ask why I was killing such pretty plants. I tried telling you that they were good for nothing other than choking up the other, proper flowers, but you wouldn't have it. You told me that your daddy owned this whole building and that I would be in big trouble when you told him that I had been killing all of his lovely plants.

Well, I said, I suppose I had better put them back then and let them grow.

Yes, you said. And ran off quickly to whichever babysitter it was that had escorted you to the office that day. A moment later there's a tapping on my back and I turn around, looking up at your little face. You were smiling this time. *Thank you*, you said, and you kissed me on the top of my head.

Just for a moment, as I watched you skip away, I wondered if Mary had been right all these years. *One day*, she said, *you'll look back at all the work you did and wonder if it was worth giving it so much of your time, when you could have had a real life*. But my heart only softened for a moment. No, I thought, there is not enough room for that.

Ten years later, on your third night with us, you were having terrible nightmares; you could, at that point, remember everything and you were clearly re-living the horror of what had unfolded. You woke up screaming. I came in to you and you were almost delirious with exhaustion and fear. I didn't know what to do with you, but you reached out your arms and waited for me to come closer. I sat on the bed and you buried yourself into my shoulder, sobbing yourself into waking sleep.

Eventually you calmed down. I hadn't uttered a word; I was sat, silent, stone-like, afraid that the slightest movement might start you back up again, but as I peered down at you, I thought you might have been asleep and as I lowered you back onto the mattress, I thought of our first meeting and without thinking, I kissed you on the top of your head. You squeezed my arm a little and I was embarrassed to have been caught showing such affection to a wretched child I barely knew.

I tell you this, knowing that you will remember nothing of either moment, not because I wish to try and warm your mind to me before I send an icy chill across it, but to tell you that even minds that are ruled by logic in almost every moment of the day can be overruled by foolish sentiment at times. It can catch you unaware and knock you sideways. Sometimes this might be the very best part of you, other times it's the darkness you try and hide from the light.

I lied, I did tell you this to try and make you think well of me.

I may as well be nailing jelly to the wall.

58

ASTROPHEL

A few weeks, or months (it was hard to keep track of time in those early days of freedom) after Dan died, I began to feel - odd. This will sound strange to you, or at least vague. But I had, I suppose, only a year or so of life experience at that point and being unwell hadn't been part of that journey. I felt like something was wrong with me. It was what you might call a headache, though it didn't ache, so much as pulsed. I found it difficult to concentrate that morning. The discomfort, or strangeness intensified for a while and I began to become anxious about what I should do. Maybe I was dying too. This seemed to be a common feature for anyone who had ever known me.

Whilst I had become immediately aware of the possibility of outside and exploration, I was nervous of it. I had explored the house timidly in the days after I had the call to say that Dan wasn't coming home. Obviously I thought I knew it well enough, having, as Dan told me, lived there for nearly twenty years, but there were rooms I realised I had never entered before.

His bedroom, the attic space, the basement. I had avoided

them all for a long time. But as the swirling in my head continued, I became desperate. I obviously understood the principle of pain relief, even though I had never needed it. I entered Dan's room and rifled through his bedside table, my eyes half closed, embarrassed to be invading his privacy, even though he would never know.

There was nothing there. Panic was rising. Nothing in the bathroom. The attic was empty except for an old sofa and a box of Mary's clothes.

I had watched enough films to know that a girl in a house on her own should never, ever go down to a basement in a house that creaked even in the daylight. I thought this to be wisdom worth adhering to, but I was freaking out and I thought that if I was going to die, it might as well be because of a psycho killer living under my house rather than because my brain exploded.

Frankly, both of those options would have been preferable to what happened next.

I made it to the slightly grainy floor of the basement. It was larger than I had expected. I would have looked around, but there was no time. I saw a circle, maybe a metre in diameter, painted on the floor. It had been there a long time. The paint was flaking, the circle was now incomplete and covered with the chalky residue that covered everything else down there. But like anyone else would, I walked towards, and then stood in the circle.

A light came on in front of me. I was almost blinded by the flood of light. Out of its whiteness, a red line, a laser, fired out and extended until it reached somewhere just above my eyes. For a moment I was frozen to the spot. And then it all vanished and I was left standing in a dimly lit, damp-smelling basement.

I turned to run back up to the light of the world above, but I didn't make it.

Hello Astrophel.

Where the hell had that voice come from? I looked around, expecting the psycho killer to jump out wielding a life-ending rusty knife, but there was no one.

Close your eyes. And then you will see.

Fuck! Fuck! Fuckety-fuck! I knew that voice and yet I had never knowingly had any memory of it until this moment.

I sat down where I was in a puff of mouldy dust and closed my eyes. As I did, a picture of a man formed in my mind. That man was my father.

I have some things I want you to know. Stay where you are and listen.

I remember actually nodding my head to the voice within me.

Fuck!

59

AUDEN

I will be remembered. This is inevitable. I have left an enormous imprint upon the world. But the full legacy of my work will not come to fruition for years to come. You will play a part in that, I am sure.

There will be two very different memories of me. Those that knew me, will tell a story that seems incompatible with the legend that has grown up around me. But, as you are perhaps coming to understand, I have been careful about controlling the narrative of every person I have allowed to come close to me.

They say that a grandmaster can think, or plan 15-20 moves ahead when playing a game of chess. I realised that I was something of a prodigy in the game at a very early age. What I came to understand, was that I could in fact see almost the whole game, laid out before me, as it were a film of something that had already happened. My victories were so decisive, so crushing, that I began to deliberately mismove, so as to keep an element of challenge.

By the time I was 15, I had become so utterly bored by the game that I put my board away for good. You see, people are unbelievably predictable that there is no surprise left in the world, except for that which has yet to be discovered.

So, I turned my attention to discovery, to the betterment of the world, to the stories that were on the very cusp of our understanding as humans. I was part genius, part lunatic to those I approached for support with my work; but this is nothing new; those who have been exceptional in the past, have faced similar reverence and ridicule.

The difference with me, is that I have lived through the proving of my own brilliance.

You must wonder at why this man, who was your father, who you barely remember, is telling you all of this now? The chain of events that my death triggered are all part of my plan. You are the next step in the building of my legend; whether you choose to listen to me or not, this is true.

60

DAN

Of all the lies that I have told you over our time together, it was the first ones, long before you would have had any reason to question the life we built, that were the biggest. What followed after that, was just a series of smaller lies, feeding the first ones.

In the end though, I think the lies became more true than anything else I did.

Let me begin with what was true.

My wife Mary suffered from something called Glioblastoma; it's a kind of cancer which starts in the brain and for which there is no cure. Mary was my whole world and when I found out that she and I would have so little life left together, I crumbled.

But this leads me to the biggest of lies. I was not a gardener at EverTech. Actually, even this isn't true. I was. I was actually a bloody gardener at EverTech, but that is not what I was or had been. I'd had a life, a really quite impressive one, but your father took that away from me.

I lived through the Second World War you know. I refused to be evacuated and when the bombs started dropping, I wasn't scared, I was fascinated. After a raid, I would get out on my bike and collect up all the bits of shrapnel I could find. By the time they declared peace I think I could have built my own doodlebug! But when I read about the Manhattan Project and the Enola Gay dropping Fat Man and Little Boy I began to better understand the complex relationship between people and the incredible things they can create. Strange really, that the bombs that literally fell in my back yard, that killed Mrs Simms next-door, that sent Uncle Frank to meet his maker too soon; none of that opened my eyes to the wasted human potential of war. Those bombs were somehow archaic; they were rude, metal bludgeons that landed without focus, but just the hope of inflicting enough damage to force a punch-drunk opponent onto the ropes. But the precision and unquestioning effectiveness of the atomic bomb was something else.

Imagine, I thought to myself, if the brilliant minds that created those bombs, had instead built an impervious shield around the Allied countries, or if they had made bullets that could turn tanks into sand; how much life could have been saved then? But that is not our way. I have learnt this in the most disappointing of ways - my own fairly pathetic failings.

Did you know, Asty, that it took us six million years to invent the airplane, but only six more to add a gun to one? This is who we are. We dream and aspire, we create and elevate ourselves, and then we realise that our potential, our genius, our beauty has been stolen by greed. But I didn't learn that until later.

First, as the war ended and unlike so many others, my father came home and made our family whole again; I was filled with hope. I was 10 years old and yes, London did not look as it once had, but I had known little else, other than war, so the meagre life of ration books and hunger, felt positively bountiful without the addition of perpetual fear at the sight of the postman and long nights spent in damp underground stations whilst war raged overhead.

I threw myself into schooling and found that I had an aptitude for it. Fast forward a few years and I became the first person that anyone on my street had ever known, to go to university. Maths at Cambridge University. I was almost famous! When I came home during the summer break after my first year, Old Mr Peters would bow to me when I walked past him. I should say that Mr Peters was my elementary school master!

Cambridge was like a different planet. I am ashamed to say it now, though I am not around I suppose, to face your judgement, but I came to think of myself as a little like Gulliver, in Swift's novel, returning home having spent time with the majestic Houyhnhnms, only to be surrounded by the distasteful, rather stupid, Yahoos. But then my mother and father died within months of each other and the community that helped raise me, wrapped me up in its arms and showed me how to grieve, whilst becoming the head of a house of one.

I showed my thanks to them by selling the house and never returning. But it wasn't spite and it wasn't because I thought myself better than them. It was simply that being surrounded by the faces of my past was too painful. That I would walk to the butcher to pick up sausages for dinner, knowing that there was no way that I could bump into my father on his way back from a lunchtime pint at The Green Dragon, was too much for me.

Cambridge was perfectly alien. I had no history there. It was a place where I expected nothing and it asked nothing of me, but that I apply my brain to problems which stopped me thinking of anything else. We suited each other perfectly.

And then, in my third year, as I had just finished neatly packing away every unnecessary emotion into a suitcase I assumed I would never need, everything changed.

61

AUDEN

I founded EverTech whilst I was still an undergraduate at Cambridge. I had designed a mechanism which could accurately pick up moving objects and place them somewhere else. I had assumed that this was to be an extraordinary breakthrough in the assembly line process and that manufacturers would be lining up to purchase the equipment I had designed. I was, after all, several years ahead of even the most basic competition. But every meeting I had seemed to end the same way - that is, it would end before it began. They would see me, a teenage boy, and think that I was out to hoodwink them. It didn't matter that one or two stayed long enough to see the prototype in action, they assumed I was deceiving them and left me with no sales and a blackening heart.

So, when I was approached by a respectable-looking gentleman as I was leaving my college one night, I was all too eager. Too eager to prove the other bastards wrong. But as it turns out, George Davis was the worst of all the sons of bitches that I would meet in my life.

Davis was a mid-level gangster, though I didn't really

know that for certain when we first met. He told me that he had heard something about a bit of equipment which might reduce the need for manpower on the assembly line. Well, I was flattered that my work was being spoken of and of course, we had a meeting. He asked to see the prototype in action and there followed a lot of very specific questions about its limitations.

In short, he offered me a great deal of money to provide him with a dozen machines. The catch was, I wasn't allowed to sell it to anyone else. Well, I was 19 years old and about to be given a lot of money for something that I could have built in my sleep. I accepted immediately.

Good, good. Said Davis. *And listen kiddo, if you need more cash to keep your operation going, then you just ask. A boy like you shouldn't have to go whoring himself out to buyers; they should be coming to you. I like to invest in talent, so you come back and find me if you'd like to discuss terms.*

And I did. I built EverTech on the money of a filthy-rich, fairly stupid drug-dealer, who managed to get me so indebted to him, there were nights I couldn't sleep for want of imagining the beating I might get should I fail to make my repayments.

But then things started to fall into place and I was able to keep Mr Davis happy with money and equipment that blew his chubby, flaccid, little mind. It has always amazed me, how persuasive something that looks like magic can be, even if it serves no purpose whatsoever. I built him something that used pressurised air to cut the end off the cigars he pretended to enjoy. He told me that this gift was in fact integral to his growing empire. When a potential customer or difficult ally would come by his office, he'd show them this mechanism and tell them that if he could use air to blow the end off of a cigar, they might want to imagine what he could do with the full-size version of this contraption, stored in the basement of his facility. There was of course no such thing, but the thought of having anything blow something off of your body, tended to be a threat that resonated. He was grateful for this gift and I was happy to use his money and connections.

As EverTech grew, I reached the point of needing new premises. Davis came to my aid right away. He offered me an old school building in central London. I asked him what happened to the school for it to close. *The headmaster owed me a lot of money; he had a terrible opium addiction. When it came to paying off the debt I gave him a choice: I take his balls, or his school. I don't much care for education myself, so I need a decent tenant and you seem like you're on the make, so don't fuck it up, pay the rent on time and all will be well.*

And so EverTech had its new home and I had the most astonishing ideas to develop. Davis was an inconvenient reality, but my plan didn't require him to be a problem forever. What I needed now, was to assemble a team of people who would be both brilliant and loyal, no matter what work I put in front of them.

62

ASTROPHEL

I had spent so many hours reading and listening and watching stories about the EverTech empire, I decided one day to go and see it for myself.

This was not as simple as it would at first seem. I was of course unpacking the kind of emotional baggage that requires hundreds of hours of over-priced therapy and/or drug addiction to get over and I was still uncertain about so many things. Going outside was by far the most stressful recurring concern that I faced. I knew it was there; I knew I needed to experience it and live within and alongside it, but it was frankly terrifying.

Once the basement had been explored, nothing else seemed as scary within the house, so I explored it more thoroughly. At the back of Dan's wardrobe was a small box with my name on it. It wasn't wrapped up in pretty paper like the tapes he left me - this one was ragged and old. Inside was a huge pile of cash and a map of London. It had a faded, curling sticky note on one of the pages. I opened it and as if he had read my mind, circled, clear as anything, was EverTech HQ.

The strange thing about my memories is that there are

plenty of things I don't remember doing which I seem to have knowledge of. I understood how to purchase a train ticket and I was stressed out by, but not ignorant of the London Underground when I finally got there after many hours of platform changes, delays and missed trains.

The building, as I'm sure you know, is just south of London Bridge, on the opposite side of the river to the Tower of London. I stood on the other side of the road for a long, long time, just staring at this place, which was presumably pretty familiar to me, but also, completely alien. I had wondered, all the way there, what I would do when I arrived.

I imagined walking in the front door without anyone paying me the slightest bit of attention. I imagined finding a way of sneaking into the gross industrial un-people friendly back of the building and finding my way somewhere interesting. I imagined walking in with a pair of sunglasses on, lifting up my arms and shouting 'Okay bitches, this is my place now! Somebody get your new boss a coffee!'

It will not surprise you to know that I didn't do any of those things. I stood and I watched.

The ground floor of the building had become some sort of museum, which was open to the public. I had read about this. It had originally been a way of making the neuro-enhancement process less threatening and more relatable. The exhibits explained how the brain worked and how the chips created connections with different parts of your brain using electrical impulses. All shown using cute characters and smiling faces. It was one of the 'top ten things to do with your kids in London on a rainy day'!

So, I could just walk up and go in. There was nothing stopping me. Nothing but the ridiculous thought that someone might recognise me. Though how that could be possible after nearly 20 years I couldn't explain.

Eventually I crossed the road. As I got closer to the

entrance, I noticed a huge, friendly-looking old man on the door. He seemed to be a combination of welcome-party and security. He smiled at all of the little kids and even gave a couple of them balloons, whilst using some sort of scanner to check the adults' bags. As I approached he looked in my direction. We were thirty or forty feet apart. Our eyes locked. I froze. Not because I recognised him, but because clearly, he recognised me. It felt like I stood there for far too long; as if the world had slowed down. But he was equally motionless. It was as if we were playing a game of musical statues and neither of us were willing to concede. Except I totally was. I pulled my shit together, turned around and ran as fast as I could back down into the underground, jumping onto the first train I could find.

I rode it to the end of the line. It took me six hours to get home.

That was why the outside scared the shit out of me.

63

DAN

My mother always told me that clever people had no common sense. Usually, she was telling me this because I had failed to notice that the weather outside required me to put on full winter-armour, rather than a t-shirt and shorts, or because I had allowed the goldfish to die, assuming that the maths problems I had buried myself in for 30 hours straight hadn't nourished it, the way they had me.

Obviously I resented the inference, but she was entirely right. It took me nearly six months of nearly bumping into the same girl, at the same time, at the same library before I considered for even a millisecond that this might require some sort of consideration. The next time it happened, I forced myself to look up from my book and investigate who this clumsy creature was.

I don't think I believe in love at first sight, but I suppose that might be because I had absolutely no idea what love, outside of a family, would look like. Actually, I think that might be complete nonsense. I looked at Mary properly for the first time that day and I knew that I would never think of anyone else again; I was just far too frightened to know what to do with such feelings, so instead of talking to her, I loped off, back to the safety of my college room and spent the next 23 hours and 47 minutes thinking about bumping into her again the next day.

You would think that with this sort of time on my hands I might have considered what I was going to say to her the next time our lives were set to a collision course, but I refer you to my mother's statement about common sense. I had no words, though Mary was often keen to tell me about a strange, almost inaudible sigh I made as I stared a little longer than was polite.

She put me out of my misery quickly enough though and began, as all great romances do, by telling a joke. *Why is it sad that parallel lines have so much in common?* She asked. I stared blankly, able to hear, but not engage any other part of my brain. *Because they'll never meet!*

She smiled wildly and awaited my reaction. It was slow to materialise. Not because I didn't think this was hilarious, which I did, but because I think my face had forgotten how to move the muscles in a way that would allow me to laugh.

When I did, I'm sure it sounded sarcastic. In fact, I know it did. Mary told me that often enough too. But that didn't seem to put her off. She began to talk and I listened. I nodded sometimes and I suspect I uttered the occasional monosyllabic word. We ended up leaving the library and getting a sandwich. She had cream cheese and mustard. I remember this because it was more or less the only disgusting thing I ever saw her do.

She was reading chemistry at the university. She liked rabbits. Her favourite colour was aquamarine. She couldn't help giggling every time she said *sweet Fanny Adams*, which she managed to do with remarkable frequency. She only ever cut her hair twice a year. She had a scar on her shoulder from falling awkwardly in a rock pool on Mawgan Porth beach when she was seven years old.

Sorry Asty, I got distracted. I miss her. There was nothing

I didn't know about her. She gave me all of herself in the most beautiful of ways. There were no secrets, no hidden thoughts. With Mary, you knew where you stood; you could see the goodness within her.

When she first got sick, I repaid her by moving out of our house.

The thought of losing her was something my mind could not compute, so I removed myself from the situation.

Of course, she found me about three days later. There are only so many places a man like me could hide without getting himself into all sorts of trouble. But I've skipped ahead too far. She didn't get sick until after I had made the very worst decision of my life. Or at least, the decision that would lead to all other bad decisions.

64

DAN

Three people changed the course of my life in impossible ways before I took you away Asty. Mary was of course the first. Your father was the second.

I had been warned, that as I was now approaching the end of my PhD studies I might find myself being tapped on the shoulder by someone from MI5. I thought this seemed entirely unlikely, as I could not imagine anybody less well suited to a life of espionage and secrecy. Nonetheless, when I was queuing at the Cambridge Union bar, Mary waiting for me at a table she had managed to nab from under a couple of drunk freshers, I was indeed tapped on the shoulder.

I turned, expecting to have an awkward conversation with some duffer I didn't want to speak to from the faculty, not to be confronted with a dapper looking chap I did not recognise.

Auden Everston. He said, reaching out a hand to complete the usual formalities.

Daniel. Daniel Allen.

Soon to be Dr Daniel Allen, I understand. And without pausing for breath, he continued. *A rather fascinating area of mathematics you've chosen. I do rather like anything with the word conjecture in it.*

I'm sorry Mr Everston, but do I know you?

We're in the process of that right now aren't we Mr Allen? Do you know what you'd like to do with yourself once your thesis is accepted?

I suppose I thought I might stay on at the university a while longer.

I don't think that is a very good idea. he said. *Wouldn't you like to do something a little more stimulating?*

This is it I thought. I'm going to be called upon to do my duty for queen and country. The thought both appalled and excited me.

What did you have in mind? I asked.

He handed me a card.

On one side were his initials, rather arrogantly displayed as the Old English character 'ash': æ on the other, an address in London.

Be there on Friday, no later than 11am. I'll show you what your life could be.

Hold on there old chap, who are you? You can barely be old enough to have finished a Master's degree; what is all of this?

Quite right Daniel. A good question. Do you know what my initials spell? He asked me, pointing to the card he had handed me.

Spell? They're an archaic character we no longer use anymore.

That's where you're quite wrong, actually. If you travel a few hundred miles north and cross the border into my grandfather's native Scotland, you'll find that my initials spell a number. 1. æ is 1. I am 1. Where there are 0s and 1s, I am 1, where there is on and off, I am on. I am go to the stop, yes, to the no. You see where this is going don't you? I am offering you a wonderful opportunity to do something that few minds could do.

I'll be at that address at 11am on Friday. I hope that you will too.

I didn't quite know what to say. I was astounded by the audacity and arrogance of this boy, who had told me absolutely nothing about himself.

Now I won't keep you; Mary will be wondering what on earth you've been up to. Goodbye.

In the pit of my stomach, I knew in that moment, that this man-boy was dangerous. That he could know of my thesis was one thing, but to know the name of the girl I was stepping out with, was quite another. And the way in which he threw her name out there, was quite impertinent. It was entirely obvious that Auden Everston was not one, but an infinite amount of trouble and I should stay away from him.

I was sat in his office on Friday at 10:59am.

65

AUDEN

Daniel Allen was a patsy. He was so goddamn easy to manipulate it wasn't even fun. But as it turns out, he was also the closest thing to a friend I think I ever had.

More fool him.

I was on my way to the top of the mountain and when I got there, nobody else was going to share that achievement. Nobody would know how I got there faster than anyone else. No one would know where the bodies were, that I would leave scattered in the permafrost on the way up. What they would see, was breath-taking brilliance and audacity.

Daniel, the poor bastard, never saw it coming.

When I approached him whilst we were still at Cambridge, he was a wet, sorry, little man with no ambition or direction. But he was decent with numbers and his PhD, whilst terribly mundane, was in just the right sort of mechanics that he would be useful, without getting in my way.

He thinks he hesitated about coming to see my lab in London; he thinks that there is a version of himself that didn't turn up that day and escaped the whole sorry affair.

He's wrong. By the time I invited him to visit, I already knew that he would betray himself and become so unbearably indebted to me, that I could get him to do anything I asked.

And of course, that is exactly what happened.

He made himself useful for a time. He was a terribly amusing little sidekick; more a willing puppy actually. I could show him things that the others would baulk at because he was so in love with the science, that he forgot sometimes to ask himself if it was okay to be doing what we were doing.

And then there was Mary.

To be honest, (which I may as well be, seeing as this is all playing out in your head, and I am dead) Mary was what made Daniel possible.

I leave very little to chance. Almost nothing in fact. I knew that the chances of Mary developing a rare form of cancer were extremely high. I knew this, because I had her bloodwork analysed. I did this, because I had a list of possible patsies and their known associates.

Knowing who you're dealing with before they know you exist, is an incredibly important and often overlooked method of achieving almost absolute control over anyone. Mary was going to get sick; this would mean Daniel would become either distracted, or desperate, or both. Any of these combinations would work for me.

I knew that the work we would be embarking upon was going to push the ethical limits of the scientific community, especially those who sit in that sad little world of regulation; that space seems to be occupied by the perennially mediocre; those willing to take science only as far as they can see and not one half-inch further. It is almost sickening to me that those with the least imagination should be responsible for capping the genius of others. But, I was also not naive enough to think that this was a world I had time to rebuild. Instead, what I needed, was someone who could allow me to infiltrate and tease them, without any risk to my reputation.

And so, as I predicted, Mary became unwell. In fact, excellent friend that I was, I helped Daniel recognise what was going on; I helped him arrive at the correct conclusions and he sought help from doctors I found, who gave him the diagnosis he needed to send him spiralling into despair.

Every day that he worked with the neural enhancements chips, I saw him dreaming of their potential to save his wife. Every successful animal implant was like a knife in his heart, because he knew that the law forbade him from using this potentially life-changing technology on someone who would genuinely benefit from it.

I did not expect him to have enough backbone to actually ask me if the procedure could be explored. In fact, he came to me with a quite brilliantly clandestine plan to use the lab when no one was around; all he wanted was my blessing. Which I denied him, knowing that he was already working on new settings and configurations for a chip he believed would obliterate the cancerous cells multiplying in his wife's brain.

When six weeks later he made a show of needing to work late, I knew that all I had planned for was coming to fruition. All I needed to do was hit record on the camera I had installed in his lab and he would provide me with the proof I needed that the BEST chips were indeed going to change the course of human history.

And that is what he gave me - the only gift I could not have given myself - actual evidence of a successful human installation, conducted illegally, without my authority, captured on VHS for anyone to see. What was even better, was that he conducted all of the follow-up work in the lab as well. He was, after all, a well-trained monkey; he recorded his results and the progress of his work with the diligence of a real scientist and I captured the whole damn story on a six-pack of video tapes I purchased for little more than the cost of a cup of coffee and a scone.

I took those tapes to three key members on the regulatory board. I showed them the quite astonishing, but illicit work that was being undertaken. I told them that this upstart crow would be admonished; his career would be quietly destroyed so that no one could ever connect their approval with this act of outrageous contempt for due process, but look, look at the wonders of what might be achieved, if only they would approve the very slow, very careful, very modest next steps and allow us to commence to official human trials and then of course, to full-blown publicly available installations. Imagine being the regulators who approved such a miraculous step-change in the course of human medical interventions.

And as they looked upon the work I had set in motion but kept my hands clean of, they were more biddable than I might have ever imagined. Each of them thought of a vulnerable relative who could benefit from such an opportunity and when the regulatory board next met, it was a mere formality that I would receive the news I wanted. BEST chips would begin human trials. All thanks to a now disgraced gardener whose name would never be associated with the scientific community again.

But, this was a gardener who would have no end of uses to EverTech; not least in becoming the surrogate father of my child. Though I must confess, even I was surprised that the child in question was you; that was the one rather interesting part of the story that was, at least at first, unscripted.

66

ASTROPHEL

The idea of Mary was really important to me. She was someone that I instinctively trusted. She was someone who deep down within myself I knew to be good and she was just another pawn in the sick game that my father was playing.

I found a load of old photos stuffed into the back of Dan's desk draw. There were a few of Dan looking much younger, with a girl who must have been Mary. Then one of him with my father. They were both younger, but I imagined the man who projected himself into my mind as a younger man, and I knew that this was true. Another with all three of them plus another woman. She was very beautiful. And she was my mother.

I didn't have the same haziness I had about Jerry, or the clarity of my father's appearing before me and explaining who he was, but I knew, without question who she was and I could feel memories of her knocking at a door inside my head. She was calling to me and it was muffled, but she was there and I was going to find a way to let her in.

I knew that doing this was going to hurt me. Nothing about any of this story paints my parents in a positive light, but she was calling to me and I could feel that there was something she would like me to understand.

I tried to find more of them all, to try and understand how they had interacted with each other, how they had grown or changed but that was the only photo of them as a four. In fact, that was the only photo of my mother.

I held her in my mind, letting her know that I was going to put her to one side for just a moment, because I couldn't deal with all of them at once. It was Mary's turn. She deserved a little of my attention. She had been a kind of mother and she had been let down by all of the people who had let down me and let down Jerry and hurt so many other people along the way.

I wanted to find something that would help me to connect with her. Dan, for all of his other failings, had loved her so much and although she had been dead many years, he was keeping her alive, by telling me about her after each memory reset. I knew about what food she liked, what music; I knew that she had kept a collection of elastic bands, ordered by size and colour, 'just in case', but there was almost nothing left of her now; nothing in my head, nothing in this house except a few photos and moth-eaten clothes.

I gathered every photo in the house. To occupy my mind and stop me from thinking about the outside for a little while, I tried to lay them on the floor in chronological order. There were probably two hundred photos in total. I could track Dan from baby to ten or years old, reasonably easily, then there was a long gap until the photos of him and Mary and my father. Then there were occasional holiday poses, a sweet one of Dan as I knew and remembered him with Mary looking quite frail. There were fewer of her. The one that stuck in my mind for a long while after was the last photo I put down on the floor. Mary, old, frail, sitting in a chair, staring sadly into a distance I couldn't see. It was such a sad thing to capture; the loss of a person before they are gone. I wondered why Dan would want to hold onto a moment so full of tragedy.

I stepped back and looked down at my work. I burst into tears. There were no photos of me.

Mother, did you have any photographs of your children?

67

DAN

There's no denying that your father was a genius. I hated almost everything about him, but his mind was astonishing. The work he was undertaking was beyond anything, anyone at Cambridge, or frankly any other organisation might have guessed at.

A year before I met him, early 1962, I remember reading about the formation of the world's first robotics company out in Connecticut. A couple of guys had built the first ever fully robotic arm. Reading that story was a kind of falling in love. It was, I imagine, a little like the moment you look upon your first child and dream of all the things they could be.

When Auden showed me around the lab he had built, it was as if I had slept through my child's entire adolescence and was now meeting the man he had been destined to be.

It was both beautiful and frankly terrifying. There was no maths, no science, barely even the imagination to do what he was doing, and yet I was looking right upon it.

He had me. He knew this. I would do absolutely anything to work alongside a man who could bend the rules of science and mathematics to do what we thought was impossible.

I was, as it turned out, EverTech's first employee. Everything he had achieved to date, had been a solo effort. *I need you to help us grow to the next level. Together we will build a company that will change the course of human history.* And I knew, in the deepest, depths of my heart, that he was right. I knew that I was in the presence of someone who could literally rewrite the rules of life.

I think the thing he showed me that made me see this most clearly, was the rat run. He had a room full of those horrible little creatures and each cage demonstrated the kinds of science I thought might be better confined to novels and trashy TV shows.

This rat has not eaten for 2 days. He is very hungry and I have made his suffering worse by putting food visibly on display behind that plastic screen. I nodded dumbly to show I agreed that this was indeed the setup we were looking at. *You will note that there is a small headset strapped to the rat's head. This is actually penetrating his skull and pressing very specifically upon part of his brain. When I remove the plastic screen, he is going to charge for the food. We will allow him to get right up to the point of having the food entering his mouth and then I will press this button and he will drop the food and move away, disinterested.* He pointed to a small console in his hand as he spoke; a simple two button panel, 'Y' and 'N' stuck on the buttons.

I watched, as the experiment played out exactly as he described. As he pressed the N, the rat dropped the food and went back to the other side of the cage. *Watch*, Auden said. He pressed the Y and the rat immediately pivoted and was devouring the food within a second. He switched between the buttons several times and the rat obeyed.

This was impressive, but I had seen electrical impulses used to teach certain behaviours. I tried not to be too won over. We moved on to the next cage. *This rat has spent more than a week learning how to safely navigate this maze. In the process of learning which way not to go, he has lost a significant part of its tail and several toes. He has been lightly toasted by a flame and lost 30% of his hair covering and one eye is no longer functional. He has now mastered the maze and can complete it without a second thought.*

I looked at this sorry, ragged creature, mutilated by what can only be described as some sort of death labyrinth. He released the rat from a holding pen and it darted into the maze. It moved with a strangely elegant ease, following the only safe route directly to a tasty reward. Auden picked the rat up and took it back to the starting point. The rat was released and completed the maze in exactly the same manner. He did this 4 or 5 more times to make his point. *You do not doubt that the rat has learnt how to navigate this place?*

I shook my head.

You see that this specimen also wears a metal cap?

I nodded.

This control, he said, holding up an even more simple, 1-button console, *will wipe away all knowledge it has of this route.*

That's impossible! I didn't mean to speak, but I couldn't believe him to be serious.

He just smiled in reply, placing the rat back in the holding pen and then pressing the button.

When the rat was released it did not move at first. It was hesitant. It emerged into the labyrinth and immediately took a wrong turn. A trap cost it another half inch of tail. It retreated quickly, moving in the direction I had seen it go on the previous runs. I thought perhaps that whatever shock he had sent through had perhaps disorientated the rat and he was now, with adrenaline coursing through what was left of his body, thinking straight. But no. Another wrong turn and this time a leg was lost. The rat rolled over, squealing in pain. Auden moved me on to the next cage.

This rat sat quietly in the middle of an empty enclosure. I thought it might be asleep.

What is special about this rat? I asked.

Watch.

He picked up yet another console, but I noticed that the rat was not wearing a metal cap. He pressed one of the many buttons and the rat awoke and began scurrying energetically around the cage. He had surely just been shocked into action in a way I could not yet see? As I watched the creature, I could not help but wonder at it. There was something just a little off about its movement. I couldn't see what it was, but I was both fascinated and confused by it.

You are looking at this rat, wondering what is wrong with it?

Yes.

Tell me about this rat.

Well, it seems to be just like the others, only with no metal cap. It's moving around freely, but it doesn't seem to know what it's doing?

My friend, absolutely none of your observations are true. He was gleeful; almost child-like in a way that frankly I almost never saw in him again.

He pressed another button. The mouse stopped and lay prostrate on its back. He pressed the same button again and the rat began to burst open from its middle. I thought at first that I might vomit, but as I watched with morbid curiosity, I saw that the guts of this rat were not as they should be. It was made of metal.

You have created a robot rat? How is that possible?

This is just the beginning Daniel. Imagine what we might do if we can bring what I have shown you today, into the realm of man. Imagine what suffering we might end, what joy we might bring, what power we could create. We will begin a new age in the history of man.

I looked at him with sceptical eyes.

In my heart, I had already taken the bait and hooked myself deliberately onto his line. He had me, and now he had but one decision left: deciding upon the fate of this floundering acolyte. But he had written my story long before we met; I just didn't know it yet.

68

AUDEN

The neural enhancement work was truly fascinating to me. But I knew that there was a strict timeline of progress that needed to be adhered to. And besides, whilst this work was remarkable, I have always enjoyed creating rather more than manipulating; though I confess that there is often a barely visible distinction at times.

So, I returned to my first love - robotics. I, however, unlike the fools who have followed, began from the outside in. I knew that the secret to success, whatever that was going to be, meant that the skin of my machines would need to be flawless; whether that was hair, or fur, or the porcelain skin of the perfect human, it had to be convincing beyond the shadow of doubt.

It took me years; it was perhaps the hardest thing I have done in many ways, but I perfected it. Well, actually I cheated. There is no synthetic substitute for skin or hair that is as convincing, so I found a way of growing it and bonding it to any surface. I could grow the leathery armour of a rhinoceros, the striped fur of a tiger, or the gossamer exoskeleton of an arachnid and infuse it with an engineered hypodermis which acted as the interface between whatever technical structure I built and a living dermis and epidermis. It was quite brilliant actually. But as a man of science, I needed to test the validity of my own hubris.

I designed the Echo Chamber to be a place where I could work outside of the regulations I was forced to put in place running a very publicly successful company. It was built off the books, as they say, so that it would not show up on any schematics of the building. It was also accessible only through a specific combination of button presses in the building's elevator. It would be almost impossible to press the buttons in that sequence by accident and thus, I created something, as I so like to do, that was hidden, by being always visible and available.

The Echo Chamber lab is where I built the first prototypes for Project Hephaestus, before I even knew how I would solve the problem of *ichor*. You see ichor, in the old stories of Greece was the blood of the gods and Hephaestus was said to use this to bring his robot Talos, to life; one vein to run from head to foot, filled with ichor, was all it took to bring him to life. I did not find my ichor for years to come, and when I did, it was not what I expected. But first, I would build beautiful, dumb machines that would fool even the most scrupulous eyes - mine.

I constructed the machines so that they would have no seams, no obvious points of entry, no visible sign that they were anything but real. As such, when I came to deliberately confound myself, there would be no way for me to cheat. I began with rats; rats are wonderfully sleek, complex creatures, but we have no respect for them and as such, I could purchase huge quantities of them and no one working in scientific supply chains would observe this as odd.

I had some simple tests that my mechanical rat needed to pass; each one would allow it to progress to the next phase. At first, I would observe it in a large colony of rats. If I could not tell which one was the machine, it progresses to a smaller group of five. Then, I would reduce this down to a pair. If it got passed this phase, I would introduce other stimuli, such as food and hazards. Of course the mechanical rat could not digest the food or feel real pain should it incorrectly meet a hazard, but that was all built into the process - it must look as if it was able to live, consume and suffer like any other creature.

The problem, which was also the finest point of the experiment, was that the only way to tell the rats apart, was to destroy them. I matched the rats for weight, for feel, everything. So, when I picked the rat I thought was the imposter, I had a robotic arm collect it from the others, placed into an isolation cage and decapitated it.

If I was right, I had failed, and a robotic rat was destroyed. If I was wrong, I had succeeded, and a little rat blood on my machinery was the most insignificant of prices to pay.

I perfected the rats quite quickly. Whilst intelligent and agile, they live simple lives and not ones that are hard to mimic.

I moved on to dogs next. This was far harder, because of course dogs do not all more or less look the same. I had to be more discerning and careful. I collected dogs from rehoming centres across the city and ended up with six mutts of different shapes and sizes. One at a time I attempted to create exact replicas. This was far more arduous and the attention to detail when copying is less satisfying than the attention to detail when one is creating an original.

Once complete, I would put the original dog and its robotic partner in a large crate and leave them for some time so that I lost track of which was which. I would return later and observe them, but hold off from making a decision. I would repeat this process 5 times in total. Then I selected the dog I suspected was my own creation.

A decapitated dog makes a lot more mess than a rat, but the satisfaction that I felt, knowing that I had cheated myself into the act of animal sacrifice, was quite magnificent. Of six dogs, only 2 robots were destroyed - number 1 and number 3. In every other case, I considered my designs superior and more life-like than the originals.

I decided to push myself further. Dog number 6 was a German Shepherd bitch I named Jazz; Jazz after Ismail Al-Jazari, perhaps my greatest inspiration. He was a Muslim inventor in the 12th Century. He made beautiful things; wonders beyond compare that stunned and entertained and made the world in which he lived, more than it was. He made automata such as hydro-powered peacocks and fountains and even a little band of musicians in a boat.

I took Jazz out of the lab one night after the site was closed and stowed him in my car. The following morning, I purchased a collar and lead and walked in the front door with him. I don't mind telling you daughter, that I have rarely been more nervous in my life. I had never before displayed my work so publicly and in a way which was so certain to illicit attention. I was after all, in charge of every person I walked past; they were obliged to pay me attention, and they did. But not as much attention as they paid to Jazz. She was a triumph.

I was nervous at first to let people touch her, but the choice was taken out of my hands when a particularly jolly employee barged his way towards me, only to drop to one knee and start petting her. He walked away happy enough and I was stunned into silence as the reality of my achievement dawned upon me.

Now I would go further. Push to the limits of what was possible. Beyond even. Go to a place on the cusp of what the gods had attempted in search of the missing piece of the puzzle; the blood of life to give my creations a true existence.

69

ASTROPHEL

Did I remember having a dog? I turned to look at Fandango who was lying patiently on the sofa behind me, waiting to be let out into the garden to play fetch for a few minutes, instead of being walked as she should be. Dan would have walked her. After the trauma of my London visit, I had stayed resolutely indoors. I even stayed clear of the windows if at all possible.

Dan told me Fandango came into his life not long before I did. Mary was not leaving the house as often as she should have been and Dan was still working full time at EverTech, so they'd decided to get her a companion. She was a good dog. She never misbehaved; she was always ready to obey; she sat when you told her to sit; she went to her bed when you told her to go to her bed. She was so good; I'd never even seen Dan put her on a lead when they went out for a walk. I'd joined them a few times and we'd crossed busy roads, but he'd just tell her to wait and she would. He never even looked at her, just knew that she would obey unfalteringly.

I knew nothing about dogs. At all. I thought about how strange this seemed strange. I sat and looked at Fandango. I knew she was a dog. That was the extent of my understanding. I crept up to the window in the front room and very slowly peeled back the curtains about half an inch; just enough to get a view of the outside world. It was pretty rural and in the distance I could see a field full of cows. *Friesians*, I told myself. I looked closer to home; nothing stirred for a while and then a very fluffy, white cat emerged from over the low brick wall between my house and the quiet road that lay beyond. *Persian*, possibly *Himalayan*; definitely not *Siberian*.

A man who lived somewhere in the village walked past, dog happily on a lead half a step ahead of him. I looked at it. *Dog*. Dog; nothing more.

What the fuck?!

It was like there was a deliberate black hole in my mind. I mean, who knows more than 1 breed of cat and doesn't know a single type of dog?

I'd written down as much as I could possibly remember from my father's freaky mind message. I looked back at the notes. Jazz. German Shepherd bitch.

I looked up bitch in the dictionary. Fun! It's always good to have a word with such diverse meaning!

German Shepherd.

What do they look like?

There was no internet at our house. Well, there was, but Dan had set it up so that it was entirely inaccessible to me; the network wasn't even visible as an option when I turned the computer on, so I was forced to search for another way of finding out.

Fortunately, or otherwise, there was an ageing set of encyclopaedias on the bottom shelf of the bookcase in the lounge. *Volume 5: Freon-Holderlin*. I flicked through from the back, past *Heraceides, Hasenclever, Walter, Hamlet, Gundicar, Gregory, Greco-Roman wrestling, Golan Heights* and so much more until there it was, right between *German National Assembly* and *German-Soviet Non-aggression Pact*: *German Shepherd*. And there was a picture. A picture of what Jazz must have looked like. A picture of Fandango.

Double fuck!

Was this really a coincidence?

Could my father have created the same type of dog as Dan decided to buy for Mary? I guess it was possible.

I sat down opposite the sofa staring at Fandango for what felt like hours. I listed all the ways in which this could be a completely plausible, annoying and weird fluke. It was a long list. It was very convincing.

But I knew that there was really only one way to know.

The thing about having a surrogate father who is a gardener (even if he was a fake one), is that you build up quite the tool collection in the shed. There was almost no horticultural emergency that I could not have dealt with, if owning the right tool for the job was all you needed.

I knew exactly where the tool for this job was.

Dan really seemed to love his axe. He had a special leather pouch for the actual cutting part and even had one of those old-fashioned whetstones that you sharpened it on. He could spend an hour just sitting doing that. I'd often wondered what on earth he was thinking about. I guess I've got a slightly better idea now.

Anyway, the axe was where he had left it; hanging on its own, labelled hook, ready for me to do what I needed to do.

I didn't know then that it was actually pretty unusual for a dog to be quite so obedient as Fandango. I told her to lie down on the patio area out the back of the house; she didn't hesitate. I did. My heart was racing. If I do this, aren't I becoming just like him; is that what I want? But I needed to know; I needed to know if this was all some sick and twisted joke; I needed to know that the things that haunted my dreams were real.

An axe is heavier than it looks. As I held it above my head, I felt it pulling back; it wanted to tip me backwards. I closed my eyes, held my breath and I swung.

Something warm spattered against my arms.

I did not open my eyes for a very long time.

70

DAN

What I didn't understand for a very long time was why he chose me. Yes, I was smart and his work spoke to the work I had been directing myself towards, but there were other people who could have done more for him, who could've advanced him more quickly. But I came to realise, far, far too late, that Auden Everston was not a man who took risks; he did not believe in chance, unless he was manufacturing it. Every interaction he ever had, was certain to have the outcome he had already decided. And so, as I stumbled blindly on; I did not see that I was just like the rat in the maze; my work had already been decided and a desirable outcome would be arrived at. Any deviation from this work was also planned. Auden knew where I would succeed and where I would fail; where I would be strong and when I would be weak.

Mary became sick at a crucial time in our work. Auden and I had, together, designed a tiny neural chip that replicated the metal mouse helmets we had originally tested with. These chips would be injected directly into specific parts of the human brain and be operated remotely, either by the user, or a moderator. We knew that because at this time, the only way to make the implant was through invasive brain surgery, we were at a point where some sort of approval would be required from an authority that outranked us. Auden knew that this would take time, but he also knew that greasing the right palms at the right moment, would lead to the inevitable outcome - his success.

Mary's diagnosis came as the secret jostling of power and favours was stalling. I had never seen Auden so deflated. He was angry and I was heartbroken. My Mary was going to die and there was no cure or treatment that would make a tangible difference. The average life expectancy of a patient with Glioblastoma is a year. Mary was diagnosed in 1973. She passed in 1999.

God did not intervene.

But I did.

I began modelling a version of our brain enhancement chip that would attack the tumour growing inside her head. The challenge was that with this sort of cancer, the tumour grows into normal brain tissue, so I would need a design that could send an impulse to destroy it before it formed, or that could differentiate the parts of the brain tissue that were healthy and the bits that were not.

It took months and Mary was deteriorating quickly. I was torn between spending what might be our final moments together and completing my work. She didn't understand why I wouldn't step away from the lab, but I couldn't tell her what we were doing. If anybody knew, it could jeopardise the whole enterprise. Up until now we had been a small, secret organisation, doing dark magic, but now we needed to become respectable, visible and virtue-driven. Any off-book work, before we were approved, would undermine that.

So she suffered twice whilst I toiled away; she was alone and she was in pain. I had to make this work, and then I had to persuade Auden to let me test it.

It was a short discussion. It involved a lot of expletives. In short he said no. *You would jeopardise everything we had been working on. You might make Mary worse. You might kill Mary. What would happen to the work then? Why would you want to complete our first human test on someone you cared about? Brain damage was a real possibility; it might be a fate worse than death.*

Everything he said was true.

I did it anyway.

71

AUDEN

It was around this time that I began to look beyond the realms of the science I understood, for answers to the questions that still eluded me.

It would be good for me to offer up a humbling anecdote about how I became overconfident and learnt to do things differently. But I cannot do that. Everything went my way. The dice, it would seem, were loaded, only I have already told you that I took no risks - I simply did my due diligence in a way that most people would think of as extreme.

After the success of Jazz, I wanted more. So, I established myself as the head of a sham conservation centre and negotiated the loan of one of the famous London Zoo gorillas. I set my sights on one of the older residents; someone they wouldn't miss in the same way as one that could still reproduce. I told them that I was studying the impact of loneliness and rehabilitation in lowland gorillas, dislocated from their troop.

After a month or so of going back and forth, and a healthy donation to their research, the gorilla, Graham, who was about 30 years old and as far as I could tell, in good health, was delivered to the handover point on the south coast, only for the driver I had paid to deliver him not to the non-existent Gambon Research Centre For Dislocated Primates on the Isle of Wight, but back into central London to the EverTech Headquarters.

The Echo Chamber was not adequately equipped to host a guest like Graham, but I had already been working on an extension, which used projection and sensors to create the idea of an outdoor environment in even the smallest, stuffiest of spaces. As such, he had run of a multi-sensory enclosure about six metres square. To him, with the adjustments I made, it felt like a small forest.

For weeks my computers captured everything about his behaviour; his habits, actions, gestures, noises; everything was recorded and fed into an algorithm that would help me mimic Graham. In a matter of weeks, I had created a masterpiece.

You'll be pleased, I suppose, to know that I didn't kill Graham. In this particular experiment I tracked which was my creation the whole time. I did however donate Graham to a monkey sanctuary on the south west coast of England, sending my version of Graham back to London Zoo. For six years, hundreds of thousands of people walked past Graham, never knowing the difference. I built him with a pre-determined expiry date; nothing that would lead to an autopsy of course; just peaceful old age. I had someone planted in the zoo to take care of the body as soon as it happened. It was rather thrilling to know that every day one of my creations was fooling its own species and the human population, and nobody ever found out.

There was really only one final step to take.

It was inevitable and yet, I will confess, even I was a little cautious at this point. It was a line not easily uncrossed and whilst I had successfully mimicked creatures, even complex ones with social habits and language of sorts, a human being would be something rather different. Not to mention how the sudden appearance of an additional, unaccounted for person was no simple thing to hide; the very existence of an android so uncannily human as to be undetectable was an exciting, but dangerous prospect. I could not get this wrong and perhaps should not have begun, until I had solved the 'ichor problem'.

That is when I read about your mother's work.

72

ASTROPHEL

Dan left many newspaper clippings for me to wade through. Most of them were glancing references to EverTech or bit-part players in this story. The one article he left me, which was all about my mother, was an obituary.

Jessica Everston née Dryden
Acclaimed cardiologist and EverTech Director
1948-1997

*Jessica Everston was a pioneering cardiologist, initially rising to fame in the 1970s after becoming the youngest...*blah blah blah.

You know that stuff already.
    This is the bit that hurt:

Mrs Everston suffered from bouts of depression during her adult life and in 1996, in a joint statement with her husband, Auden

Everston, the founder and CEO of EverTech, she stepped down from her duties at the company they had navigated to extraordinary global success for nearly twenty years. This follows the death of their son, Jericho, two years earlier, in a tragic accident involving an experimental driverless car that rocked the family and Mrs Everston was said to have been irrecoverably wounded by the loss.

Mr Everston commented that whilst her death was tragic and untimely, it was not altogether unexpected as Mrs Everston had become dissociated from reality in recent months and had frequently been admitted to hospital for psychiatric treatment. 'Our son's name was never far from her lips and I hope that she has found peace by joining him in the next life.'

She leaves behind an extraordinary legacy of progress, intellectual daring and raw talent. Many lives have been both saved and improved by the work she pioneered before and after joining EverTech. Many hearts owe their soothing rhythmic beating to her and they will beat a little slower knowing that she is no longer with us.

Mrs Everston is survived by her husband.

Where am I? Why am I invisible and unmentioned? Jerry's death led to my mother's suicide; but I was here the whole time. She must've known I was here. But I wasn't enough. I wasn't Jerry? Was I not special enough?

So I am left without a family and all I have to remember them by are the testimonies of strangers, a couple of newspaper clippings and a bat-shit crazy recording in my head.

If I wasn't so afraid of leaving the house, I'd be going to find myself some therapy. But what would I say? Who would believe anything I have to say?

I could show them the dog I suppose.

But then what?

I sat for a long time, feeling sorry for myself - which I think I was more than entitled to do, by the way. I mourned the loss of having roots in this world; I wanted to feel connected to something or somebody, but there was no one left who knew me.

Well, maybe someone. But did I really want to venture out there again?

In the end I decided that I did. There were still too many unanswered questions and I was getting pretty damn sick of other people's stories. I needed to find my own.

So, I packed my bag and once more headed to London.

I'd like to tell you that I wasn't completely terrified and that this time I didn't linger forever on the opposite side of the road, out of site of the doorman. But I was. And I did.

I held an untouched coffee in my hand, imagining that this prop was all the cover I needed to remain incognito and unnoticed whilst I stared intently at every person who went in and out of the EverTech building.

Eventually there was a lull in people walking past; whilst I liked the idea of blending in, I didn't much care for the thought of creating a scene as the next part of my really-not-thought-through-in-the-slightest plan unfolded. I crossed the road and headed straight for the door.

The same old man was there, just as I had both hoped and feared. He saw me coming from a long way off. This time he didn't freeze. Neither did I.

From twenty yards away I could see his name-badge. It said exactly what I had suspected: Rufus.

Here was the link to the past I had been looking for.

I'd hoped you were going to come back, miss.
You know who I am?
I do.
Prove it.
Well, your name is...

No! Not like that. I turned away from him and stuck my fingers in my mouth to whistle as hard as I could. A few seconds later Fandango came racing out from behind a tree, across the (fortuitously deserted) road and right up to my side. She sat down next to me.

Jazzie! Oh my, is that you? I didn't ever know what had happened to you.

So you know this dog?

Of course. I used to walk her every day. But what happened to her tail?

I cut it off.

Why?

I took the tail, now stripped of its fur and layers of fake tissue, to reveal a sorry looking articulated, metal, snake-like tail. *I wanted answers.*

I see. Well, I have some of those I suppose. He reached for his radio. I was ready to run. *James, this is Rufus; I'm taking my break early today. Can you please cover the door?*

I relaxed a little; though I still didn't know what was coming next.

You better follow me, miss. I guess you've got a few things you'd like to see.

73

DAN

I explained everything to Mary. I held nothing back. She knew me better than anyone and I vowed to give her the odds as they were, not as I wanted them to be.

She agreed.

In the dead of night, I launched the robotic arm I had developed to perform the first part of the procedure. It then planted the chip into the required location, all whilst Mary was awake and talking to me.

It was another month before she had healed enough for me to command the chip into action. The lead up to that moment was the most frightened I think I have ever been.

I pressed the button, whilst my whole body shook silently. I watched Mary for any sign of something being wrong. But she just sat quietly in my armchair, in our living room, looking back at me with the serenity of someone who has put all their faith in you.

She closed her eyes. For a long time.

I didn't dare say her name.

Had I just put her to sleep forever?

She looked so peaceful.

But of course, you know that she survived. She beat that bastard cancer for more than a quarter of a century. If I'd known then, what Auden knows now about the composition of materials required to endure in the human body, maybe the chip wouldn't have failed and I would have kept her longer.

If I had though, I think she would have discovered the truth about you sooner. Then I would have lost her anyway. She would not have drifted quietly out of this world with love in her heart for me. She would have raged against me; she would have taken you away from me.

And it would have been only what I deserved.

74

AUDEN

She had an article published in *New Scientist* in June of 1975. She'd been named the youngest deputy-chair of cardiac surgery in the country and I think Imperial College London wanted to make sure a sufficient fuss was made.

There was a picture of her in scrubs, looking every bit the active surgeon, but what struck me was something she said in the interview: *I believe that the heart is, in many ways, a second brain; it has the power to make decisions for the body that will protect and better it. The accepted wisdom of science suggests that the brain controls the heart; I would suggest that the heart is the forgotten part of our nervous system and that it lives in a sympathetic and co-dependent relationship with the brain.*

She was lambasted for these words and nearly lost the position for which she was supposed to be celebrated. The hospital kept her well away from the press for many years after that, but I was astonished by this thinking. It was outrageous, foolish even to make such assertions without decades of research and data to support your thesis, but nonetheless, as I pictured this strange and untested back and forth between heart and brain, I called to mind the ichor tube Hephaestus installed in Talos to make him live.

I put all my other work to one side. My attention was now squarely on Jessica Dryden and ensuring that when I made contact it would be in a way which meant she would give me everything that I wanted. In order for this to happen, I would have to create something spectacular. But I assume you already know about Mia Svobodova's heart? Of course you do. I know that you do.

That heart was perhaps the most beautiful thing I had created. Unlike the automatons, I had to blend human life seamlessly with my own work. I can tell you that a lot of rats died getting that symbiosis to happen. But it was worth it. Not because of the life I saved, but because of what it might mean for my work. Jessica was going to be astonished; she would do anything I asked just to be near this miracle. To her, as a sentimental creature, she would see the possibility of ending the organ donor lottery, the years of waiting, the uncertainty of organ rejection. For me, she was lining up to be my next patsy. She would order research to be conducted because I suggested it, and it would be entirely untraceable back to me. When I had it, I would take her lab and all of its data and we would begin the next phase of my work.

You see, I knew that Mia was going to apply for a job in Jessica's lab; I knew about her heart condition and I knew exactly when to contact Jessica and tell her all about the ground-breaking work I was doing. When Mia's surgery was complete, she was indebted to us in a way that was irrefutable to her own ethics. She would do anything Jessica asked, and I ensured that we pushed this loyalty to its limits. When she 'discovered' the heart's magnetic field she sat on her findings for several weeks and I wondered if I had miscalculated her character. But sure enough, she then presented the report, demonstrating the findings I expected her to uncover when I had that boy's doctor transfer him for further testing at Jessica's lab.

The report was beautifully pieced together; full of the surprised optimism and naive hope of a young researcher. Mia had found what other cultures had innately known for thousands of years; that the heart can transfer, interpret and respond to energy around it. But the report allowed me to have a conversation with Jessica about what might happen next.

There was one failure which threatened to derail my work; it was the one result I had not accounted for, and that was the realisation that Mia's EverTech-created heart would not replicate the magnetic field of a biological heart. Well, this is not quite true - it did create a magnetic field; I built that into the design, but she had no control over it whatsoever; the connection between brain and heart was nullified by the technological invasion. I had assumed that a human body, laced with a robotic heart would create the optimum environment in which to generate a more powerful, controlled magnetic field. I was wrong. And that does not happen often.

A good while later I came to understand that I had simply been looking at the problem in reverse. In fact, my other work had been there all along, to show me that the answers to my problems had mostly been resolved. In that moment I felt as if my mind had been playing games with me, hiding that it had foreseen the outcome of this setback all along, preparing for the real, inevitable outcome years in advance. As the fullness of my plan began to take shape, I saw that my whole life had been shaped to create something more astonishing than even I had realised. That my unconscious had plotted a course towards immortality and all I would need to complete the work, was one good heart.

75

RUFUS

I've worked at EverTech, for your father, for a very long time. I didn't much know what it was I was being hired to do at first, but I was a young man in need of a job. I'd got a girl, soon to be wife, in the family way sooner than we'd expected and I had absolutely nothing to offer her or our child. I heard that there was a job to be done here through a friend of a friend. All I knew was that it was for some scientist who wanted to keep his privacy and that if I kept my mouth shut and made sure no one bothered him, there was half decent money at the end of each week.

We met; he was pleased I was a big fella and I understood that he was the sort of bloke you simply couldn't afford to upset. There was something about him that I knew was dangerous, but as time passed, he was always nice to me and I did the job he wanted.

When the operation started to get bigger, he let me bring in a few more people and I felt like I was a boss. It was more than I had ever thought I could do.

I knew that something big was going on, because Mr Everston told me that there was going to be a lot of people leaving us and I needed to be sure that they didn't hang about or try to come back. There were a lot of pretty unhappy people walking out the front door for a few days and one or two wanted to make a fuss. But most of them were scientists and they're not really the sort to cause trouble with the likes of me.

Then a few weeks later they invented those brain computer things and Mr Everston told everybody that wanted to stay working here, that they needed to have one shoved into their brain. Well, I nearly shit my pants when he told me that. I went right up to him that day and I said *Mr Everston sir, I have liked very much working for you, but you ain't shoving nothing inside my head that God didn't put there, so thank you very much, but I will be done here.*

Well, he tells me that with the greatest of respect, perhaps God could have afforded to put a bit more in there for me to work with, but on the other hand, he knew I had been loyal and he respected my discretion. He told me that he wanted me to stay on without a computer in my head on the understanding that he would kill my son in front of me if I ever crossed him.

The movies would like you to think that there are essentially two types of bad people: those who are bad, but actually quite nice and those that are bad and are crazy, stone-cold killers. I grew up around a lot of bad people and I did some pretty dumbass stuff as a kid; sometimes people do bad things, and sometimes they enjoy them and sometimes they don't, but mostly they do it for a reason. Mr Everston was a dangerous man because I didn't know what his reasons were. He could easily of gotten rid of me and found some other big, dumb guy who would have run his security. But he didn't and that was frightening. He made a point, every time we spoke, of letting me know that he knew where my son was. *How's your boy getting on at St Saviour's? Is Mrs Bingham being nice?* He knew every teacher he ever had and even right up until he died he didn't let up; *how's that shift work going over at the supermarket. That supervisor of his, Benny, sounds like a piece of work.*

He knew everything without needing to put one of those things inside me. He had me right where he wanted me and even now he's gone I check in with my boy every day; he's 37 years old and his old man calls him every day like he's a baby. That's what your father did to me.

But that's enough on that. You ain't here to hear about my problems; you've got your own. You want to know what I know? Well, I know bugger all about science, but I know too much of the other stuff that happened.

I saw Dr Allen getting humiliated when he tried to help his missus. I had to escort him to a shed so that he could be shamed in front of me. I seen your mother getting more and more desperate, trying to find a way out of the mess she had found herself in. I seen what your father was building. I seen what they did to your brother. I seen everything and I don't want to see nothing more like that.

But I need to show you what you need to see, just so that you know what it is you need to know. I could tell you a hundred sad stories, a hundred stories of weird stuff that I've seen; that pup you got there is nothing compared with the stuff that came before it.

There ain't much left of it now, but you want to see the Echo Chamber I suppose? It went up in smoke within minutes of your old man dying. I thought that such a thing might happen, but there weren't no warning he was going to go, so I couldn't do anything about it until there wasn't much left.

It's not a happy place down there. No good will come of you seeing it, but I can see that you're not here for a fairy tale. Which is for the best, as there ain't no happily ever after here.

76

DAN

Auden called me into his office six weeks after I had performed the secret procedure and told me that he knew everything. Actually, I should mention, that he was rather one for showmanship, so he demonstrated that he knew, by playing a VHS of me performing the operation.

You've put everything we have worked on at risk.

I was ready for this. I knew somehow it would come out. *I don't care.* I told him. And I didn't. Early tests showed that the implant was working and that there was 93% less tumour than pre-installation.

Do you know how many regulatory bodies I am having to coerce into even meeting with me to discuss the possibility of doing something like this?

I don't care. It works.

Of course it works. That is not the point. The very existence of your wife's head with an implant in it is enough to destroy this whole operation. Nobody cares whether it works at this point; they just want to know that we aren't going to kill everyone, either by doing the surgery, or by blowing up their heads afterwards.

I'm sorry Auden.

Sorry! You have performed an illegal surgery on a person with potentially compromised mental capacity using technology which is also illegal, in my laboratory! Being sorry is of no fucking consequence!

I understand that you need to be angry about this, but nobody will ever need to find out about Mary. She is not a public person; I am not a public person. We are invisible in all of this.

Not invisible enough. He moved behind his desk and sat down. *Do you know what I keep in this draw,* he said, pointing to the top right draw. I shook my head. *A gun. From the very first day I moved into this space, there has been a gun in this draw. In fact, I'm rather embarrassed to say, that it was in the draw when I moved in. The whole place has been rented on favours and promises from people we cannot afford to let down. When I first saw the gun, I wanted to throw it away, but then I was worried someone would find it and trace it back to this lab and somehow it would be my problem. You see I don't know what this gun has been used for before I came to be its keeper. It may have been used in defence of someone's honour. It may have been nothing more than a security blanket for whoever sat at this seat before me. Or, it may have been used to commit terrible crimes. Whatever the truth, I didn't think it worth risking follow-up questions from the outside world. You see old chap, our work is secret and our work is going to change the world when it becomes known. I cannot risk anything changing that. And so, as these thoughts have been on my mind, I have come to understand why even the most reasonable people may keep a gun. Sometimes a mess is made that cannot be unmade and so it must be got rid of. At least, that is, I'm sure, what the owners of guns must think.*

He took the gun out of his draw at this point just so as I knew that he was not bluffing (I never, have ever thought of Auden Everston as a man who bluffs).

I'm not going to kill you Daniel. He said, pointing the gun at me. *Because I still need you, and of course, you are my friend. But things will need to be different for us going forwards.*

When I arrived at work the next day, I was not allowed to enter the lab. *I'm sorry Dr Allen, but you no longer work in the lab.*

Rufus, what do you mean? You know me; I have worked here as long as there has been a here to work.

I'm sorry sir. I've been asked to escort you to your new office.

I see.

I followed Rufus, who looked almost as embarrassed as I did about the whole situation. We walked all the way through the building and ended up in the grounds behind the building. He stopped when we arrived at a shed. He opened the door. Neatly folded on the floor was a green EverTech overall and polo short, along with some boots.

I understood the punishment. It was the sort of sick joke I have no doubt your father found terribly amusing.

I picked up the polo shirt and laughed out loud. It had been embroidered with 'Dan' on the left breast.

Fuck you, Auden. I said, noticing a camera in the corner of the dilapidated outbuilding. I began taking my clothes off then and there. Rufus backed away, embarrassed.

Yesterday I had been on the cusp of history. Today, I was gardener Dan. And so I stayed until the day I pulled you from the car.

What I became after that…well, you'll decide what you call that.

77

DAN

I adjusted to my new life surprisingly easily. In fact, it was Auden I think, who struggled with it more. He would regularly summon me to his office and I would sit there, more or less silent, as he told me of the company's progress.

The regulators had approved the Brain Enhancement & Stabilisation Training chips. The beginning of his bid for world domination was underway and he was lonely enough to have to bring in a shabby, old gardener to share his excitement with. It was pathetic really. And yet every titbit he threw men was nourishment to my lost soul.

It was also how I kept Mary believing that everything was ok. I knew enough of what was coming round the corner to ensure she didn't suspect that I had been left, quite literally out in the cold. She would never have forgiven herself, even though it was not in any way her fault. I guess that's the difference between the good ones and the bad ones - the good ones feel bad even when they aren't the reason you're hurt, the bad ones are quite happy to keep ramping up the pain.

But the truth is there were times where I didn't think I could keep up the charade - not to Mary and not to myself, but it was always at just such moments that Auden would reel me back in and throw me something that kept me hanging on. He implied, over and over again, that one day, perhaps, I could win his trust back and undo the hurt I had caused. One day I might be by his side and things would be as they should be.

I knew he was lying. I knew a man who kept a pistol in his desk could never forgive. And I knew that a mind such as his was incapable of forgetting. But I played my part. When he showed me plans for enhancements to the chip, I gave comments. When he invited me to observe a chimp he had smuggled in for testing, I watched in awe, as Auden's ever-expanding team created an extraordinary metallic copy; it was quite literally impossible to tell them apart in any way.

When he severed the arm off the living chimp and used the created arm of the other to replace it, I began to understand how far he had advanced his work.

I observed the bonding of synthetic and living tissue at a molecular level and within a week, when I was invited to return to observe the chimp cyborg, he had full and complete control of his new limb, as if nothing had ever happened.

When he met Jessica, I was kept away for longer. I saw, from a distance, that Auden was wooing this remarkable woman and I believe it was only I who could see that it was all just another game. Your mother was a prize to be won and then she was turned to do his bidding.

When their rapid, whirlwind romance ended in a quick wedding, I was not surprised. Auden had begun to talk to me about new research he was conducting which was demonstrating a previously unknown connection between the brain and the heart. *If I want to have complete control of the body, I need to have complete control over the head and the heart.* he told me. Jessica Dryden understood the heart in a way that no one else did. His seduction of her was what I believe you call a no-brainer.

But to really understand what you're up against when you think of your father, you have to believe me when I tell you that he really did have a quite remarkable mind. He had the ability to look into the future and predict the movements and decision of other people with an uncanny degree of accuracy. He plotted a course towards a direction that others had not even considered.

BEST chips went to market and made him an extraordinary fortune and yet they only performed a tiny fraction of the functionality they were capable of. They were used to suppress anxiety and increase concentration. It was almost insulting, even to me, the one-time co-creator, now gardener, that the miracles we had been building, were little more than electronic antidepressants! But, despite his meteoric rise to fame,

when one of Jessica's assistants filed a report about the heart's magnetic field shortly after the chips went on sale, it began a period of time, over a decade long, that I called *The Darkness*.

Auden segregated himself away from almost every aspect of the business. The chips sold in unthinkable quantities, but he was a recluse within his own company. Ironically this is the time in which he and I spoke most often. I was intellectually capable of understanding his wildest musings, but in no position to challenge or stop him.

If you're keeping up with the timeline though, this is also when you first entered the world.

I would like to tell you that you were born out of love; that the one thing that held Auden accountable in the real world, was his family, but that would be a lie so grotesque, it could only ever have come from his mouth.

Dear Asty, you were a miracle. Not in the way that all new life is, but because you were designed to be so. You see, Auden read what Mia Svobodova had discovered and he saw the opportunity he had been waiting for; he saw what no one else would see - an inbuilt ability to empathise and understand each other's existence, could be used to deliver almost anything from one human being to another on a microscopic level. In essence, he had found a way to weaponise our kindness and you were to be the vehicle of delivery.

Mia's research was quite beautiful. Auden let me read it once and the personal narratives she told of the invisible connections between people, were more inspiring than anything I had created at EverTech. But Auden needed a heart with more power. The magnetic fields, he understood, could transfer a payload from one human to another, but only if it could be amplified.

I just need one good heart. He told me. *Someone must have a heart with the magnetic reach I need.*

Why not make one? I asked.

I did. That patsy Svobodova has one of our hearts. So do half a dozen others. They don't emit anything. It's biological and I can't recreate it.

How do you know?

Know what?

That they don't emit a magnetic field.

I've had hidden magnetometers installed all over the building.

What?

Not just the building actually; shopping centres, tube stations, even a few buses.

My god. Auden, that's unbelievable.

What is unbelievable, is that of the tens of thousands of hearts I have monitored, not one of them reaches the levels I need.

Then maybe, whatever you want to be possible, simply is not.

That's exactly the sort of bullshit I'd expect from a failed scientist.

I didn't stick around for the rest of the conversation that day, but of course I came back; whether he summoned me or not, I was hooked on the Auden Everston drug and I could not help but lap up the scraps he threw at my feet. I ached, deep within my core, to be back by his side. But he would never have me. He enjoyed my pathetic, fallen state far too much.

It was a few weeks later that I learnt that you were to come into the world. Because you were the answer to his problem. He could not make a metal heart to replicate the human magnetic field, so instead he would rebuild human nature and create life, not in his own image, but in the image he wanted. You were born to have the good heart he wanted. You were born, not to be his daughter, but to be his next guinea pig.

78

AUDEN

The most difficult part of the path which lay ahead, was gauging how Jessica would respond to my proposal.

I would like to think that I at least attempted to take the high road, but I doubt that you will see it this way. Jessica, like every other EverTech employee (which is what she was, despite her job title and the press coverage about us running the company together), had a BEST chip installed. The mantra was that we were representatives of this cutting-edge technology and if we weren't comfortable using it, what sort of example was that setting to our potential customers. I inevitably lost some good talent because of their reservations about having a synthetic interface connected to their brain, but ultimately it was a position I enforced and my employees willingly bought into.

It was my ultimate fail-safe.

Nothing in their minds would be out of my reach.

I used it against your mother.

I told her that I wanted us to have a child who could change the world. She thought this an endearing sentiment at first. However, when I began to explain that this would not be because of parental optimism, or even the unrelenting pressure to achieve, but that we would craft someone born to be special, she began to get anxious. By the time I explained the extent of my plan, well, she became so angry that she threatened to have me committed to an asylum. You see, my daughter, she thought me insane. She thought that my desire to create a life that could reimagine the boundaries of human ability, was somehow insane.

I had, of course, assumed that this was a possible reaction. As such, I had added a sedative to the wine she was drinking as we had this uncomfortable conversation. By the time she awoke in the morning, I had removed the memory of the previous day from her mind and at the same time, I had implanted suggestibility triggers in her subconscious. I would place items in front of her over the coming weeks and months that would ignite these triggers and she would begin to agree with my plans before having even heard them.

Now suggestion, is far from an exact science. Suggestion is almost as much magic and hokum as it is knowledge and strategy, and the truth is, you cannot ever fully make someone do something they absolutely do not want to do, but I had spent a lifetime manipulating the odds of success in my favour, and given the fact that I could so tightly control the experiences of my wife, I was confident that the next time we sat down to review the future work of EverTech, the latest incarnation of Project Hephaestus would seem less challenging to her.

In fact, once I took her to the Echo Chamber and showed her where Jazz, our now faithful companion, had actually come from, the triggers were complete and she was open to the idea of our future child being a landmark in the evolution of the human story.

To make things easier for her, I had laid much of the groundwork for this eventuality early in our relationship. I had told her that I was unable to provide her with a child naturally, but that I could still provide the materials necessary for a genetic heir. Thus, in her mind, our child was always going to be something created with the aid of science. When she was impregnated using artificial insemination, it was because this is how it had been destined to be.

The truth of course, is that I could have given her a child, but the leap from this, to a person crafted with such precision, with so much riding on its success, with a fate so different to that of a naturally conceived child, was too much. I saw her struggle with the news that she was pregnant; I watched as her brainwaves threatened to interfere with the chip in her head; I should have foreseen then, that there are limits to the stress you can put a person under before they can overwhelm even the most beautiful technology, but she held steady and bore me the daughter I had designed. You, Astrophel, were to be the future.

But your mother intervened.

She stopped me before we had really begun. She loved you. I tried to make this difficult for her, but biology, nature, whatever it was, got in the way. Got in *my* way.

And so, Jericho was created. He was supposed to be my fool-proof backup plan. He turned out to be something quite different.

79

ASTROPHEL

When we got to the Echo Chamber, I found myself in an almost completely empty space. It had clearly been damaged by fire, just as Rufus said, but there was nothing to see at all. It was a shell.

I was afraid for a moment that Rufus had lured me down here to ensure I never asked any more questions, but as I turned and saw this hulking, old man approaching me, I could see that his face was kind, despite the things he had seen and done.

He knelt down slowly in front of me. *This is the only place I know, where no one can listen in to what we say, because that's how your old man built it. I don't much care if they hear anything I got to say about him, or the past; ain't too many round here that will be missing him and the others got some sort of brain-wiping thing happening after he died; it was damn near the most strange moment; people all round me just paused for a couple of seconds, then they look around, slightly confused, like they forgot where they was going and then they carried on. Couldn't say for sure what happened, except that after that, I never heard no one mention your father by his name again.*

Anyway, I'll say what I want up there, to anyone who asks and some that don't, but there was something I promised I would do that no one can get in the way of.

He reached into his jacket pocket and pulled out a flash drive. Been carrying this around for a long time. Won't be sorry to be rid of it, because I can rest easy knowing that I did what I said I would do and now I don't have to come back here no more.

What's on it?

I didn't ever do anything other than hold on to it miss, but if I had to guess, I'd say it was going to be love. Filled with love. Now you need to get you and Miss Jazzie away from here as soon as you can. This isn't the right place for you to be.

That was the last time I saw Rufus, almost the last time I visited EverTech, nearly the last time I went to London. It marked the end of many pieces of my life in fact, but I walked away knowing that I wasn't mad, or at least I was no more mad than a big, friendly monster of a man who had held onto a secret for me, for nearly twenty years. And I held in my hand another piece of the puzzle that was my quest to know why so much of my life had been stolen from me by the people who are supposed to protect you.

80

DAN

By now you must surely know enough about Jerry to wonder at what I have told you. How could you have been the chosen one, when such things have happened to him?

The answer is quite simple - the answer is in fact, what the answer always is. When faced with perfection, and you were, according to all the metrics that mattered to your father, perfect, the only thing that can create a problem is people. People and their ability to have feelings.

It will probably not matter to you now to know that Jerry was brought into the world because your mother was too attached to you. Against all the odds, and all of Auden's plans, Jessica Everston enjoyed motherhood. When he saw this, he knew that using you for what he had intended would be impossible.

Jerry was designed just as you were. An almost identical copy in fact. How would this time be any different you might wonder? Why would Jessica not love her son as much as her daughter? I didn't understand myself at first. I thought maybe he had manipulated her through reprogramming her neural chip, or perhaps he had done something to the baby at a genetic level to stop it bonding with her, or perhaps, I wondered, he would make it so that the baby was born sick, just so that he could propose to save the child and in so doing he would get his way.

The truth is more sad. The truth is, she didn't need that much persuading, not when they realised what they had created.

You see you were, as I mentioned, genetic perfection; he had built you a heart that radiated power in a way no naturally-developed heart could. Jerry should have been the same. But he wasn't. When they first scanned him, Auden went bat-shit crazy. He began smashing things, screaming, he walked up to Jessica, who was reading the results of the ultrasound they were performing on the infant Jerry, and slapped her hard across the face.

You defective bitch! Look what you've done?

A ventricular septal defect is a flaw in your design, not in the mother's ability to birth a child. She grabbed at Jerry, even then, in that moment of crisis, a natural mother, at least until she became unnatural. She held him close to her.

Don't you dare try to blame me for this, this monstrosity! I designed it to perfection and yet still it flops out into the world with a fucking hole in its heart!

He went to hit her again, but missed. He hit a pile of equipment on the table next to where his wife and child stood. In crashing into it, he turned on a new mobile magnetometer he had been designing to amplify the sensitivity of the SQUIDs (superconducting quantum interface device) but in a noisy environment. Immediately it began pumping out results to a screen both Jessica and Auden could see.

You understand where this is going Asty. Jerry's readings were a miracle. He was radiating a magnetic field at the sort of level your father had only dreamt of. Within hours he had had ECGs, EEGs, in fact, every test you could imagine. When Jerry was touching another human, his readouts switched to match the other person within seconds. He was demonstrating what Mia had described at Quantum Empathy. His brain and heart synced with whoever was nearby.

I was in the room when all of this happened. They needed someone to assist with the machinery and even the most loyal employee would surely have had questions about what they were doing, so they chose someone who was guilt-bound to comply.

As it dawned on them both what they were witnessing, Auden was like a pig in shit. Your mother smiled when he looked her way, but I could see her grip on the baby tighten and tears rolling down her cheeks.

They both knew what this meant.

The clock was ticking.

One child was spared.

The other child would die.

Their father was both creator and executioner.

Their father was now more powerful than God.

81

AUDEN

I hadn't wanted to involve anyone else in this project. Frankly even your mother knowing was proving to be an almost impossible barrier, but reproduction was a seemingly unavoidable element of my plan. I needed to create a human being with an optimised heart that would radiate a magnetic field beyond anything possible within the current realms of human potential. Jessica had proven herself to be a doting and loving mother. This was an unexpected and challenging problem. So, against my better judgement, I outsourced the issue to someone else.

I found a woman who had already had a number of children. She was on the margins of society, but she was clean, her children were healthy and she was desperate for the sort of stability a briefcase full of money could offer. The DNA was still mine and Jessica's, and the heart was an exact replica for the one we had modified for you. This woman carried Jerry whilst Jessica faked a pregnancy for all the world to see. This time she knew, this was not going to be her son in the way that you had become her daughter. Jerry was destined for a

ONE GOOD HEART

different fate and I believed that I had done enough to ensure that this was easier.

The woman delivered Jerry safely. She was paid. She disappeared. I never met her. She has no idea what she helped to bring into the world. Jessica had no childcare duties; we hired a live-in nanny and doula to take care of almost all of his needs. He never slept in our room. Jessica was forbidden from soothing him when he cried. Clean, clear and total detachment.

A few weeks after his birth I took him to the lab to run the first scans of his heart. When the results came in, I will admit, I was less than composed. You see Jerry was born with a ventricular septal defect - a hole in his heart. I lashed out at Jessica; in that moment, with literally millions of pounds worth of work trickling through my fingers, I would have killed her. She had the audacity to blame my design; but I knew that was nonsense - it was the same design I used on you.

In my anger, I grabbed at the baby, but Jessica moved him out of my reach. I accidentally set off a series of magnetometers around the room and immediately I saw that my work was not defective; it was better than I could ever have hoped for.

Jerry's readings were remarkable; they were powerful and definitive. Even allowing for the fact that babies are naturally more sensitive to subconscious empathy, these readings made yours look like a failure.

Jessica saw those readings and held him tightly in her arms, but I knew that this was going to be the push she would need. Jerry's journey was inevitable now. He was destined to give up his mortal body to demonstrate the next phase of human existence.

I could not have been more excited.

In my wildest fantasies I could not have imagined that a

human heart would be able to be so powerful. What I could not reconcile yet, was that the defect was in fact a benefit.

Your mother and I spent years arguing over this. Every test I ran suggested that it was somehow accentuating the electromagnetic conductivity of his quantum empathic ability, but he was also far more fragile that you were.

I had records of almost every moment of your life; data that was feeding into the narrative I would need to consult in order to make sure we timed the organ transfer at the optimum moment. As I compared you to Jerry, there was no doubt that you were stronger, healthier, better in every single aspect of physical health. But his heart! His heart was miraculous. It was both flawed and perfect.

I knew that there would be a cost to proceeding with Jerry over you. I knew that if I didn't allow Jessica to heal the hole in his heart that he would be vulnerable, but despite my desire to make this experiment work, I could not risk changing any of the circumstances of the setup we had.

I admit to you, Astrophel, that I knew Jerry would not survive for long with what I proposed to put him through. In fact, he exceeded my expectations. In so many ways.

82

AUDEN

In many respects, I suppose you and Jerry grew up fairly happily. You knew nothing other than the life we gave to you and the two of you rather doted upon one another. Jessica understood that Jerry should be thought of only as your playmate and if she could agree to this, then I would allow the two of you to grow up as siblings - with the understanding that one day this would need to be removed from your memory.

She agreed to the price of this offer. I see now that she was in fact a rather old-fashioned and traditional person. She wanted to experience what the world called a normal family. She wanted to be a mother, even when the cost of this would be enormous pain. I did not engage with any of you in the same way. I understood that bonding with you was likely to cause a sub-optimal outcome for the experiment. I was unwilling to allow this.

Once we had decided that Jerry was indeed the route we were going to explore, your future became less certain. Jessica loved you like a real daughter. This sounds unkind. I know that you are our daughter, but I rarely thought of you in this way and I was frustrated that she had shown such weakness. Nonetheless, she understood that you being around once Jerry went through the procedure, might prove to be a distraction. We agreed that you would be sent away. We agreed that Daniel and Mary would be the appropriate hosts for this matter. Daniel was permanently indebted to me and Mary had always desired to be a mother. This would provide a satisfactory solution.

We agreed that the procedure would happen once Jerry was 10 years old, as his body would be suitably stable and developed at that point, but we did not particularly want to run the risk of the complications of puberty if at all possible. He would be suitably small enough to always require a chaperone, who outsiders would imagine to be a parent, thus meaning that the age discrepancy between those monitoring and working with him, and Jerry himself, would be nullified.

This was decided by the time he was two years old. That gave me eight years to perfect the procedures, form the right team, establish a secondary laboratory and of course, invent the technology required to complete the extended central nervous system transplant and android integration.

The reality of what happened once these plans were put in place differed somewhat in my memory to those of Jessica.

This is because I deceived her in the most extraordinary way. Over and over again.

I regret much of this, because in the end I believe that her grief, much of which I caused, was a significant contributor to her suicide. And I did care for her. I did not love her in the traditional sense, but she was my wife and she was a quite astonishing and insightful scientist. She deserved better. I am sorry for you too - I deprived you of a mother who cared deeply for you.

But I was a man on a pilgrimage to immortality and I was unquenchable in my thirst.

I remember an evening, perhaps four years into my eight-year window; I brought Daniel down to the Echo Chamber to show him the work I had been developing. I showed him the chambers where I kept my automatons. He was impressed by the chimp and the dog, who was actually a less developed version of Jazz. When he came to the third chamber and saw a young girl waving back at him, I could see his panic. When I ushered him on to the fourth chamber and he saw an exact replica of me, I almost laughed. I thought he might shit his pants then and there!

He asked me who the girl was. I could see that something was pulling at a thread in his mind, but I told him she was the creation of an algorithm. She was not. She was you. You as a girl of five years old. You were ten years old by this point, so looked quite different. I changed a few details, like the colour and style of your hair, but it was you. I told myself that I was being sentimental. Then I told myself that as we had easy access to you and photos of you, it would be straightforward and obvious for me to use that data to build my first human automaton. It wasn't simply vanity that I built one of myself either - I could verify its accuracy far more easily, given that I had the original with me at all times!

But none of this is the truth.

The truth is that in my mind, I had not yet moved on from all of this being about you. You, Astrophel, were supposed to be my magnum opus. You were destined to be the next step in the evolutionary tale. In building you as my first human-mimicking robot, I kept that timeline of events alive. I am not heartless either, despite what you will be thinking. I did so enjoy building you; you were a sweet little girl and I spent much time in the Echo Chamber talking to your synthetic twin about the work I was doing. She did not understand anything; she could not speak; she couldn't do anything other than smile and wave, and sit and stand, but you, she, was so contented. It brought me joy to see what might be possible. It brought me joy to keep my dream of immortalising you alive.

That should have been the end of it. I should have let you go. I should have been content with my homage to the work we would have done.

But I'm gone now. Daniel is gone. Your mother, Mary. Even Jerry is gone now. Eventually you would have discovered the truth. And if you didn't, then someone else would and that would be so much worse.

83

AUDEN

Everybody thinks they are special. It is one of the most ingrained of human attributes. If you give a dog praise it will wag its tail; if you praise a human it will do what you already had it doing, but with a little more willing, thinking that you somehow value it more than you did before.

Each person working on Project Hephaestus happily wagged their tail at me as I told them that they were doing the work I wanted them to do. Each person assumed that they were somehow uniquely qualified to do what they were doing and each person thought they were the only ones working on the project.

The arrogance of the freshly elevated, is astonishing.

I had a dozen different teams of people working on every element of the project. None of them met, so they assumed that no one else existed.

In the entire project, there were only two people that were irreplaceable. Me and Jessica. And at a push, I may have been able to replace her.

Everybody else was fodder.

In the end, it was a mere boy who performed the extended central nervous system transplant on Jerry. It shouldn't have been him. There was actually someone better qualified. Someone who had already successfully performed the procedure.

You see, much like my rats, there were different phases and stages to the testing. Stage one was to identify humans with the appropriate latent skill and desire to perform groundbreaking, ethically challenging surgery. This was basic psychology and dexterity. Step two was to put them under extraordinary pressure, to implant a BEST chip in their brain, to track their every movement, to test their allegiance to the cause. Step three was to have them rehearse the procedure using the finest virtual reality technology available. They would do the procedure again and again and again until they could do it in their sleep. Step four was to harvest every bit of data we had to see who should progress to Step five - human testing. Success here should have been a-given and this victor would move to Step six - operating on Jerry.

Step five was complicated by the fact that we would require a live human being to operate on. It's remarkably difficult to remove a human being from society without someone noticing. Even the most worthless grunt seems to find a connection that makes a sudden withdrawal from the world noticeable. And besides, I did not want just anybody to have the surgery. If it was successful it would be entirely lifechanging; indeed, it would be the sort of change that could destroy a mind if it was not well prepared and suited to such a procedure.

I had many people seeking out prime candidates. A few came close, but ultimately there was one fundamental barrier which remained insurmountable. I have already told you that our neural enhancement protocols are partially reliant on people accepting the suggested changes. This is why it has been so easy to find success with mental health issues - people want to feel more confident, happier, hornier, whatever it is they want and so they do not fight the chip at the point of implant. In order for this procedure to work a neural implant would need to be in place to maintain consciousness at the point of transplant, to nullify any pain at the moment of bio-tech integration and to assist with the psychological trauma of changing body. This would be viable if the candidate was willing. However, any viable candidates would never have been willing to sacrifice their human bodies; their mental strength being an asset, but one that was linked to good health and a certain joy in their own self which they at least partially defined through their human form.

As I widened the search, the answer came into focus. Actually, this is a lie. I knew, as I have always known, what the answer to this particular question was, because it was entirely obvious.

You.

You were the answer Astrophel. You were the perfect candidate. You were in fact, born to do this very thing. For perhaps no one in the history of mankind, can that statement be more true.

You were the one. You were the first recipient of a successful extended nervous system transplant into an entirely synthetic body with full biological integration. You are the girl who will never grow up. You are the immortal embodiment of perfection. You are the future of humankind and you have been so for decades without any clue as to what you are and what you can be.

I knew that you would agree to the procedure. I knew this because I knew you. I knew that if I turned my attention to you and treated you as my daughter that you would do anything I asked. Perhaps this honesty sickens you. You will wonder at how such a monster could live with the choices he has made. You may think that I have wronged you, manipulated you, hurt you. Perhaps in some perverse way you think that I have killed you.

But I know the truth.

I have made you a miracle.

84

JERRY

My beautiful sister; I so wish that we were meeting face to face, rather than this sad message from a past you don't remember. But if you have this, it means that Rufus outlived everybody else, which is as it should be.

Don't worry though, I didn't leave finding you to chance; there were countless other ways I would have found you; this was just the one that made the most sense.

I know you don't remember me; how could you; this face is not even mine, but I want you to know that you were a great sister. You were my favourite person in all the world and not coming to find you after it all happened, was the hardest decision in the world.

If you made it to EverTech, you must know nearly everything; or at least, you will know what everyone has wanted you to hear.

I spent my second life trying to right the wrongs of our father; I hope that you do not feel that you will need to do the same. I visited so many people touched by the depth of his ambition and I used the little power I had, to help ease them past the pain that he had caused them.

I hope that you have met some of them. So many troubled souls; so much kindness and guilt and sadness and joy; it was beautiful being able to be with them and hear their stories. I'm sorry that you won't get to meet Harry; he was the detective who was looking into the accident which exposed the secret. He was a good man. Maybe you found Evie? She is so sad to have lost him; she is angry but not at you, no matter what she says. She was one of the few people I met who truly wanted to hold on to their pain; she said it kept Harry close and that was what mattered to her, not how it made her feel.

She was brave. They all were. Mia, José, Ovi, Kibibi, Jack, Daphne. So many stories - have you found them all? I wonder if you will find comfort in them as I did?

We have our own story to tell too. But I will not be here for very much longer. The body our father built for me, is much like the one that clothes you as well, and it is strong, but my heart was not up to the job of being long in this world. I so often heard our father talking about his search for a good heart and of course, in the beginning I had no idea what he meant; then I understood that he would look at me with hungry eyes and I knew that he had found what he wanted within me.

I was not a child to him; I was an experiment, but I tried to love him anyway. I wanted him to know that even though my heart ached when I touched other people, if he thought it was good enough, then I wanted it to be so. In the end of course, I betrayed him, because I could see that he was cruel. I could see that I was not to be a thing used to heal, but to harm, so I turned his creation upon him and when I ran away to try and fix what he had done, I planted one of his robots and told it to sit and bide its time and when the moment was right, to stop him from causing more harm.

I meant to run away and find a way of destroying this shell, so that I could not be put to other uses, but I had also already witnessed what I could do to help. I had returned the mind of a man who was lost to the world. It saddened me that this man had done terrible, terrible things, but it was not for me to judge him. I did not feel the same way about our father's sins.

So, I ran, knowing that every time I found someone I could help, that it would help me along the road to oblivion.

I can't think of a better way of spending a life than listening to the stories of others, laughing and crying with them and helping them move on from their pain.

I wanted you to know that our mother is not who they will tell you she was. She was brilliant. She was kind. And she loved us both. She was manipulated and controlled by our father. He didn't just put a chip in her head to do it either; he was her captor and when she had a chance to escape, she helped me instead. She let me escape when she should not have. She did die, but she did not kill herself. She was punished for her disobedience. I don't tell you this with the facts, only with the knowledge of what I saw before I left. She was good. A little broken by the journey she found herself on and then she became different. Cold, as if she stopped seeing us. I knew that our father had done something to her, but I didn't know how to help her. You saw it too. You knew that it was all wrong. I miss her.

We were almost a family for a little while. There were times when I was searching for those who had been hurt, when I would daydream about a life where we were who we had been born as and our mother would take us away to the beach. We would play. We would have a dog just like Jazz, but made of flesh and bone. And we would laugh. We would walk along the sand dunes and you would find a dandelion lurking in some grassy scrubland where the beach meets a park. Before you could blow it apart, I would run up to you and explode its fluffy seeds in your face and run off laughing, hoping you would chase me all the way into the ocean.

I have one more secret, Asty. Did you know that they sent me to school for a year, before all of this happened? As scientists they thought it was important that I was well socialised and our father wanted to ensure that there was an official record of my existence so that when he ended my first life, there was a narrative that made sense.

St. Jude's Primary School. It always made me smile when I looked back upon this, as St Jude was the patron saint of lost causes; such a strange person to name a school after! It was quite wonderful, being surrounded by other children, but it was exhausting. Every time someone would tag me, bump me in the corridor, hold my hand as we lined up for assembly, I felt my heart racing to connect with theirs. It is a connection filled with joy, but one which is overwhelming. I appeared to be a sickly child to the outside world, because I so often looked tired and pasty, but in truth, I was flooded with the love and joy of others and my body found it hard to process so much feeling. In the end they took me out of school, cover story intact; clearly I needed to be home-schooled, as mainstream education was too much for a delicate little chap like me.

But those were happy days. And I would come home and you would be waiting, eager to hear about what had happened. You relished the stories of history and literacy as much as the dramatic tales of friendships won and lost on the playground. You lived a life through my experiences and I wanted to make sure you felt as if you had been by my side the whole time. It was never enough for you; you always wanted more; every night you would reach out and hold my hand and I would try to let you feel what I had felt, but you saw how tired it made me and so you would hold your teddy bear instead and I would know that you loved me.

Before my body completely gave out, I found Mia and she promised to help me disappear quietly. I knew that she cared for me and I knew that she felt a deep well of guilt about what happened. She believed that she was the catalyst that begun our transformations. But our father had been laying the groundwork for his masterplan long before Mia stumbled across a beautiful truth; we are all looking to reach out and connect with each other all of the time, even when we are looking the other way. Her work is what should inspire hope in humanity; our father took nature's poetry and did something terrible with it. I suppose we shouldn't be surprised; there are always people who will look to reimagine perfection; this is how we evolve, but choosing how and when, is something we so often get wrong.

He nearly did something remarkable, but he misunderstood what his life's work should really have been about. We are the collateral damage in that learning. But your heart is strong; it is more than good; it is the one great gift that you have been given and I hope that you will try to live a life.

There are so many things I wish I had time to pass on to you, but Mia is waiting to take me and I am in a hurry to go with peace in my faltering heart. So, I will just tell you this: listen more than you speak; people are full of beautiful stories that can change your life. Trust that you can help most by being kind and don't forget to pretend to eat food and go to the bathroom occasionally - it's amazing how much of human life revolves around these things!

I hope you still have Jazz with you; she's programmed to defend you and that might come in handy one day. But I hope, more than anything, that you will eventually be able to settle somewhere; that you will be able to be yourself and rest.

I am so tired Asty; but in a way that makes me happy to be going to sleep now. I feel like I am inhaling jasmine and honey under a warm summer's evening sky. I lived the best life I could, at least, the second time, and now my only regret is that we did not get to grow old together. I think I would have been a very good uncle! You were destined to become someone amazing. So, I leave you with one final gift, now that our lives are different to the ones we may have uncovered for ourselves: if you unscrew the drive that this message is on, you will find two inhalable BEST chips, hacked and reconfigured by me! They are very delicate, so please be careful.

You'll probably need a magnifying glass, but one is inscribed with the word *sleep* and the other *awake*. You can choose what happens next. It's what you deserve. If you choose sleep, then you'll have 24 hours to find a safe place to be, get yourself to sleep and then the chip will send a huge surge of electricity through your heart initiating a sudden cardiac arrest; you will painlessly and quietly fall asleep forever. If you choose awake, that chip will knockout the one our father planted and actively restore all of the memories of your life. You'll remember everything from before the crash, before you were transplanted into this body, everything between each reset while you lived with the Allen's. Or, you can crush this flash drive and find your own path.

Whatever you choose, it will be the right thing, because it will be your choice alone.

I am leaving this world knowing that I helped right some wrongs. And I will be thinking of you, me and mum on the beach, dandelion seeds and laughter floating through the air as I drift away in another direction.

85

DAN

Despite the fate that lay ahead for Jerry, he was allowed a normal life for a little while. I know so much of your memory of growing up has been scrubbed, but I saw you as happy children. You ran around EverTech as if it were your personal playground. But I suppose those occasional visits are not much of an insight.

Your father was reinvigorated by the discovery of Jerry's situation, though he and Jessica argued almost daily about whether or not they should operate on the hole in his heart. He was paranoid that changing anything about his biological make-up could destroy the miracle he had created. Auden was never going to lose that argument and so, when he was not looking, I saw you mother smother Jerry in the love that comes with anxiety and fear.

And he had too much work to do to waste on such things. He distanced himself from all of you, to focus on the next phase of his plan - the body that Jerry would need to occupy.

You see he had built something quite astonishing - something which at the time didn't even have a name, but that we now come to call nanobots. He built these independent of any other work that was happening around the globe and still, to this day, no one has come even close. The bots were microscopic, but the technology to miniaturise or control them was nowhere near good enough. When he read the work Mia had done on the heart-brain connection and the empathy fields created with electro-magnetic energy, he knew that he had found an answer.

If he could create a vehicle, or a body, made of nanobots, the heart-brain connection would be able to power them, using nothing more than their own electrical impulses. This was relatively simple actually. Where he created magic, was in understanding that if the heart could generate a strong enough magnetic field, with the right discipline of mind, the nanobots could be directed by the host's empathy field. This magnetic field should be able to identify pain or disease in another person, and then carry the biologically charged nanobots from the host to the recipient, directing their actions and allowing them to heal a person on a molecular level. When the host moved away from the recipient, the nanobots would become inactive and be expelled from the recipient over time.

He had been building uncanny lifelike creatures for decades. On several occasions he invited me to the secret lab within his secret lab - he called it the Echo Chamber. There was a line of glass-sided prison cells along one wall. There were 5 in total. 4 were full. They were all in the dark. They lit up as you stood in front of them. It was all wildly dramatic. In the first was a chimp. She was jumping up and down, seemingly quite agitated. The glass deadened her cries, but her face was pained. In the second cage, a dog. I'm no expert, but it was big and quite handsome. It sat patiently and as I approached, its large golden tail began to wag rhythmically as it made eye contact with me. The third enclosure frightened me the most. It contained a human child. I don't know how old it was, less than a teenager, more than toddler. It, she, stood silently and still, unmoving until I stepped closer to the glass, then she looked at me and slowly, with sad eyes, she waved. It was only now that I turned to Auden, imploring him to do something.

What is this place? What have you done?

There is still one more enclosure. You will enjoy this one, I'm sure.

I hesitated but knew better than to disagree. As the final cell lit up, I jumped back. I turned to Auden. *How is this...why?*

He smiled. In fact, he smiled twice. Once, the real him, standing behind me, looking ridiculously pleased with himself and then again, as I stared upon a perfect copy of him behind the reinforced glass.

Is it...real?

For fuck's sake Daniel! Has spending so much time tending to flowers and fox shit left your brain so decrepit? We're not a circus; I'm not some petty geneticist after a cheap thrill. Of course they're not real. They are perfect, robotic replicas. They think and feel nothing other than the basic mechanical programming I installed.

So, you've done it then? You've created a shell for...Project H?

Not quite. They look perfect now, but nothing yet will both host and integrate the full, living brain-heart system.

Who is the girl? I asked, pointing at the robot.

No one. A fiction created by an algorithm.

I shuddered as I watched it continue to wave sadly at me.

He was relentless in his pursuit. I saw countless creatures killed or maimed as he experimented for years, spending almost every penny of profit the company made to prove himself a genius.

And eventually he found a formulation which worked.

I was summoned, as so often was the case, to Auden's office. There I was greeted by a large cage, with a chimp listlessly pacing within its confines. *This is Lucy. I'm currently having her body incinerated in the furnaces at the back of the campus. That is, with the exception of her heart and brain. Those have been installed into this version of Lucy.*

And has the original Lucy transferred in terms of behaviours? I asked. Too astounded to be afraid for what this meant.

She behaves exactly as her biological version did. With the exception of her body being renewed, she is the original Lucy. If that is who I choose to allow her to be. You see I have added an unregulated neural chip to her brain; I can switch her natural behaviours on or off as I choose. I can have her be whatever I want and most importantly, she could, if only she were intelligent enough, launch the nanobots that are integrated into her skeleton.

I had no choice but to congratulate him. It was an astonishing scientific achievement. As I walked away however, all I could wonder was how long Jerry had left.

AUDEN

When I realised that you were the answer, the final problem confronted me - I needed your mother to agree. She was essential to the success of the procedure. And whilst you may not believe me, more than anything in the world, I wanted you to survive. In the end, it was this very thing that persuaded Jessica to perform the procedure. I told her that I would have the transplant carried out with or without her, but that without her it was far more likely to fail and you would be lost to the world forever.

She threatened to run at first; to take you and Jerry with her and disappear, but I reminded her that with a BEST chip in her head, hiding was not an option. Before she calmed down she threatened to kill you all instead. I played her at her own game: If you're going to do that, then why not let me have a go anyway? What difference would it make to you? In fact, surely if I gave the order to perform the procedure, then the blame is mine if anything goes wrong?

I will not repeat the words she screamed at me; she had quite the temper your mother; I rather enjoyed that side of her. Ultimately though, she knew that I would prevail and she knew that she would want to oversee the procedure.

And so, it was done.

I had already built the body you would inhabit. It was the most perfect replica of you in that moment of your life. You at 14 years old; ready to take on the world, but now never to become a fully-fledged adult, at least in body. Our top candidate was primed and ready to perform the transplant and Jessica was there to tackle the intricacies of connecting the heart into the biotech body.

Everything worked perfectly. My God, Astrophel you kissed your mother on the cheek before the surgery and told her not to worry! Even I was astonished at your compliance. And the procedure itself could not have gone better; it was textbook. Which was of course exactly the point. There was nothing happening in that operating theatre that each participant had not rehearsed a thousand times before. If every one of them had been struck blind I suspect we could still have completed the work.

When you woke up, you were you. You were exactly who we had seen willingly hop onto the operating table. It was this, in fact, which began the slow destruction of your mother's mind. You see, you did not know that anything had changed; at the point of surgery a chip was implanted to ensure that you had no recollection of the transfer and to suppress the exploration of your body. It never entered your mind to consider why you did not go to the bathroom, why you did not wash, why you did not eat; you bore witness to these things, you understood them, you had prior knowledge of them, but you never noticed that you no longer did them.

Perfection.

Honestly, I should have stopped with you; nothing could have improved upon what we did. But I wanted more. You were perhaps too perfect; you made me arrogant; you made me believe that I was the god I had expected myself to be.

But of course, your existence posed some problems that needed resolving if we were to move the project forwards.

If it had been up to me, you would never have left my side. I loved you now in a way I never had before the transplant; you were more my daughter than you had ever been. I had crafted every bit of who you were and made certain your survival. But you would never be any different now and that, at some point in the not-too-distant future, would become difficult.

There were mechanisms I had already put in place. For example, Daniel aside, no one at EverTech knew you existed. You came into the building hundreds of times, often with your mother, sometimes with me, almost always with Jerry at your side, but if you asked anyone at EverTech who you were, they would not know. Every employee had their chips adjusted to make you invisible to them. It had started as a game actually; Daniel had not believed me when I explained how easily the brain could be fooled, so I wrote some new code for the chip and deployed it to 3 of my employees who I knew arrived at roughly the same time each day. I had Daniel join me on the second floor to watch for their arrival. We looked down from one of the labs which overlooked the central atrium and waited. As they entered they began to scream and ran back towards the entrance, but one of them seemed stuck; paralysed with fear, looking to all the world as if they were about to fall over. I used a handheld computer to deploy an update to their chips which would wipe the code and that same employee suddenly stopped crying out. She looked around, confused. I had Rufus, our head of security collect her and the other two and escort them to my office where Daniel and I met them.

What did you see? I asked them.

There was no floor. The floor had fallen away and there was a huge, terrible gaping hole.

I thought I was going to fall; I thought I was going to die. I was terrified.

And then?

And then there was a floor again. I don't understand. Mr Everston, what happened to me?

What happened, was that Daniel witnessed that as ever, I was right. It is so depressingly easy to tell the brain what it is seeing. Or not seeing. When you were born, I decided to take no risks. You were hidden from the eyes of every employee; your destiny was too important to have other people monitoring you.

After the transplant you remained hidden, but there were gaps, or lapses in the illusion. More than once, mildly traumatised employees reported seeing a girl in the building. Of course, I had enough coverage to be able to sweep such foolish talk away, but your biotech body did not resonate at the same frequency as your original body and it was more complex to remove from the world.

That alone was reason enough to reconsider my plans for Jerry.

Your mother was a bigger problem.

I realised that the uncanny existence of your body was too much for her to cope with. She had in fact overwhelmed her chip and nothing I did to soothe or persuade her had any effect. She was breaking and this was simply unacceptable as she needed to be functioning at the highest level for the final procedure.

She couldn't bring herself to touch you; she barely looked you in the eye; she sobbed daily, telling me over and over again that you were different. When I asked her how, she couldn't tell me. *Just different*, she'd say. You, who knew no better, assumed you had done something wrong and the whole household became dysfunctional.

I decided then, that I would build a body for Jerry, that was totally different to the one he had. Everything would be new; skin colour, hair, eyes, voice; the essence of Jerry would be as it always had been, but that is where the crossover would cease. I needed to ensure that his mind would be able to cope with this change; there are many examples of cognitive dissonance nearly driving people to madness when they cannot reconcile a replacement limb, or reconstructive surgery, but this was a small challenge, given the extraordinary range of capability the BEST neural chips allowed. He would still need to be a boy of similar age, but his emergence from the lab would be explained through the referral system we have long had in place with many medical institutions, including Jessica's former laboratory.

Jessica understood that Jerry as he was, would need to die, publicly, so that no questions were asked. She understood. But she only agreed, because I also built in your removal to the narrative. She loved you, but she could not bear to look upon you. You would be hidden away from the world, and as she lost Jerry, she would grieve for you too.

I was happy with this arrangement. It meant that you would be safe from harm or investigation and as far as I was concerned, you were too precious to endanger. After all, you were my first creation and you were also the back-up plan should anything go wrong with Jerry. You were living proof of what I had achieved. You still are.

I knew that Mary's chip was failing. I knew that Daniel was getting desperate. I knew that if I dangled hope in front of him he would do whatever I asked. Taking you away was an easy ask for the promise of my help. And so, you lived with fools who would do anything to protect your secret and those fools were little more than a hindrance in my daily life, so I was glad to be rid of Daniel and his moralising bullshit.

I accept that you lived a strange half-life that I have monitored from afar, but now that I am gone, I free you from that imprisonment. Each year I have reset and wiped the memories of the year before; that way you could never begin to piece together too much of your past, or ask questions which may have led you to answers I did not want you to uncover. You never thought of yourself as anything other than the 14-year-old girl you were so very long ago and looking in the mirror each day, only confirmed your belief that you were who you thought you were. But now you can walk out of the door of that sad, little house that has held you captive for so long and you can explore the world.

I will not take anything else away from you.

87

ASTROPHEL

After I watched Jerry's message I looked in the mirror. We were nothing alike. We looked like we came from different places, had different lives, had no reason to ever meet. He was not the boy in my hazy vision. And yet he was. Even on film, I felt that he had reached out and connected to me. But everyone I had spoken to had said that same thing. Maybe he was just special.

I was a freak.

Untested, discarded, alone.

Indulge my pity-party a moment won't you - I just found out that I'm made of fucking metal, having been manipulated into some sort of pseudo-suicide by my own father!

The people I needed were dead; the people I wanted to scream at were dead; anyone who could give me answers was dead. They'd all played a blinder in that sense! No one could hold any of them to account. And that just left me.

Well fuck that! I tore open the flash drive Jerry had left me and found the two microchips. I could sniff them both without looking at the labels and this could all be over within a day. No one really knew I existed, so it would be weeks, months, maybe years before anyone found me. Presumably I would look unchanged, whenever that was; a perfect, frozen-in-time freak, who rotted away on the inside.

I cried. Except of course I didn't. I couldn't. I had never had enough awareness granted me before now to notice this. I had all of the emotional turmoil, but could not produce any tears. I didn't even make the noises that people make on films. I silently, invisibly, sobbed about this new reality.

How could knowing more help me now? How could remembering not being this way, make things better? Surely Jerry was joking; he couldn't really imagine that I had the possibility of a real life?

I was ready to stop existing. In that moment, as the truth of my being lay before me. My father's message, Jerry's, Dan's; they wanted something from me I could not, or did not want, to give them.

If Jerry had been here, maybe I would have been able to be stronger; maybe he could have helped me. He was clearly tougher than I was. He spoke with a wisdom that far exceeded my own. He had the power to heal others. Could he have healed me, even through the metal casing that guards my heart?

And that was when I found hope. That thought. My heart. My heart had been built to do something. Perhaps I could do what Jerry did? Maybe my skeleton was made of those tiny robots. Could I learn how to do that?

Could I live a life that did some good? That might make the loneliness worth something.

But I had no people to teach me and no one to touch. Even the dog, was of no use. I thought of Mia's studies, with the boy and her dog; how they had revealed the magic that led to our creation. The thought of holding Jazz made me sad; she would feel nothing as the tiny part of me which maybe kept me human reached out to try and find meaning.

I resolved in that moment, to opt for hope, just temporarily. There was always a back-up plan. Test this method, then use another if it doesn't work out. I'm sure my bastard creator would be pleased with such logic.

I chose to be awake.

I inhaled deeply and felt the tiny chip fly silently up into my brain stem. Jerry's tech sent to play off against my father's. Cyborg child healer against mad scientist, battling out for control of my brain. What could possibly go wrong?

DAN

As far as I could tell, you were now largely irrelevant to them. You were free. Well, more free than Jerry. But I have lied to you; when I proclaimed to only realise later about the chip in your head. I did know. It was me who put it there.

You see despite the success of EverTech and BEST chips, they were, as I mentioned, operating only at a fraction of what we could do and, irrespective of this, they were very much illegal for people under the age of 21. We had almost no data on what our chips might do to a brain that had not finished developing and I knew already that Jerry would, should he survive the procedure, have a chip implanted.

Auden did not want to take any risks. So, he asked me to implant one in you. You, who had been born to be the star of his strange and twisted show, were now reduced to the part of understudy; you were the testing ground upon which Jerry's life would be weighed against. And of course there was only one person he could drag in to further dismantle his own reputation; only one person who would baulk, but comply when asked to do something so foul as to tamper with the free will of an innocent - me.

Our nasal application process was still awaiting approval and did not yet fully meet our own required level of success, but we had found that there was another, less appealing way of delivering the chip payload without open surgery.

I had to drive the chip directly through your ear drum and cochlea to implant onto your brain stem, which is a suitable alternative to the other more usual locations used for the installations being done in EverTech Brain Sync Centres around the world. It was more brutal, it would destroy your hearing, but there would be no trace of the installation. Once it was there, your father would be able to erase your memory of it ever happening.

I don't know under what false pretence you came to EverTech HQ that day. I don't know when he gave you the sedative that made you fall asleep in the chair you found yourself. But I do know that I did the procedure and at least in some way, I did so willingly.

Your readings confirmed that you were a suitable back-up and that a child's brain could comfortably cope with the technical intervention of the chip. With that established, your father decided you were now only an inconvenience which needed to be preserved, but kept out of sight.

The solution was to deal with both you and Jerry at the same time and create enough witnesses to make it a secret worth hiding. All I had to do was play my part convincingly enough that nobody wanted to ask questions.

I should apologise, but I can't. Not in a way that would be entirely true. What I did, I think, saved your life in some way. You may think that the life you've had is one that has been mangled and dismantled, but you could be free now to live something more real. Installing that chip, in some ways made that possible.

I can hear the desperation in my voice as I'm saying these words to you. I am sorry Asty. I'm sorry that I was too cowardly to tell you the truth in person. I'm sorry that you're hearing this when there's no one left to confront; no one left to spit fire at; no one left who knows your story. You'll need to create a new story now. Please have a life Asty. Jerry had his stolen and I can't do anything about that now. You could live for a very long time indeed. I want you to be happy.

I know you know that I haven't told you everything, but there's plenty you already know and maybe some things you don't ever need to know.

I was a weak man. I loved my wife and I loved Auden Everston. And I loved what both of them made me, even when it tore me apart. I came to love you too Asty, but by then I had done too many awful things and lost more than I could ever regain.

You are a miracle. Please do not waste that truth on hating me and your father. We were not worth it.

89

AUDEN

The rest you know, or suspect.

I choreographed the car crash. Daniel was in place to rescue you. I had vetted the security team and knew from intense psychological profiling that the security detail was made up exclusively of men who would betray EverTech if they thought they were heroically saving a child.

The paramedic was an annoyance, but Daniel played his part well and once she was gone, everything settled into a routine.

Jerry's surgery was an extraordinary success.

He proved that the nanobot skeleton could indeed be activated and controlled via the magnetic field of his heart and its biologically encoded messaging system. I watched as he deployed these bots via the lightest of touch, sending them to build, heal, destroy and replace; whatever was needed.

He was the future of medical care and espionage in equal measure. He could save or destroy. And all I would need to do, was retain a clear and vigorous control of his thoughts.

And then the little shit betrayed me. Everything I have

worked for, disappeared off into the world to perform party tricks dressed up as miracles.

We knew where he was for a little while, we heard snippets of the stories you have discovered, but he evaded us more often than not.

He is dead now. I know this, because his final act was to leave a message for me, filled with lies and hate and ingratitude. He destroyed perfection when I had offered him a life of meaning and purpose. I will never be able to forgive or forget this betrayal.

I hope you are made of tougher stuff, my daughter.

I leave you with nothing. Except an almost invulnerable body. Upon my death EverTech will create a board of directors and this project, along with several others, will be wiped from the company servers and indeed the minds, of anyone who knew about them. My untimely death slows the course of human history by three quarters of a century, but I am not there to care or bear witness to the folly of others. It is not arrogant to say that I was born with messianic potential, but at every corner there was a barrier, forcing me to the shadows, encouraging me to take the paths that would hide my true ability and in the end, yes, I have cured the mental health crisis for the world, but I had so much more within my reach.

It is not too late for you to pick up my mantle. You, who will live for who knows how many years; you who will see everything from the vantage point of a demigod. You could do something Astrophel. I named you not just to be a lover of the stars, but to reach out and claim them for your own.

Do something with the gift I have bestowed upon you Astrophel. You owe your creator that much at least.

90

ASTROPHEL

My surrogate father and my real father tricked me into having the brain version of a back-street abortion.

Jerry allowed me a rebirth.

I felt complete. That is not to say that I no longer had questions. I did. So many. But I saw who I was in its entirety for the first time. I saw my mother had loved me the way I could only have hoped. I saw a brother who was so kind and yet seemed to know his fate long before it had even been decided. I saw Dan, a nearly-father who was broken by the iron grip of my not-really-father. I could see that Auden Everston had been the Pied Piper in all of our lives, leading us to a conclusion only he saw, and I pitied them all.

But mostly Jerry.

Jerry, whose life was destroyed to spare my own; Jerry, whose life could have been lengthened and strengthened if only one of the world's leading cardiologists had been allowed to perform a simple procedure. Jerry. Jerry. Jerry. Maybe it was all about him after all and I am just a bit part player, left behind to tell you how unfair it was that he was taken instead of me.

I needed to know if I could be like Jerry, but I didn't know where to start. I now had the complete picture of the road upon which I walked to get to this point, but the road ahead had not yet been built. So, I did the only logical thing I could think of: I walked back to the beginning and looked for inspiration.

I found our house and watched its new owners come and go for days. I went back to EverTech; Rufus had retired literally the day after my visit, so there was no one left to notice me. I wondered their public gallery for hours at a time, watching the employees sign in and disappear into the labs and offices beyond. I even found the school that Jerry went to.

I stood by the school gates when children were dropped off and collected. As someone who looked like a sibling, no one paid me much attention. Well, until they did.

Excuse me? A blonde-haired lady, who looked to be about forty years old was marching towards me. Despite being weighed down by multiple school bags, a handbag the size of a small country and what looked like a watermelon under one arm, she seemed to slide through and around the crowd of other parents with a ballet dancer's ease, never breaking the eye contact I had accidentally allowed by looking up, somehow knowing that the voice was calling out to me.

Excuse me? She said, now within touching distance. *I know this is going to sound very strange, but you're not related to Jerry Everston are you?*

Shit! Bugger! Crap! I was not prepared for that!

Only...well this is going to sound a scary kind of crazy, but I knew him you see and I...well you look just like someone I saw once, in the car that used to take him home.

I did some basic calculations in my head. What is a safe answer? No. No, would have been a safe answer. But I think my face already told her enough to ensure this wasn't going to fly. *Jerry was my mother's cousin. They used to play together sometimes I think.* That was a shit lie. But it was enough. She looked at me in a way I couldn't quite understand, but this woman had something she wanted to say. And as it turned out, it was something I really needed to hear.

91

MOLLY

I saw you standing there and I was struck dumb. You are the absolute spitting image of your mother! I mean I never met her properly, but I saw her through the car window a few times, and I so wanted to speak with her. I wanted to know what it was like to be around Jerry away from school!

I'm not making much sense am I? I'm sorry. I just have been hoping for a moment like this for a really long time.

People love to exaggerate the influence of others on their lives. It sounds cool to say so-and-so changed my life, or doing this-and-that changed my life, but it's often just a way to get someone to complement the changes you've made, the weight that you've lost, the partner you ditched. But Jerry and I were just children; we met fleetingly really, but every single day of my life, I think of him and I thank him, because he saved me. Not in a fake life-coach sort of a way, but literally saved my life.

Jerry joined in Year Two; he had started halfway through the year, so everyone was making a bit of a fuss of him. He was so quiet, but when he spoke, everybody would listen. And when you're talking about a room full of seven year olds, that is pretty amazing in itself.

I was grateful as his appearance stopped me from being the most interesting curiosity in the class for a little while. You see, I had started to get sick and children can be cruel without meaning to be - they would point at me when I came in looking pale, with bloodshot eyes. They would laugh if I would vomit. But Jerry never did. He was kind, without ever speaking to me. I wanted to talk to him; something made me want to be his friend, but it was hard for me to do much more than be in school and exist. I remember watching him go home each day; it was so different to everyone else, which is why I paid it attention. Everyday a car would arrive, the door would open and he would get in. Then it would drive off. No one ever got out; no mum or dad ever came to greet him and he never seemed to utter a word to anyone as he was swept off. But there were a few times when I saw someone inside the car. I always wondered who it was. And then one day, the person was sitting on the side that Jerry would normally get in on, and the window was open. My goodness, you look just like that person; like your mother I suppose she was?

Anyway, I struggled through the rest of the year, but when Year Three started and Miss Hogan was our teacher, I had become a lot more ill and I was diagnosed with something called Blitzen Disease. The doctor's first noticed it when I was about five years old, as my eyesight suddenly got really bad. At first they just thought I needed glasses. But then I started having seizures. We saw a lot of specialists and eventually they ran enough tests to diagnose me. By that time, I was on anti-seizure medicine, I had gone almost totally blind and we all knew the prognosis - I was going to be dead by the time I was twenty and the decade leading up to that moment would be filled with pain. You see there is no cure for Blitzen's and my brain was beginning to atrophy. I was going to school only for a few more weeks, just so that I could play with my friends a little bit, but I had a full-time carer and I was barely speaking because of the pain.

I know this is going to be a lot. I know you'll think I'm mad, because I would if I were you, but when we came back to school that year, I couldn't really see much more than outlines, and I wore big black sunglasses just to make sure everyone knew it, but when Jerry came in that first day back, I could see like a ball of light, wherever he was. It was like he was some sort of human lighthouse that only I could see. It was beautiful. The first few days I just observed quietly from my corner of the classroom, but I was desperate to reach out and touch this light that had come into my life.

On the third day, when it came to break time, the ball of light did not leave with the other children. It waited, until they had gone out to play, then it began to move towards me.

Hello. he said. *My name is Jericho Everston, but you can call me Jerry.*

My carer was going to speak for me, but I beat her to it. *I'm Molly.*

It's nice to meet you Molly. I could hear that he was moving a chair from under a desk so that he could sit down in front of me. *I'm sorry that you are in pain. Please would you let me hold your hand? I would like to comfort you.*

That's very sweet dear, but Molly isn't really supposed to get too close; she's quite poorly and she's just here to listen in and say goodbye to her friends. My carer read from the script she'd been forced to memorise in order for my parents to agree to this.

That seems very sensible. I think that rules like that are very helpful. If you like I can sit here with Molly while you get a cup of tea. I will make sure that no one comes near her and that she is safe.

I spent a lot of time as a teenager wondering if Jerry was some sort of real-life Jedi, because my carer, whose name was Val, was not particularly interested in caring or indeed anything much other than sitting down, but seemed somehow to think that this was a good idea.

As soon as we were alone in the classroom Jerry said, *I'm very sorry Molly, but I actually lied to that lady, because I am going to hold your hand.*

That's okay. I whispered.

That's good.

He was so gentle, but as our hands touched, I felt as if I was falling through the air at a hundred miles an hour. I looked at him, a little panic rising in me. And I saw his light was changing. It had become a thousand different colours and they were dancing; they were warm and they began to reach out to me. My hand, where he held me, was hot; I looked down towards it and watched as most of the colours streaming around Jerry were heading down along his arm and then disappearing through his hand and into me.

My chest felt full of the most wonderful, clear, mountain air. My heart was thumping excitedly in my chest. I thought in that moment that Jerry had come down from Heaven to take me to God and I was full of joy for it. I could not imagine a more perfect way to be delivered to the next life. There were tears in my eyes as I prepared myself to bid the world farewell. I could feel myself floating away from where I was sat. I had closed my eyes, ready to be greeted by a new life in another world, but when I opened them I was in my classroom and in front of me was a sweet looking boy who was smiling with his eyes closed, looking to all the world as if he had fallen asleep in his chair. His hand still held mine, but the heat was fading.

And it was only then that I realised that I could see. Everything. Properly. Clearly. And if I had wanted to, I could have stood. I felt full up with life and I wanted to jump and dance and sing and cry and laugh and bounce all at the same time.

Perhaps Jerry sensed this, because his hold on my hand tightened just slightly and he opened his eyes to look at me.

You feel better?
I feel wonderful! What did you do?
I just wanted to help you feel better.
I have never felt better than this!
But please don't tell anyone yet.
What do you mean?
I think I will get in trouble if they think I did this to you.
But you made me better, why would anyone be cross?
Sometimes grown-ups don't like it when they get things wrong.
But this is a good thing?
Yes, but sometimes they don't like good things that they don't understand.

He looked frightened and tired. I was just a little girl, but I knew that he was right. I knew then that something magical had happened and that grown-ups didn't believe in magic. I didn't want anything bad to happen to this incredible little boy who had made me feel better.

Okay. I won't tell them I'm better until in the morning.
Yes. That is good. They can't get mad with the morning.
You're funny.
I'm very tired.
Did making me better hurt you?
No, it made me as happy as it has made you.

I was little, but I wasn't stupid. I knew that whatever he had done, came at a huge cost to him. I wanted to reach out and hold him, but that was the moment that Val came back with a cup of something and a fist full of biscuits.

Jerry got up slowly; I could see through my no longer needed sunglasses, that he was holding onto the desk behind him far more than should have been necessary, but Val was not a careful observer of people. She didn't really see him at all.

It was very nice to spend playtime with you Molly. I hope that we can play again another time.

You know that bitch Val actually mumbled *Don't bet on it,* under her breath. We both heard it. But she was behind me, so she couldn't see me smile at Jerry; the boy who saved my life.

I never got to see him again. When I woke up in the morning, apparently cured of all my woes, I was then subjected to many months of tests. I was prodded, poked, injected; stuff was pumped into me, stuff was taken out of me, but I didn't mind. I never said anything about Jerry, but with every test and with every puzzled-looking doctor, I just smiled.

I was cured of something that no one has ever been cured of. And now I have a whole life I was never meant to have.

When I saw that Jerry died in a car crash a couple of years later I was devastated.

I had promised myself that one day I would find him and I would give him something special to thank him for his magic.

But I never got the chance.

And as I grew up, I found it too hard to move away from this place where a miracle happened. It was a way to be close to him, to pay my respects to him. My daughter is in Year Three now. And she is fit and healthy and thriving, but nonetheless, every day I pray that a Jerry will walk into her classroom and change someone's life.

I have never told anyone that story. Not even my husband. I just assumed he would think I was crazy.

But I look at you and I see Jerry. I see something about him, lingering around you; like a tiny flicker of his light has made its way back to me and I had to tell you.

92

ASTROPHEL

They had given birth to a miracle and in trying to exploit what they saw as a loophole in his genetics, they destroyed him. They took something that was nature's unparalleled design genius and they manufactured a cheap and nasty alternative; they built a grotesque fake that ushered him to his death when he should have been protected and nurtured and loved.

My brother was something bigger than my father could have ever predicted. He was a miracle, long before he became a product of a man who had read one too many science-fiction novels. He healed people. He made the world better, not because of what Auden Everston did to him, but in spite of it.

I think perhaps Mia was right. He was an angel. And we let him escape. But then why would an angel wish to stay in a world so full of people willing to do terrible things?

I remember him now. I remember him as he was; as a boy with a heart that was full of love and a gift that did immeasurable good.

I knew, once I had met Molly, that there was no point trying to find out if my body could do what Jerry's did. It didn't matter if I was made of nanobots or tin; it was all a nonsense. My father invented toys; he built weapons to control and manipulate; he never made anything that could heal the world. That was what Jerry could have been, if they had only looked a little closer at what they were doing.

Now that I knew Jerry's story; now that I knew that he was a miracle, not of my creator's making, but of his own, all that was left for me to do, was find a path for myself. Who was I now that I lived in a world where my brother's magic would fade into folklore and fairy tales, and I was a wholly different story altogether?

I felt that with each step I took, I could hear the clinking and grinding of my body weighing me down. The brutal architecture of my being felt so clumsy in contrast to his poetry. I would not light up a room until they got my hands on my body and dissected me for their own entertainment and morbid curiosity. *Could we make another one of these* they'll ask. No one will ever say that of Jerry. There will never be another and no one would dare try to recreate his wonder.

OBITUARY
THE TIMES

Auden Albert Spenser Everston | 1942-2012

The man the world came to know as Mr Mental Health, Auden Everston, passed away at a private hospital on Wednesday of this week, following complications from a routine surgery, according to his own private physician. Mr Everston, the founder of the world's largest medi-tech company, EverTech, was a pioneer in brainwave manipulation and biotech integration.

By far the company's most successful product, the BEST chip was designed by Everston only a few years after being kicked out of his Cambridge University college for failing his first-year exams, twice. Everston spent many years lobbying various medical councils to approve his technology and to allow minor brain surgery to be undertaken by specially trained technicians, who would insert the chips to activate their 'brain harmonising technology'. Once approval was given, an elite network of high-net-worth individuals took the first batch, wearing their scars as a statement of their power and new-found mental health.

Eventually Everston made the technology less expensive and less invasive, with the most recent iteration being ingested through the nose, for a quarter of the original asking price. This led to EverTech expanding globally at a pace not seen before by any company in any sector. By the time Everston passed away last week, EverTech had offices in all but 3 countries in the world and a market share of 87% in the biotech industry.

Everston's personal life has been one marred by tragedy. His son was tragically killed in 1994, in what is considered to be the first fatality involving a driverless car. The car was one of EverTech's first forays into other tech-related industries and the project was abandoned almost immediately after the death of Jericho, Everston's only son with his wife Jessica, a world-renowned cardiologist.

Only a few years later Jessica committed suicide, despite Everston ensuring that she was supervised by medical professionals 24 hours a day at a specially created unit that he had built at the family home. Jessica had suffered severe depression following the death of their son and had been in and out of various psychiatric facilities whilst Everston was left alone to run the company, that she had been a co-owner of.

For the last 15 years Everston has been hidden from public view, but has been no stranger to controversy in that time. A number of former EverTech employees have launched legal action against him, claiming that they were only allowed to remain in their jobs if they agreed to BEST chip implants with unlimited ad-hoc updates provided without warning. Claimants reported that they had been experimented on without their consent and that the chips were used as a method of control by Everston and his inner circle. Whilst no legal ruling was made in Everston's lifetime, the case continues.

Other rumours about the secretive billionaire have been

more wild. Some have claimed that his wife was in fact a robot of his own creation, others announced that Everston himself was only partially human. One employee told this newspaper that Everston actually had a secret daughter who he kept locked away to perform experiments upon, but no public records exist to support this claim.

Whatever the truth of Everston's personal life, he will be remembered as the founder of one of history's great companies and the man who used technology to cure our mental health crisis. For that, we thank him.

EPILOGUE
ASTROPHEL

The pain of not becoming the thing you could have been, is only exceeded by the pain of discovering the potential to become was never there in the first place. It took me many years to accept, but I now wander the world, not with the hope that I will heal the sick, or ease the burden of the broken mind; I have chosen simply to experience it. I hope to become utterly lost in it.

I am a miracle of sorts, just a secret one, that is of no use. I am impervious to pain, my body is as good as invincible, I do not need to eat, I do not feel the cold or the heat. I do need to sleep though; I need to give my mind and my heart time to rest, but beyond this, I have limited needs. I am not cyborg-strong, I don't seem to have particularly exceptional eyesight or hearing, but I have made peace with myself.

I can go almost anywhere; when I need to be treated like a child, I can channel that; when I need to be an adult, I can speak with the sort of authority that comes with years on earth, not the look of a face. Dan's money has helped, and I am now plugged into the internet, which was a bit of a revelation and there are skills I have learnt to help me get by. I have a bank account, a driving license, I own a house. But I'm never there, so I rent it out and live off that money.

Jerry was a miracle forged in the fires of self-delusion and the desire for fame. And yet what was created was not entirely what was meant. He was something that could not have been imagined and they broke him. They corrupted what was perfect. I was created alongside him. Apparently superior, but never to reach the beautiful heights of his fleeting achievements.

Jazz and I are explorers now. Aimless perhaps, but I hold Jerry's words in my heart. Wherever we go, I listen to people's stories. I help them only by being willing to be nourished by their lives. It is enough for most people. And it is enough for me. For now. I am a slightly damaged shell who both does and does not have faith. I still carry the second chip that he made me; *sleep* is never far away from my mind, but I'm not ready to give up on finding the world he told me about.

I cannot now prove that anything you have read is true. The actors in the story of my life have all fled the stage and I am left to my lonely monologue, imploring the audience to suspend their disbelief a little longer.

All I can do is ask you to believe in Jerry. A boy who had two bodies, but just one good heart.

POSTSCRIPT

The rise and fall of EverTech has been well documented by others. Its short-lived journey to global domination is only slightly less remarkable than its almost immediate and total collapse. Once BEST chips began malfunctioning, a panic spread across the world. And that was before the deaths began. By 2019 it was estimated that 12% of those who had a nasal-delivery chip had died of haemorrhaging on the brain, with a further 19% suffering irreversible brain damage. Needless to say, the red tape EverTech has so skilfully navigated and cut through on their way to the top, reappeared with a vengeance almost overnight. And that killed the neural enhancement industry. Maybe for good. Though I doubt it. There was too much money invested for it all to be for nothing. There are plenty of people who will still expect to get paid, and more who will think they can do better next time around.

Auden Everston has a loyal cult following, though the received wisdom, 10 years after his death, is that he was a very smart man with a deep, moral deficiency. Rumours about the murder of his wife dogged him in his final years and several individuals have attempted to have the case tried posthumously, but the evidence has remained scant and is yet to compel any judge to take action.

The cynical amongst you will note how convenient it is that this story emerges only when all of the players in Astrophel's story are dead. It has been difficult to verify much beyond the recordings of the interviews that she sent me, along with a box full of tape cassettes left to her by Dr Daniel Allen. Given what she compiled during her research, after what she calls her 'reawakening' it's easy enough to piece together a story that makes sense, but the lack of verifiable witnesses is of course troubling.

The fact that she does seem to exist as a registered person, is even more challenging. But she has stood in front of me and recited many parts of her story almost verbatim as they appear before you. She existed, but out of what she was made, I cannot tell you. To be honest, it seemed rude to ask.

We first met in 2013. I was playing in a park with my daughter who was not quite two years old; my wife was at home resting, trying desperately to find the energy to bring our monstrously-sized son into the world, and so I had taken off our daughter to engage in a wonderfully wide-ranging and intense game of 'eye-spy', laced with all of the best bits of 'tag' and a sprinkling of hysterical giggling for absolutely no reason. She was dressed as a princess, but as I watched her climbing the wooden walls of the playground castle I remember hoping that she would never need a prince to save her, because she was already perfectly complete.

I sat on a bench watching her watching out for pirates, dragons and taxis from the top of her tower. Out of the corner of my eye I noted that someone had sat down next to me. It was late in the evening, and the summer sun was setting. My daughter was the only child in the playground.

I turned, not very subtly, to see who was next to me; a girl, no more than 15 or 16 years old, staring at me. 'Your daughter is very sweet.' She said quietly.

'Thank you.' I replied. I turned to the aforementioned daughter and did what I often wondered if other parents did - look at their children very intently in the hope that the conversation you don't want to have might evaporate because you choose not to look it in the eye. But, as I would later discover, Astrophel was nothing if not persistent.

'My parents are dead.'

'I'm sorry.' I said, feeling increasingly uncomfortable, wondering if I could deliberately butt-dial my wife for back-up. I managed to do it often enough by accident - how hard could it be?

But no matter how much shifting around I did, it turns out that the butt-dial is a kind of magic, a little like fairies, that only makes itself known when you're not looking for it.

'My foster-parents are also dead.'

I had assumed then, that my daughter and yet-to-be-born child were to be raised without a father, so certain was I that this girl was the reason that four adults who had been charged with her care were no longer alive and that for whatever reason, I was to be her next victim.

'Do you like your daughter? You seem like you do.'

'Of course. I love her.'

'How do you know?'

'Because...' I thought for a moment about the situation I was in and I saw, as I looked into this strange girl's eyes, that she was not a threat and yet I was wary of her intensity. 'Because sitting here, talking to you makes me nervous. I want to protect her. To be honest, I want to grab her now and run away so that I know she is safe, but I'm worried that this might not be the right thing to do.'

'That's love? Running away?'

'I think love is wanting to protect someone when there's danger, yes.'

'I'm in danger. I have a dog, but I think she only loves me because I let her sleep on my bed. I don't think she would protect me.'

She sounded so utterly lost, that I turned away from my daughter to look at her. 'What sort of danger are you in?'

'I know a secret that I shouldn't.'

I didn't say anything. What could possibly be comforting in this situation? A patronising: *We all know secrets we shouldn't sometimes - when you grow up, you'll realise that navigating when to share and when not to, is what will define your relationships*? I didn't think so. Asking further questions also seemed like a bad idea. But I didn't have to wait long for more.

'It might be something wonderful, but I don't understand it fully. And it could be something terrible. And I think there are people that don't want me to be okay.'

It's hard to predict what one might say when confronted with unexpected and frankly uncomfortable conversations that don't make a lot of sense. I suppose we like to imagine that we are all conversational wizards who have a witty or sage response to any scenario. That's certainly how I like to imagine I would handle these things. The truth is though, there are moments that we are just wildly unprepared for because they aren't supposed to happen in real life. I would like to report that I said something kind and comforting that also removed me from the situation in a calm and classy way. But that is not the case. The truth is my daughter came over and wrapped herself around my knee, staring at this girl whilst more or less sucking on the leg of my jeans. This blindsided me. I looked from one to the other, and just as I hoped that my daughter would never need rescuing, I hoped that if she did, it would be from someone who would be kind and not use her vulnerability against her.

I turned to this wild, unblinking girl and asked her if I could help.

She smiled for the first time, but it was not a look that radiated happiness; she was relieved, but still alone. She passed me a cassette. I hadn't seen one since I was about thirteen years old and I upgraded to a 'Discman', long before the advent of digital music. I couldn't believe that someone her age would have any clue what this was! 'Would you listen to this? If you think you can help, maybe you could meet me here tomorrow.'

She got up to leave. I asked her name before she began to run. 'Astrophel.'

'As in the poem?' I called after her.

'I knew that you were the right person.' She said, smiling in earnest as she disappeared.

We met on three further occasions after this. She met my wife, and on the final time we met, our newborn son.

That was many years ago now.

What you have read is the compilation of our correspondence and the tapes and papers and old newspaper clippings that she sent me.

Each word has been transcribed from boxes of cassettes she gave me over time, with very specific instructions about how they should be compiled.

I have made no additions or changes other than to occasionally note when the recordings were unusual because of long pauses, or to try and give words to sounds that the interviewees made.

I was ordered not to include Astrophel's questions as part of the transcripts.

Dr Daniel Allen's death is what sparked all of this. He opened Astrophel's eyes to something he was unable to deal with in life. It was his idea to use the cassettes. His was the cassette Astrophel gave me in the park the first time we met.

Mia Marković recorded her words more than 15 years ago into the voice memo app on an ancient smartphone. The phone was sent to my home anonymously. The very arrival of this artefact nearly made me burn everything that I had so far collected. If it hadn't been for the truth I found in Mia's words, and my wife's gentle encouragement and calmness in the face of my own nervousness, that would have been the end of it.

Jack Lewis died many years ago. After some pretty impressive detective work Astrophel tracked down an old lock-up he owned just off of Huntington Street, about an hour south of Los Angeles. She purchased the lock-up without ever seeing it and had the contents shipped over to England. Half a dozen surfboards later, we found a box full of letters that Jack had written to his mother, spanning years. He had never sent one of them and he had kept on writing them long after she died. I have reprinted those letters, where they are relevant to this story.

This is not my story.

It is a story that I lived just on the very farthest outpost of. It shook me to my very core. It has made me wake in the middle of the night, fearing for the world in which we had brought children, and filled me up with hope in a way that seemed impossible.

After the final box of cassettes arrived, several years after we first met, I had my last conversation with Astrophel over the phone. "You have my whole story now, right up to this moment. You will understand how much has changed for me since our first meeting. I live in another world now. It is not better or worse, just different. It is one that is okay because at least I now know what is real. I don't think that anyone will read what you put together and believe that it is anything but a story, and that's okay. I needed to find out what happened to my life and I needed someone who wasn't me, to hear it and tell me that I'm not crazy."

That was more or less the entirety of the call. She told me that she was going off on her own adventure and she would send me an update some time.

She never did.

ACKNOWLEDGMENTS

Like so many, I began writing a novel in the strained moments of 2019, but my journey with writing has been a long and happy one dating back far longer. I am beyond grateful to my wife who has supported, nudged, critiqued or ignored my scribblings in exactly the ways I needed, to get me to this point.

I would also like to thank Gaelle, David and Ed for being the first people to give me feedback and encouragement outside the family home.

And of course, my love and thanks to my parents and my beautiful children.

ABOUT THE AUTHOR

A J Webster is an emerging author of Science Fiction and Fantasy. *One Good Heart* is his debut novel.

To get updates on his work, use the links below or sign up to his newsletter on ajwebster.co.uk

Follow @iamajwebster

Printed in Great Britain
by Amazon